"Full of breathless blood-and-guts action, hairpin twists and turns, Miller's cocktail of murder and dirty business is potent and compelling." —*Publishers Weekly*

"An explosive new thriller."
—*Mystery Lovers Bookshop News*

TOO FAR GONE

"*Too Far Gone* offers terrific characters caught in the grip of kidnapping, murder, and a deadly storm. Every moment is real enough to touch. The twists are truly surprising, and the pacing never lets up. It simply doesn't get better than that." —John Gilstrap, author of *Nathan's Run*

SIDE BY SIDE

UPSIDE DOWN
Nominated for Best Paperback Original
for the International Thriller Writers Award

"Riveting. John Ramsey Miller is an accomplished word-smith whose readership should grow as his body of work increases. Winter Massey has the strength to become an easily recognizable hero, one even discussed at the literary water cooler. Do yourself a favor and make it a point to meet Winter Massey." —*Mystery Reader*

INSIDE OUT

"*Inside Out* is a great read! John Ramsey Miller's tale of big-city mobsters, brilliant killers, and a compellingly real U.S. marshal has as many twists and turns as running serpentine through a field of fire and keeps us turning pages as fast as a Blackhawk helicopter's rotors! Set aside an uninterrupted day for this one; you won't want to put it down."

—Jeffery Deaver, author of
The Vanished Man and *The Stone Monkey*

"A compelling and exciting action thriller starring a likeable protagonist." —*Midwest Book Review*

"Nonstop action . . . Miller has created a hero the reader cares about." —*Mystery Reader*

THE LAST FAMILY

"A relentless thriller." —*People*

"Fast-paced, original, and utterly terrifying—true, teeth-grinding tension. I lost sleep reading the novel, and then lost even more sleep thinking about it. Martin Fletcher is the most vividly drawn, most resourceful, most horrifying killer I have encountered. Hannibal Lecter, eat your heart out." —Michael Palmer, author of *Silent Treatment*

"The best suspense novel I've read in years!"
—Jack Olsen, author of *Son: A Psychopath and His Victims*

"Martin Fletcher is one of the most unspeakably evil characters in recent fiction. . . . A compelling read."
—*Booklist*

"The author writes with a tough authority and knows how to generate suspense." —*Kirkus Reviews*

"Suspenseful . . . Keeps the reader guessing with unexpected twists." —*Publishers Weekly*

"From page 1, you'll be caught in this gripping, taut thriller. . . . Five stars." —Larry King, *USA Today*

"First-time novelist John Ramsey Miller's *The Last Family* is another attention-grabbing thriller that likely will find a home in Hollywood. The briskly paced page-turner pits former DEA superagents against each other in a taut dance of death and revenge." —*Chicago Tribune*

"This is a right fine debut thriller based on a great idea."
—*New York Daily News*

"Miller provides enough action for any Steven Seagal movie. . . . Some of Miller's plot twists look like a long, easy pop fly coming at you in center field, only to dart around and pop you in the back of the head."
—*Charlotte Observer*

ALSO BY JOHN RAMSEY MILLER

Available from Bantam Dell

THE
LAST DAY

JOHN RAMSEY MILLER

A BANTAM BOOK

THE LAST DAY
A Bantam Book / January 2009

Published by Bantam Dell
A Division of Random House, Inc.
New York, New York

This is a work of fiction. Names, characters, places, and incidents
either are the product of the author's imagination or are used
fictitiously. Any resemblance to actual persons, living or dead, events,
or locales is entirely coincidental.

Bantam Books and the rooster colophon are registered trademarks
of Random House, Inc.

ISBN 978-0-440-24311-3

Printed in the United States of America
Published simultaneously in Canada

www.bantamdell.com

OPM 10 9 8 7 6 5 4 3 2 1

The Last Day *is dedicated to*
Kate Burke Miciak

ACKNOWLEDGMENTS

I specifically want to thank Randall Klein, an extremely talented young editor without whom this book would be much less than it is. I have been blessed that I have always worked with the best editors in the business, and a great publisher, Bantam Dell. Special thanks to Irwyn and Nita, and to all of the professionals at Bantam Dell, who have been so remarkably supportive and have all worked so hard to see that my books over the past years are as good as they can be and find their way into my readers' hands. The house has always made me feel appreciated and an important part of the family.

A very special thanks once again to Anne Hawkins, my agent and good friend of many years, and the captain of my team.

With each book I write, the list of people I want to thank grows, and invariably I leave someone out who should be included. The truth is that a lot of people help me out with research and support me one way or another every day. My friends and family are important to me, and they know who they are and hopefully what each means to me and to my continued stacking of words. I have decided not to list them, but they know I love and appreciate them one and all.

ONE

OUTSIDE CONCORD, NORTH CAROLINA
THE THIRD SUNDAY IN AUGUST

Sitting cross-legged on the cool clay floor, the watcher used the tip of his survival knife to carve another letter into the wall of his hide. After he inspected the letter—an *O*—he ran the sharpening stone against the blade, holstered the knife, and set it down gently by his side.

The midday sun cooked the still air outside the hole. He looked out at the rear of a sleek, modern house through the four-inch opening in the trap door. When the interior lights were on, and it was adequately dark, looking through the large windows reminded him of peacefully watching fish in a tank. The house's two occupants—a man and his wife—swam from room to room like trout. He often watched their big TV screen through his binoculars, over the back of the leather sofa. Rarely were the residents together for more than a few minutes. Their conversations were short ones, and the obvious emotional distance gave the watcher great pleasure.

The sound of a motor's purr caught the watcher's attention as he looked up in time to see the wife's Lexus coming around the house while the garage door opened. He felt a rapidly growing sense of arousal watching the SUV roll slowly into its bay. The woman was not perfect, but nevertheless a beautiful and desirable creature.

Watcher switched off the iPod, opened his rucksack, drew out a jar, and held it up, illuminating six large dark-shelled beetles he'd found under a rotten log that morning on his way to the hide. In the sunlight, their ebony armor had the iridescence of raku pottery. The bugs ambled along, content, creeping like tanks over the bottom of the jar he had brought to urinate into while he was in the hide. The insects would walk around in circles, try to scale the walls, and climb over each other for the rest of their lives, constantly looking for a way out. The man knew this from experience. He knew a great deal about captive behavior. While it was true that the bugs were docile, he had experience with beetles and many other creatures whose de-

meanor seemed fixed . . . until outside forces in-
tervened.

Finding a drinking straw, the man opened the
jar and set the lid aside. He used the end of the
straw to jab at the insects, prodding each once or
twice before going to the next. After a few seconds a steady hissing sound, like a leaking tire,
erupted from the jar's inhabitants. He smiled,
knowing that before long the seemingly docile
beetles would attack each other and begin using
their powerful jaws to dismantle their mates,
leaving severed appendages in the jar's bottom.
And he would release the victor—the bug with
the most limbs left—and crush the losers under
his boots. His grin widened as he watched the
garage door close, the hissing of the insects
reaching a frenzy.

TWO

Dr. Natasha McCarty slipped on her reading
glasses and gently pressed the abdomen of Josh
Wasserman, a four-year-old whose appendix
had ruptured early the previous evening. As

usual, she'd done a first-class job both on the re-
moval of the defective body part and in the even
spacing of the sutures. Across the room, a bright
bouquet of tulips stood centered in the window,
and Mr. and Mrs. Wasserman sat quietly in
chairs on the other side of the bed where the
small child lay. Mrs. Wasserman, a petite, round-
faced woman, appeared to be about eight months
pregnant. She stared at the child as though he
might vanish should she blink.

"How are you feeling this morning?" Natasha
asked the bright-eyed boy as she checked the
chart hanging at the foot of his bed. His color
was good, his vitals strong. She wouldn't know
he'd been at death's door less than twelve hours
earlier if she hadn't performed the operation herself. Children could be amazingly resilient.

"My stomach hurts," he replied sullenly.

Natasha smiled sadly as the small face twisted
in on itself and tears streamed down his cheeks.
She set the chart down, put her hand under his
chin, and sat on his bed, careful not to jostle his
small body.

"You're going to be fine very soon," she told
him tenderly.

"You've been such a brave boy," his mother added with forced cheer.

"He's worried that his soccer career is over," his father said.

"That's not a problem, Josh. You'll be back running around and playing ball in a couple of weeks like this never happened." Natasha handed him a tissue from the bedside table and waited until he wiped the tears away.

"What about peritonitis?" Mrs. Wasserman asked. "Complications."

After smiling reassuringly at Josh, Natasha looked over at the parents.

"We cleansed the site and we'll monitor very closely, but the antibiotics he's on are very effective. Josh is a very strong young man. There's no reason to worry."

"Can I have it?" Josh asked.

"Have what?" Natasha asked.

"The palendix," he said. "In a jar. So I can have it to keep."

"Josh," Mrs. Wasserman said, "you do not need your appendix."

"We could use it for bait next time we go fishing," Mr. Wasserman joked.

"I'm sorry, Josh," Natasha said. "We didn't keep it."

"What did you do with it?" he asked, curious.

"We incinerated it."

A look of confusion grew on his face. "What?"

"Incinerate means we had to burn it up. When we remove things from people, we are required by law to burn them up in a furnace."

"You *cremated* my palendix?"

Natasha smiled. "Yes."

"Like Buster," Josh said.

"Buster was our Labrador," Mrs. Wasserman explained.

"A vetanarin cremated Buster," he went on. "In a hot, hot fire."

"He was nine," Mr. Wasserman added.

"Mr. Murphy runned over Buster in a car," Josh said with a tiny sneer.

"Ran over," Mrs. Wasserman corrected.

"He ran over him. I wanted a new dog, but I'm getting a new sister instead. I wanted to bury him, but Daddy said our yard was too little. Our yard is all brown and crunchy because the police won't let us put any water on it."

"It's very dry where I live, too," Natasha said.

"Where do you live?" Josh asked.

"I live way out in the country north of here," she replied.

"Do you have a dog?"

"We don't have any pets. But we do have deer, squirrels, raccoons, and possums, and lots of birds."

"You live on a farm and you don't got pigs and cows?"

"We don't live on a farm. We live in the woods."

"You got many snakes?"

"We have a few. Mostly harmless snakes, thankfully."

"Do you live with your daddy and mommy?"

"My mommy and daddy live in Seattle, Washington. That's a long way from here. I live with my husband." Natasha braced herself for the next question.

"Do you have any little boys and girls?"

"No," Natasha said, smiling.

"Why come?"

"Josh," Mr. Wasserman said, "you shouldn't pry into Dr. McCarty's personal life."

"I'll see you tomorrow morning, Josh," Natasha said, rubbing his head.

"When can I go home?"

"In a few days."

Natasha was near the nurses' station dictating her notes for transcription when she saw Dan Wheat walking toward her. One of her partners, Dan had the bedside manner of a mortician. She didn't know why he'd gone into pediatric medicine, since he seemed to view children as troublesome monkeys. He was rail-thin with a roving eye and a legendary bag of tired pickup lines. Natasha had once overheard one of his young patients tell him he had stinky breath. Dan immediately ordered a spinal tap for the offender before he went off in search of mints.

"Natasha," he said, waving her down. "You see my new wheels?"

"No."

"I broke down and treated myself to a top-of-the-line Benz SL five-fifty—that's a two-seat convertible—in jet black. It's a bitch to keep clean, so I run it wide open to blow the dust off. I figure, hey, I work hard for my money and

I deserve it. You know, he who toots not his own horn risks leaving it in a state of untootedness."

"Lovely, Dan," Natasha interrupted. "How are your patients?"

"Claire is making me buy her a new car as an act of revenge because I won't let her drive the Benz, so I was thinking maybe a simple Lexus SUV like yours so she can haul the kids around in fair style. You buy it or do you lease?"

Natasha sighed. "Ward bought it for me."

"I lease strictly for tax purposes. I drive it free, basically." Dan barely paused for breath. "Oh, did Edgar talk to you about my little brother? I was thinking he'd be a great addition to our practice. The boy's got hands like mine, and he aced medical school. We should get him here before he gets an offer he can't refuse in a major city."

"I didn't know we needed a sixth partner," Natasha said.

Natasha had met Dan's younger brother. If such a thing were possible, Bill Wheat was half as impressive as his older brother. He was short and stocky, and his half-open eyes made him look like he was in the process of passing out. Natasha hadn't wanted Dan brought on board, but she hadn't felt like opposing her partners. Dan was typical of what was coming out of medical schools: very intelligent, aggressive, competitive, and greedy. He saw each patient as a business opportunity and his billings were off the chart because he ordered every test he knew the insurance company would pay for.

"Perhaps we should discuss this at the next partners' meeting," she said noncommittally. "I hate to break this off, but I haven't slept in two days."

"Does Ward get fed up with your hours? It drives Claire crazy that I'm always working."

"Ward doesn't complain."

"Well, keep my brother Bill in mind. We're getting busy as hell and it would help you and Ward to spend some more time together."

Natasha realized to her horror that Dan Wheat was staring at her right hand, which was tingling like it was asleep. And that hand was shaking ever so gently.

"Are you all right?" Dan asked her, the note of concern ringing false.

"Fine," she said, shoving it into the pocket of

her gown. "Fatigue, I guess." She turned and headed for the bathroom.

After she'd finished at the hospital, Natasha got into her Lexus SUV and headed home. Although it was just after noon, she was exhausted; she hadn't been able to fall asleep after the Wasserman surgery, which had ended around ten-thirty the previous evening.

Twenty minutes later Natasha was turning into her driveway. The McCartys' twelve wooded acres had been a wedding present from Ward's father. Ward and Natasha had selected a wide ridge for their house site, cleared the trees from it, and built a four-thousand-square-foot split-level modern house. Other than the asphalt driveway and the mailbox, there was no sign at all that a house sat back in the woods. The asphalt driveway wound through the trees, and curved in front of the house. The home's façade of raw textured concrete and floor-to-ceiling windows had been built with its back facing a tree-lined and elevated ridge.

Natasha used the remote to open her bay in the three-car garage, and pulled in. She went into the kitchen, poured herself a glass of Pinot Grigio, and carried the bottle into the den, where she turned the large-screen television to the Food Network. She put the bottle on the Noguchi coffee table, drank a long swallow from the glass, went into the bedroom, and took a hot shower. After slipping into a robe she got a blister pack of Ambien and went back to the den.

Natasha popped a pill out and held it in her palm for a moment, staring out at the grounds, feeling again the unease she'd become all too familiar with. Her eyes caught a motion in the shadows as she searched the tree line for the source. A chill ran up her spine. Her discomfort grew. A wild animal, or perhaps a house cat foraging for field mice. Of course, with the new subdivision up the road, it was possible that kids were playing in the woods. Over the past two years she and Ward had seen evidence of people having been in the woods—beer cans, soda bottles, and candy wrappers—but had never caught anyone close to the house. Ward had the standard POSTED signs on the property line, but they knew that such signs were just suggestions, respected only by the reputable.

Due to the woods, and since the house faced

north, there had been no need for curtains to block the sun or to give the McCartys privacy. For the past weeks, though, she'd been considering having blinds installed. She had even gotten an estimate, which had been staggering since the curved thirty-foot-wide wall was comprised of four-by-eight double panes of thick glass.

Natasha sat down and put her feet up next to the bowl on the coffee table. The bowl held a baseball she'd put in it the night after Ward left for the trade show. She'd been almost asleep when she put her hand under his pillow and was startled to discover the baseball. She brought it out to the den as she paced, holding it like the egg of a strange bird, trying to figure out why Ward had placed it there. It had to have been a message about Barney, but the meaning hadn't been apparent, unless Ward simply wanted her to think about him. When had she not thought about their son? The incident had stunned her and she'd fought the urge to call Ward and yell at him, but she had taken a pill instead and had gone to sleep angry. It seemed cruel, and not like the old Ward she'd fallen in love with—had lived with all these years.

Natasha reclined on the couch and chased an Ambien with a glass of the chilled wine. She held up her hand and stared at it, daring it to shake.

THREE

LAS VEGAS, NEVADA

The hotel shuttle deposited Ward McCarty at the airport to catch his flight home after three days of overfilled tote bags, crowded sales booths, and insincere smiles. He hated trade shows but had to attend them in order to keep up with new suppliers, new materials, gimmicks, manufacturers, competition.

After standing in a long line, Ward showed his North Carolina license and ticket to a bored female guard, slipped off his shoes, belt, cell phone, and watch, and put them all in a plastic tray. He took the computer out of the briefcase and placed it, his briefcase, and his carry-on on the conveyor belt, watching them vanish into the X-ray machine. He felt naked in his sock feet and he hated holding his khakis up with one hand so the cuffs didn't drag.

At the other end of the conveyor belt, a burly guard with a buzz cut opened his briefcase. Ward glanced over to see an elderly woman standing calmly while a guard ran a wand up and down over her stooped body. Satisfied, Ward's guard lifted out a bubble-lined envelope from the briefcase and slipped out a small blue die-cast race car. As he studied the toy, his eyes grew comically larger. He looked at Ward as if asking permission.

Ward smiled. "Go ahead," he said.

"Man." The guard whistled. "Richard Petty's Road Runner die-cast in near mint. You are one lucky devil. That was a one-year deal, that car." He looked at the underside. "It's not marked on the bottom."

"It's a prototype. It was never produced. One of a kind."

"One of a kind?" The guard placed it back into the envelope with care. "What's it worth?"

"No idea. It's been in my family since before I was born," Ward said.

"Have a good day, sir," the guard told him, as

he put the padded envelope into Ward's brief-case beside his computer and closed it.

Ward reached his assigned concourse through a maze of temporary signs, Sheetrock dust, scaf-folding, plastic sheeting, and constructive pande-monium, accented by the shrill buzzing of power drills and electric saws. At Ward's insis-tence, the travel agent had booked his and his un-cle's flights so the two business owners wouldn't be on the same plane. Ward had spent a few hours of his time in Vegas with Mark and his sec-ond wife while they were being entertained by manufacturers' reps, only slightly more pleasant than visiting the dentist.

At his gate Ward spent the time waiting for his flight staring at an open novel he'd bought be-fore leaving Charlotte, trying to absorb the words and make sense of the plot. When he traveled with paperback novels, he always tore out the chapters as he finished them and threw the pages away, which served to both mark his place and make his load lighter. After he finished the chapter he was working on, he ripped the pages out and put them on the seat beside him, then slowly realized that he had no idea what had happened in the discarded chapter.

Ward was bothered by the lack of clocks at the gate, which meant that passengers had to have watches or cell phones in order to know how long they had until their planes boarded. Of all of the things Ward didn't like about Las Vegas—and there was nothing he did like—he most disliked the city's denial that time passed there. Sitting in a leather chair with his carry-on bag and briefcase at his feet, he looked out through the windows at the Strip—easy to spot from the monstrous black glass pyramid and the giant sphinx with its lion ass backed right up to it.

Ward called his wife on his cell phone to explain the delay, but got their home answering machine. He had spoken to Natasha only once in the past few days, when he'd arrived at the airport for the memorabilia-suppliers' trade show. Of the six or seven times he'd called since, he'd left short messages. He wasn't alarmed, because Natasha often turned the phones' ringers off, or ignored them. She carried a cell phone but rarely turned it on unless she needed to answer her emergency beeper.

Sudden jazzy notes of youthful laughter froze Ward and he turned slowly to see not the young boy he expected to see but a young girl of eight or so playing tag with a smaller child. He exhaled loudly and looked down at his paperback, feeling the sudden tears running down his cheeks. Several times each day for the past year, something brought Barney into his mind, and, with that trigger, a choking gloom descended over him like a wet curtain. It could begin with a familiar odor like iced tea, a flash of a red shirt, a sudden movement in his periphery, a flag snapping in a brisk wind, a child with blond hair, a bicycle lying on a lawn—just about anything at all. Any thought of Barney brought Ward back to the memory of clutching a small, limp body in his arms as hell closed in on him.

Barney's given name had been Ward McCarty III, but he chose the name Barney himself at the age of five because he so admired that insipid purple dinosaur. At first, Ward and Natasha humored their beautiful boy. Soon, he stopped answering to anything but his newly chosen name.

Ward often dreamed—some dreams included a cameo by his son, or, if Ward was very lucky, a starring role. Those double-edged dreams were sweet torture, leaving his soul lacerated and leaking some essential nectar. He always woke with an odd feeling of being both full and empty at the same time.

What consumed a great deal of Ward's waking hours was the thought that every decision a creature made led to a path with unknowable consequences. An animal's choice of an action—or path—might find it a mate, shelter, or food—or the possibility of becoming another animal's dinner. By the same token, some bean counter with a sharp pencil might choose to install a less expensive—not ground-fault-interrupted—electrical outlet near a pool, and then not properly insulate a connection which, if the ground was saturated, could lead to the tragic death of an angelic child. Ward thought about this faceless man in some generic office day after day and saw no relief to being forever haunted by the avalanche that had begun with the simple decision of a budget-conscious drone.

Sometimes, when Ward McCarty looked at animals, he wondered if they ever dreamed alive their dead the way people did.

It was cool inside the wide-bodied craft. When Ward arrived at his assigned row, he found the center seat already occupied by a young girl with blond hair accented with bright red and blue streaks. She was plugged into an iPod. He opened the overhead compartment and managed to wedge in his carry-on.

The girl looked up at him, and when he met her green eyes, she smiled, showing small teeth accented with silver wire braces. Ward pointed to the window seat beyond her, whereupon she unplugged her earphones, got up, and moved into the aisle to let him pass, leaving her cloth tote bag on her seat.

Ward spent the first two hours alternating between watching the movie on a small screen in the ceiling over the aisle, and, out of the corner of his eye, observing the electronic activities of the girl beside him.

He figured her age as somewhere between thirteen and seventeen. Her freckled skin was clear. She wore an ebony pearl stud in her small earlobe. She was five five, and the yellow too-large-by-a-mile sweatshirt had the famous "Welcome to Las Vegas" sign screen-printed on it, which contrasted with her red shorts and blue flip-flops. He couldn't help but notice that each of the nails on her fingers and toes was painted a different color.

The black tote bag in her lap contained an assortment of electronic devices, and like a child with a short attention span she went from her iPod, to a Game Boy, to plugging a set of airline earphones into the armrest to watch the movie, then back to the iPod. And when he had decided that she was closer to seventeen than thirteen, she took out a DVD player and watched a cartoon clearly geared to very young children. She watched intently, laughing melodiously here and there as the cartoon played.

Thirty minutes out of Charlotte, he dropped his tray, reached into his shirt pocket, and pulled out one of the monogrammed index cards he carried to list things to do. As he lined up his thoughts, Ward began sketching a small familiar face in one corner of the card.

"Hey," the girl said suddenly, interrupting his drawing.

As she stared down at the card on the tray, she pulled her earphones off.

"Whacha doing?" she asked.

"Thinking," he replied.

"You're a good drawer," she said. "Could you draw me?"

Ward studied her round face and reproduced

her likeness in less than two minutes, all the while her eyes moved from his face to the drawing and back like someone watching a tennis match. Ward had the ability to sketch what he saw, and faces were what he drew best.

When he finished the sketch, she smiled. "Cool. Are you a professional artist?"

He answered, "No. I do some light designing."

A confused look briefly took over her features. "Like what kind of lights do you design?"

"Oh," he said, smiling. "My company makes and markets NASCAR memorabilia. Cars, hats, T-shirts, mugs, key chains."

"No shit?" she said, too loudly. The word earned her a frown from the man beside her. "My mother is a race-car fan."

Ward reached down, took out his briefcase, and opened it, taking out the model car to show her.

"You, what, painted it?" she asked, beaming.

"My father had it made in Japan. Nowadays they're made mostly in China. See, we take pictures of a real car from several angles and a factory makes the model from the pictures, which they produce, box, and ship to us, and we distribute them from our warehouse. We just change the art on the car depending on whose car it is, since every race team has different sponsors."

"This is so fucking cool. Could I get one?"

"Well, not this one. This one is the first one my father had made," he explained. "This is the prototype. He didn't have a lot of money and that car only raced one year. As it turned out, he made other models and they did sell and so he ordered more, but this one was handmade. Mostly he used it to show to bankers and investors, who weren't all that impressed. In those days NASCAR was only popular with relatively few people."

He started to tell her why he had it with him, but didn't. What he did say was, "I can get you a new one—driver of your choice."

"No shit?"

"Absolutely none." He took another note card and scribbled his office number on it. "Call and ask for Leslie, and she'll send one to you for your mother. We have thousands of them in our warehouse."

She narrowed her eyes, suspiciously. "How much will it cost?"

"My treat."

"No shit? Thanks. That is so sick."

"Sick?"

"Sick as in cool."

"Who's your mother's favorite driver?"

"I dunno. I can find out." She ran the wheels back and forth on her lap and made a motor noise as she did this. "Is this you on the card?" she asked, pointing at the card he'd given her with her inked likeness. "Ward McCarty. That's you?"

"It is," he told her.

"Why were you in Vegas?" she asked. "Gambling?"

"No. Work. You?"

"I fly back and forth a lot," she said. "My dad lives there and I live with my mother in Charlotte. You married?"

"Yes."

"What's your wife do?"

"She's a pediatric surgeon," Ward said.

"What's that mean?"

"Pediatric means children," Ward said.

"I know that. So she like cuts little kids open?" Her eyes were wide, her mouth a circle.

"Yes, but I think it's more complicated than making cuts."

"Y'all got any kids?"

"No," he said.

"You're like too old?"

"I expect you're right," he said, trying to smile. This wasn't true . . . as far as he knew.

When she handed the car back, Ward put the padded envelope back in his briefcase, closed it, and placed it under the seat.

"I need to slip out past you," he told her.

"Why?" she asked.

"Visit the little boys' room."

After the man beside the girl unbuckled his seat belt and stood in the aisle, she tucked her feet up in her seat so Ward could get out.

After he'd finished in the tiny bathroom, Ward left the enclosure and found a man in Bermudas waiting his turn. When Ward returned to his row, the girl, who was back again listening to her iPod, smiled up at him and pulled in her feet to let him get to his seat.

When the plane landed ten minutes later and parked at the terminal, the girl grabbed up her bag of toys and was off the plane before Ward got his carry-on and filed out.

He thought about what the girl had said about him being too old to have children, and realized it wasn't true. He and Natasha hadn't talked about having another child since Barney's accident, and the thought comforted him. For the first time in a very long time, Ward McCarty felt a degree of optimism about the future.

FOUR

While standing on the curb, waiting for the shuttle, Ward spotted his young seatmate climbing into a dark green Porsche Cabriolet. The driver, a woman with blond hair and pale skin, wore a flowery scarf and dark glasses that obscured her features. Perhaps the woman was the girl's mother, the NASCAR fan.

Six minutes later he climbed down from the bus, walked to his car, and frowned at the thin film of red dust coating the original black paint. Leaving the car in the open sunlight wouldn't do anything to prolong the paint's life. The vehicle, a pristine 1994 BMW 740i, had been his father's

only admission to the world that he was a man
of above-average means. Ward climbed in and
started the engine. Aiming the heavy sedan
toward the exit he pressed on the accelerator
and felt the powerful V-8 respond.

Ward turned on the radio, which was always
set to NPR. He didn't listen to music much when
he was driving. He had never felt the need for a
soundtrack in his life. Natasha had joked on
more than one occasion that her husband
danced to the melodious voices of liberal com-
mentators.

Although it should have been just the opposite, Ward's heart seemed to grow heavier as he
drove north on I-85. After leaving the Interstate
at the Concord Mills exit, Ward drove past
the racetrack, up Highway 29, and entered
Concord on Cabarrus Avenue, using the new
roundabout. He drove out Highway 73 and
turned left at the Exxon onto Gold Hill Road.
Two miles later he slowed for a doe and her two
spotted fawns, which ran across the road near a
farm owned by the grandson of a mill owner
whose last name was synonymous with bath
towels.

Turning onto the asphalt driveway a mile far-

ther down the road, Ward drove through the
woods, past the front door, and on around to the
side of the house, where he used his remote to
open the center garage door. He parked beside
Natasha's Lexus, the hood cool to his touch. His
other car, a dark blue Toyota Highlander, was
parked in the third bay. He rarely drove the
Toyota, preferring his father's old BMW.

Ward paused in the kitchen where the answering machine blinked a red 4. Natasha hadn't
bothered to listen to his short dispatches from
the red-hot West. Ward held his finger over the
button and hesitated before he finally hit delete.

A stack of unopened mail on the counter lay
beside a bottle opener with one cork still impaled
on its screw and another nearby. It was Natasha
who'd said you never leave a cork impaled on the
screw. He hadn't asked what law of winery that
violated. Strains of canned laughter drifted into
the kitchen from the den. Since the wall of windows overlooking the woods behind the house
was dark and there was no moonlight, the television screen was the sole illumination.

Natasha, wearing a light robe over her night-
gown, lay sleeping on the sleek sectional sofa.

An empty bottle of wine stood on the coffee table, and a blister pack of Ambien rested nearby. Ward frowned to see that of the original eight tablets, only two remained.

He frowned at the empty wineglass standing on the stone floor beside the couch. She appeared pale, but at least her chest was rising and falling. Ward stared down at her delicate features, washed by the uncertain light of the screen. One of his fears was that he would arrive home and find her dead.

Life was fragile.

Death happened just like that.

This he knew far too well.

Natasha was even more beautiful than she'd been the day he met her in Seattle a dozen years earlier. She had been a surgical resident attending a party given by a college friend of his— an artist whose paintings depicted a perfect, though surreal, rural world. There had been an immediate and mutual attraction, and they'd been married three months later in her parents' living room. Hastily arranged, the service was attended only by her three brothers, her best friend, their parents, and his uncle, Mark

Wilson. Gene Duncan, his best friend, who'd been in law school at the time, had flown out from Duke to be his best man.

Natasha Crossingham had just entered her last year of residency at a children's hospital, and Ward had remained in Seattle until she'd completed her term and, as soon as a group of pediatric surgeons at Carolinas Medical Center in Charlotte made her a partnership offer, they'd moved back to North Carolina. Ward had gone to work for his father's company, Raceway Graphics Incorporated, just in time to find out that his father had lung cancer, which despite the best available medical treatment took his life less than two years later. Ward had taken over as the company's president; he'd worked there during the summers for most of his life and he knew the business and the majority of their clients.

Natasha was in her eighth month of pregnancy when the McCartys moved into the newly completed house and within a month their son, Ward Crossingham McCarty, was born and their lives had settled into a sort of perpetual perfection that had lasted right up to the afternoon of the electrocution.

When Ward sat down on the edge of the

couch, Natasha opened her eyes slowly and looked dreamily up at him. As the real world came to her, she pulled the robe around to cover herself as she would if he were someone there to wash the windows.

"What time is it?" she asked.

"Eight-fifteen," he told her.

"When did you get in?"

"Just now," he said. "Oh, an hour ago."

Frowning, she said, "I should go to bed. I have rounds at six A.M. Have you eaten?"

"Not hungry," he said.

"There's leftover lasagna in the fridge," she said, sitting up. "I thought you were supposed to be back this morning."

"My original flight was canceled. I took a later flight," he told her, his heart sinking. "I left a message on the machine."

"Did you?" she slurred, exhausted. "I didn't check the machine. Sorry. I had a long day at the hospital. Emergency appendectomy last night and I couldn't sleep. I came in from morning rounds and . . ."

"Nothing to be sorry for," he said. Ward couldn't mask his disappointment that his calls home had been totally unimportant to the woman he loved more than anybody on earth. He wished he could say that to her, but for some reason the words were stacked away in some mental cubicle he couldn't locate. She had not said "I love you" since Barney's death, and it was possible she no longer did. Perhaps that love was forever gone—a victim of their grief. Perhaps Barney had been such an integral part of their passion for each other that, now that he was gone, there was nothing at all to bind the doctor to the toymaker.

"I put fresh sheets on your bed yesterday," she told him.

"Thank you," he said, feeling as though someone had turned a rheostat that had increased the gravity in the room. *My bed*.

"If it's all right with you, I'm going to order curtains for this room this week." Natasha stood and looked out the windows into the dark. "I know it's weird, but I feel like I'd like to close them at night."

"Whatever you want," Ward said. Although he hated the idea of curtains covering the windows, if she wanted them, what the hell.

She yawned and stretched. "I'll see you in the morning."

Ward sat back on the couch and watched as Natasha picked up the blister pack containing the sleeping pills and the wine bottle, then bent to retrieve the glass from the floor.

"I'll get that. Leave the bottle, too," he told her.

"You sure?"

He nodded and watched as his beautiful wife set down the bottle and, moving in a more or less straight line, floated toward the hallway before vanishing into the darkness.

Like a lone egg in a nest, one of Barney's baseballs sat in the ceramic bowl on the coffee table. He picked it up and turned it in his hand, imagining him and Barney playing pitch with it in the backyard on a spring afternoon. He supposed Natasha had been holding it to better remember Barney. He put it back and looked down, spotting, between the sofa's cushions, a flash of white. He came up holding an envelope addressed to Natasha at her office. The return address belonged to the head of pediatric surgery at the Seattle children's hospital where she had done her residency. He lifted the flap, took out the letter, and read an offer to join her surgery professor at the University of Washington School of Medicine. Dr. Taylor

Patten, who practiced at Seattle Children's Medical Center, wanted her as a partner in his practice. Ward's face grew hot as he sucked in a long breath and contemplated the letter's significance.

Ward had once wondered if the association between his wife and her mentor had been more than the usual student/teacher relationship, because of their familiarity when they were around each other. The idea now revolted and alarmed him. He'd never asked her about their relationship, just as she'd never asked him about his previous girlfriends. What he wondered as he read the letter was whether she had written her mentor first, or if he had sought her out. And his heart pounded because it reinforced his belief that, aside from Natasha's patients, there was nothing of substance holding her in North Carolina. It didn't make him feel any better to discover that the letter was dated two years earlier, because that meant she had kept it. Why had she? She had been born in Seattle, grew up and had friends and family there. She had never mentioned wanting to return, but in keeping the letter she must have been thinking that she might pursue the offer. She must have been thinking of getting out.

Ward folded the letter, replaced it in the envelope, and put it back where Natasha had left it.

Crossing to the wet bar, Ward opened the liquor cabinet and selected a bottle of Laphroaig. He poured three inches of the golden liquid into a crystal glass, clouding it with a little water from a plastic bottle, and, picking up the remote, sat down, put his stocking feet on the coffee table, and started surfing TV channels as his mind grew dull from the pleasant effects of the Scotch.

FIVE

After Natasha left the den, she walked down the hallway, the slate cool against the soles of her bare feet. The combination of chilled wine and Ambien was an effective white noise generator. Natasha was confident that she knew enough about her own body and the drugs to ensure that she wasn't in any real danger of overdosing.

There was the time, a few weeks earlier, when she had awakened in the tub half filled with cold water, dried vomit in her hair, with no memory of either throwing up or getting into the tub. She mixed the drugs only occasionally, she thought, as she ran her hand along the wall.

She had been lucky so far that her hands hadn't started shaking during surgery. The duration of the tremors so far was short—usually a few seconds—but they seemed to be coming more often. She would have to have tests run to see what was causing this, but there was no explanation for the tremors that was good. If she had a nervous system disorder, like MS, she was screwed—her career would be over. With the diagnosis of any degenerative disease, she would have no choice but to quit performing surgery. She knew she would have to seek a diagnosis soon.

Walking by Barney's bedroom, Natasha reached out to brush the knuckles of her left hand gently across the smooth wooden door. For nine years of nights she rarely walked past this door without pausing to visit with her son or to open the door quietly, take a peek in, check on her sleeping child. The room had not changed in a year. Six months earlier, when she had mentioned to Ward that it might be time to begin thinking about boxing up just the clothes in their son's closet and few drawers, he'd started screaming at her like a lunatic. It was as though Ward expected Barney might return as long as his room wasn't altered. As often as not Ward didn't remember discussions they had, to the point that often she wondered why she bothered to talk to him at all.

The one thing she was sure of was that Ward hadn't loved their son any more than she had, and he couldn't possibly miss him any more than she did. If he wanted to think he had a corner on that, fine, but it would never be the truth. If it were possible for her to trade her life to bring Barney back, she'd die in the next second with a smile on her lips. But he couldn't come back, so she was determined to live the rest of her life. If Ward decided to live his, then they could do so together. If not, he'd have to make his own way to its end.

She went into her bedroom, closed the door, dropped her robe on the floor, flopped down across the bed, and stared up at the ceiling.

Natasha picked up a small stuffed bear that she'd had made for her son while he was still inside her womb, and still lying on the bed, pressed his hand. The recorder inside the animal said in her voice, "Little guy, Mama loves you so very much." Her own voice brought tears to her eyes, and she hugged the bear to her chest.

She reached over to Ward's side of the bed and felt his absence. She put her hand under his pillow and a dreamless sleep overtook her.

SIX

Watcher sat in his hide in the woods, sipping a sports drink to stay hydrated. When he heard the tone, he opened his pack and saw on his GPS receiver that the black BMW was leaving the airport lot in Charlotte. Thirty-seven minutes later, it pulled into the garage. Two months earlier, Watcher had duct-taped a GPS transmitter to the big car's frame near the gas tanks, and had placed a second unit inside the engine compartment in the Lexus SUV Dr. McCarty drove. He could see at a glance where the pair was at any given time.

Watcher was a shadow, a bad situation that would grow and grow until Ward and Natasha

McCarty were as doomed as hooked fish cast up onto a grassy, sun-baked slope. Watcher was a reckoning. Watcher's patience was a rapidly emptying hourglass.

Toy Boy—a fitting, albeit whimsical, nickname he had selected for his quarry—was a man hanging onto his life by a rope that had been fraying steadily since the day his son died. In three days the McCartys would endure the first anniversary of their son's death, and, Watcher would ensure, their last day on earth.

SEVEN

Alice Palmer had called her boyfriend twenty times and had left five increasingly angry messages from the time she arrived back home from the flight from Las Vegas until eleven that night. Either Earl was high, his phone's battery was dead, he'd left it somewhere, or he was punishing her for visiting her dad. "Fuck you," was the final message she left, but added, "It's your baby doll. I love you. Call me as soon as you get this . . . asshole."

She and her mother had argued all the way from the airport. Upon arriving at their home in Dillworth, her mother had come into the house with her, tossed her keys on the kitchen counter, and said, "Put your dirty laundry in the chute, and make your own dinner when you get hungry. I'm going to lie down. I have a splitting headache and I have to show four houses to some damned impossible-to-please Yankee couple in the morning. And clean up your room. The maid's off this week. And brush your teeth. Your breath smells like shit." After saying that, she'd gone into her bedroom and closed the door. Only the sound of her TV filtering under her door evidenced her presence in the house. Alice knew her mother was never going to be up for Mother of the Year.

Alice opened her carry bag to take out her Game Boy and saw the blue toy car she'd taken. She studied the portrait the man drew against her mirror. It wasn't at all bad, and she wished she could draw people as well as he did. The name embossed on the card was Ward McCarty, RGI, Inc. The address was one she wasn't famil-iar with. It wasn't close to school or home.

She pushed the model car around on her sheets, making motor noises. She'd lied about her mother being a race fan. Earl often talked about NASCAR drivers, and the obscene amounts of money they made. Her mother didn't like anything but the "look at all the pretty houses" channel on TV, which she watched religiously in high-def like a cult member. Alice and her mother's relationship was based on mutual animosity, and their conversations were hardly ever more than a swapping of sharp barbs and insults punctuated by long silences.

The remarkably heavy toy was maybe six inches long and three wide, and the rubber wheels rolled easily. Growing bored, she placed the car on her dresser beside the large pickle jar filled to the rim with pennies.

She undressed, and gazed at her body in the mirror. The raised but faded scars that crisscrossed her thighs were the result of cuts she'd made. A single-edge razor blade when she was younger and solidly in her Goth period had left the marks. On her stomach, the tattoo of a butterfly with its wings removed and lying beside its bleeding body was another reminder of that period. She hated it, and couldn't wait to have it removed. Her mother had offered to pay to have it taken off, but Alice had refused on principle.

She fought an urge to get into her car, a beater Toyota, and go find Earl. He'd come around in a day or two, with his head up his ass, give her excuses, and she'd forgive him. He depended on the money her mother gave her, or she stole, for his subsistence. She doled it out as she saw fit. It was the only control she exerted on him, and was a very effective rein.

Her mother was like some kind of parrot, cawing the same words constantly about Earl being dirty, unattractive, stupid, worthless, and a bad influence on her daughter. Okay, Earl had his faults, but he alone needed, understood, and cared about her. She took out a picture of herself and Earl taken in a dollar photo booth at the mall and smiled at his image. In the shot he was wearing a T-shirt with "Fuck you very much" on it. His eyes were crossed comically, and his long fingers were making a gang sign, funny because what gang would want Earl?

Alice thought about the man she'd sat beside on the flight and wondered if he could draw Earl from a picture. She took up her Game Boy, smiling as she imagined him opening his little briefcase and discovering the toy was gone.

EIGHT

At six A.M. on Monday Natasha was at the hospital in her scrubs. She had just finished sterilizing her hands for a hernia operation on a nine-year-old girl. As her surgical nurse was slipping on Dr. McCarty's left glove, Natasha's hands began to tremble gently, almost imperceptibly. Panic filled her as her nurse, Gloria Ready, fixed her with a look of concern.

"Are you all right, Dr. McCarty?" Gloria asked her.

Natasha managed to smile reassuringly. "I'm fine, Gloria."

"Your hands are shaking."

"Pre-op jitters," Natasha told her.

Natasha heard something behind her and turned to see that Dr. George Walls, the senior partner in her practice, had entered the room. There was a snap as he pulled off his glove. "Hello, Natasha, Nurse Ready."

"Good morning, Dr. Walls," Gloria said, looking down.

Walls stared at Natasha, scrutinizing her. She dropped her hands to her sides.

"I'll be in the OR," Gloria said, leaving.

"Natasha, is everything all right?" George asked, frowning with concern.

"Fine, George."

"Hold out your hands for me."

"My hands are fine," Natasha said, feeling fear and embarrassment well up inside her.

"Please, humor an old friend," he insisted.

She held out her hands and her fingers trembled slightly.

"Your hands are uncertain," he said firmly.

"I don't know what this is about," she said, on the verge of tears.

"I'm sure you are perfectly fine, but not to perform surgery."

Natasha said, weakly, "It's probably nothing but pre-op jitters. I didn't sleep very well last night."

Walls smiled reassuringly. "Let's do this as a precaution, Natasha. Let me take this one and you can assist. If that's all right?"

"Of course. Thank you." Natasha could have argued the point. She was sure the trembling would pass as it always had. During the last operation her hands had been certain. Being replaced was humiliating.

"Has this happened before?" he asked. "These tremors?"

"No. Well, not during surgery. And it passed in a few minutes. I would never . . ." She exhaled loudly. "I should see someone. I'm sure . . . I've been under a lot of stress lately."

"Why don't you schedule something with Walter Edmonds? It never hurts to be certain."

Dr. Edmonds was a neurologist.

A neurologist can diagnose neurological diseases.

A neurologist can end a career with the truth.

"I will do that today," Natasha said weakly.

"I don't see where it could hurt a thing," Dr. Walls said, smiling kindly. He turned to the sink and began to wash his hands meticulously.

NINE

For the past month or so, Ward had been able to remember his dreams only in piecemeal. While he'd been in Vegas he had dreamed, and his dreams had included a recurring nightmare, that he was lying in warm water as thick as motor oil. There was pressure on his chest like someone sitting on top of him. Above him, moving into view like a cloud, was Natasha's face, abnormally white—bleached of its normal color—and there was a bright red line on her neck behind her collarbone. Ward could feel her hands on either side of his face, and he could see that she was crying. And over her shoulder he saw Barney materializing. Barney's face was illuminated a golden hue. And his son reached over his mother's shoulder and Ward reached up and took his hand, and he felt a remarkable lightness, and was floating up, up . . .

Ward McCarty awoke slowly to slits of bright sunlight being fractioned across the landscape of the guest bedroom wall like the stripes of a loping zebra. He heard the dull bumping as the hard-cloth vertical blinds swayed against each other, powered by the cold air rushing silently from the register below them. He closed his eyes and knew he hadn't dreamed at all.

Slowly Ward drew his strength together, sat up, moved his legs so his feet were on the hardwood floor, and yawned. The large red numbers on the alarm clock read 7:32. A white-coated Natasha was by now working her way through the hospital rooms. Or maybe she was already in a suite operating on some parents' child, those perfect hands moving deliberately to open and remove some part gone bad, to make a repair, to heal, to fix.

After showering and dressing, on his way out, Ward stopped in the hallway outside the door to Barney's bedroom. He pressed his ear up to the door quietly, as if to not wake his son. For long seconds he stood staring at the pattern of the hardwood.

After Barney died people had related to Ward differently—his old friends standoffish or guarded in their conversations with him. Friends with their own children had stopped calling after a few weeks, and Ward and Natasha's socializing had slowed to a crawl. They stopped going to the country club, and no longer attended services at

the First Methodist Church in Concord. It wasn't
that Ward blamed God for Barney's death; it was
just that he and his wife had lost interest in par-
ticipatory worship, just as they had lost interest
in a lot of other things they'd done as a family.
Ward hadn't lost his faith, but he didn't believe
that God was paying attention, believed that His
interference was as random as the flight of a discarded plastic shopping bag on the Interstate.

Something always drew him to open Barney's
door. He always approached the room shrouded
in the feeling that he was entering a tomb, and
entering was something he did with increasing
reluctance. Finally he reached down, pressed the
lever, and opened the door to what could have
been a museum exhibit dedicated to the beautiful boy. Barney had handled the objects on dis-
play, and his collection was open only at the
whim of the curators, only visited when they
felt a need to touch base. At that moment Ward
knew something was off, something he was supposed to do that he couldn't put his finger on.

His eyes went immediately to the wall that
held four wooden shelves, where colorful
NASCAR die-cast models were lined up, angled
with their grilles facing out like vehicles parked

and awaiting tiny drivers to jump in and roar away. There was an open slot in the center, like a missing tooth.

Ward hurried to the kitchen, located his briefcase, placed it on the counter beside the sink, and popped it open to discover that the prototype race car was not in its padded envelope. He felt sick to his stomach.

Jerking up the phone, he was already dialing Natasha's private number when he realized that she would not have opened his briefcase, much less taken the car from it. The receptionist answered on the third ring.

"Piedmont Pediatric Surgical. How may I help you?"

"Mary Katherine, it's Ward. Is Natasha in?"

"She went into surgery an hour ago. Can I have her call you when she gets back? Do you want her voice mail?"

"No, I'll talk to her later." He pressed the off button and, feeling hollow inside, replaced the phone in its charging base.

Ward's mind raced over the last time he'd seen the car and he remembered taking it out on the plane, but he'd definitely put it back after the girl looked it over. "God damn her!" he shouted.

After grabbing his car keys and briefcase, Ward took off for his office with his mind racing. He had told the girl to call his secretary, Leslie, for that free car he'd offered to give her for her NASCAR-fan mother. If she followed through, he would talk to her, or at the least have an address so he could find her. He felt a wave of fear and uncertainty. Accusing her of stealing would be awkward, but he had to get the prototype back. As he got out of his car in the parking lot in front of his building he wondered how many of the electronic devices in her bag were pilfered from other unsuspecting people she'd run across.

Just wait until little Miss Bad Hair finds out that lifting that little toy was grand larceny.

TEN

Watcher was in the kitchen of his rented house drinking coffee when the GPS showed McCarty's BMW two miles away, getting farther. A minute later, Watcher left the house and moved rapidly through the woods, down the hill behind the McCartys' house and up the slope, carrying his rucksack. He passed beside the swimming pool and, first using a device to fool the house alarm system, he opened the far left garage with a multifrequency transmitter. He closed the door behind him. The McCartys had good reason to believe their alarm system was impenetrable, and it would have been for any but the best professional burglars. Watcher wasn't interested in taking anything but their lives.

Using the spare key he'd predictably found hidden under the doormat months before and copied, he entered the McCartys' kitchen and strode down the utility hallway. Passing the laundry room, he went straight into the large storage room.

Metal shelves loaded with cardboard and plastic boxes wrapped the room. Watcher went to the box marked "Christmas Decorations" that he had selected and took it down. It was unlikely to be opened. He took the digital recorder from the box and downloaded the audio and video into his laptop computer. He had audio-only bugs that transmitted to a recorder in the home he rented nearby, but he didn't depend on those. He needed to visit the house anyway. He walked through the rooms, read the mail, and used his senses to gather intelligence that even the expensive cameras and sound microphones couldn't pick up. And most important, he had to come inside to fuck with things.

In the doctor's bedroom he paused only long enough to pilfer the stuffed bear. Perhaps he would take more than life.

In the kitchen he looked at the calendar and used a red pen to circle the anniversary of their child's death. After capping the pen, he noted the glasses in the sink and sniffed the highball glass, detecting the odor of Scotch. He smiled, imagining the gloomy void Ward had been trying to fill the night before. He checked to see if the doctor had purchased any new bottles of the juice she drank, and saw that she had purchased two since the last time he'd visited. Watcher used a syringe to penetrate the cartons and add a thin stream of liquid.

Watcher lifted the Scotch glass and set it carefully upside down in the sink beside the wineglass. He left the house the way he'd come, the small stuffed bear tucked under his arm.

ELEVEN

The year before Ward was born, his father purchased eighteen acres of farmland three miles from the Lowe's Motor Speedway complex, which despite being technically located in Concord, was then called the Charlotte Motor Speedway. His father bought the land figuring that even if his business failed, or if NASCAR turned out to be a flash in the pan, Concord and Charlotte would eventually grow together and the land would be a solid long-term investment. In those early years most racetracks were going through tough financial times because ticket sales often failed to cover track expenses. In those days, the big names in racing were, were related to, or were trained by the ex–moonshine runners who had begun racing each other in their over-powered coupes—fitted with tanks for carrying liquid contraband—on small dirt tracks throughout the South. Ward loved the illicit history of his legitimate business.

The crude structure that had housed Raceway Graphic's first three employees—a two-thousand-square-foot Quonset hut built as an equipment garage in 1937—had since grown into a fifty-thousand-square-foot complex of offices and design studios, an employee cafeteria, the stock warehouse, and shipping dock.

A tree-lined parking lot in the front was for office employees and visitors while another larger one to the side served warehouse workers and delivery trucks. Picnic tables, protected by a roof, allowed employees to eat lunch outdoors when the weather was pleasant. Ward's father had personally planted a number of the trees.

Ward had hardly gotten to the reception desk when his uncle waved at him from the mezzanine stairs.

Mark Wilson, sixty-three years old, had a full head of white hair and a neatly trimmed beard. Ward McCarty, Sr., called Wardo by everyone who knew him, had started the company alone. But after a few months, when he'd needed both operating capital and help, he had sold his brother-in-law—then a successful car salesman—forty-five percent of the company's stock for five thousand dollars. Ward Sr. had been a thoughtful introvert with no marketing or sales experience, and no interest in learning any. Mark was the opposite, and together they'd made a dynamic partnership for thirty-eight years.

Mark and Ward's father had spent most of their workdays together, as well as countless long days and nights on the road during race season, peddling their merchandise at the race-tracks from a small trailer.

Wilson played tennis and golf and knew the names of the coaches and players and the rankings of every professional and college baseball, football, and basketball team in the country, one of which was always sure to break ice with both suppliers and customers.

"How was your trip?" he asked, slapping Ward's shoulder paternally. Ward had always been the closest thing Mark had to a son, and for the past few years Mark was the closest Ward had to a father figure.

"Fine," Ward said. "Same old bunch. My feet hurt as much as my eyes."

"Always the same. Bunny enjoyed the slots more than seeing Wayne Newton." He lowered his voice. "How did your meeting with the video game designer go Saturday night?"

Ward smiled. "Great. I saw the beta version of

Driver's Seat and even got to play with it for an hour. The accelerator and braking are perfect, but the steering and suspension controls have to be adjusted. The handling is still sort of sloppy, but it has even better graphics than I'd imagined. Unk, it's so real on the monitor I swear I could smell the tires burning when I made my way around a six-car crash on turn two."

"I'm glad to hear it. It's going to make you rich, nephew. Beyond rich. Look at Grand Theft Auto. Tens of millions. And with the race downloads available."

"If people buy it, it'll make us both rich."

Mark grinned, shrugged. "RGI was always your father's dream, and I know you came in because Wardo and I needed you. The game is all your dream, kid. And the first of many, I'm sure.

"So, how's your mother?" Mark said, furrowing his brows.

"No change," Ward said. "At this point that's real good. She still thinks I'm my father."

"I'm sorry, Ward. Hey, Bunny is excited about spending next weekend with you guys. My gal loves the spa, and it shows. Am I right?"

"What?"

"Next weekend. In Asheville at the Biltmore Hotel."

"Sorry?" Ward asked, tilting his head.

"You said you and Natasha would join us. I made the reservations right after we spoke last night."

"Yes," Ward said uncomfortably. Bunny Wilson was Ward's age and she treated Mark more like a rich elderly uncle than a husband. Natasha believed that Bunny was far smarter and conniving than she let on. After the wedding, when Ward had made a "trophy wife" comment, Natasha had said, "I wonder who got the one for first place."

Mark had met Bunny at the Speedway Club, where she'd been a bartender who'd spent her time flirting, mostly with men who should have been old enough to know it was their bankbooks that she found attractive. Natasha resented the fact that Mark and his wife of twenty-four years hadn't had children only because Mark hadn't wanted any. So naturally, when he left Ward's aunt because Bunny was pregnant with his child, it pissed Natasha off. Women took intimate betrayal personally. A week after Mark proposed and set a certain date, Bunny suffered a miscarriage while visiting an old friend in San Francisco. When Ward told Natasha that Bunny had lost the baby, she shook her head in amusement. "Surprise, surprise," she said. "Imagine how she'd have looked pregnant in a wedding gown."

Ward had never been close to his aunt Ashley because she'd openly resented the fact that her brother hadn't made Mark an equal partner in RGI. She had believed that Mark deserved to own the majority of stock in the company because he did most of the "real" work. And Ashley McCarty Wilson had acted as though she was somehow superior to Ward's mother in every way. When they were together the tension was palpable, but Ashley had been kind to Ward and Natasha and had spoiled Barney with expensive toys and lavished him with her attention. Since Barney's death she had all but stopped communicating with Ward and Natasha. Ward supposed it was because she couldn't face being reminded of her only nephew, and because Ward loved the man she now hated.

"I'm going to give you help with your golf game next weekend while the girls bond in the antique shops," he added. "You need something to get your mind off work."

"I don't have a golf game," Ward said. "I'm surprised the PGA hasn't asked me to sell my clubs." Ward decided that he would wait a day and tell Mark his wife had surgeries scheduled, or some such excuse. And, truthfully, he didn't believe Bunny actually wanted the four of them to spend a weekend together any more than Natasha would. "I still have to run next weekend past Natasha," Ward said.

"You didn't clear it with her?"

"She was already asleep, and she was gone when I got up. If she has conflicts, you guys will understand, right?"

Mark looked disappointed, and Ward felt the way he always felt when Natasha refused an invitation to be with Bunny.

Ward went up the stairs. Checking his cell phone's log he saw that Mark had called him at ten-thirteen the night before. They had talked for eleven minutes. And Ward did not remember it.

TWELVE

Leslie Wilde had worked for RGI for two years and had been Ward's secretary for fourteen months. Anna Bost, who had been his father's secretary, was seventy-eight when she'd finally retired and moved to a condo in Charleston. Leslie had been the first applicant. She was bright, efficient, attractive, and quick-witted, and since she already worked for the company and had a reputation, he'd hired her.

Leslie was busy at her computer terminal when Ward entered her office, which was just next door to his.

"Good morning, Leslie."

"How was the trade show, Mr. McCarty?" she asked him, smiling.

"Busy," he told her.

"I put the order sheets on your desk," she said. "I also have a stack of letters for your signature, and the new inventory report. The calls you need to return ASAP are on yellow Post-its, the should-be-returned-at-your-earliest on blue, and the standard sales calls on green. No personal calls."

Ward had resisted installing an automated messaging system because he hated listening to a recorded voice and punching numbers to navigate to an actual person. He did have voice mail, but Leslie always asked the caller if she could take a message, or if they wanted to leave a message on Ward's voice mail. Most left a message with her, which further reinforced his belief that given a choice, people preferred to interact with living, breathing humans. *Please listen carefully, as our options have changed. Please press one because we're insensitive assholes who are too cheap to hire an employee to answer your call.*

"Very good," he said. "Listen, Leslie. There's something I want to mention. If a young lady calls to ask for a die-cast car that I offered her for her mother on the flight home, get her name and mailing address."

"You don't know her name?" Leslie asked, reaching for a pen.

"No. I told her I'd give her a die-cast car if she'd call. Get her name and address for me."

A look of concern crossed Leslie's features, as

she made a note to herself, then stared at Ward with alert brown eyes.

"Do you want to talk to her?" She was familiar with Ward's slipping memory, and she, like everyone else in the offices, knew of his mother's illness. It had crossed his mind more than once that the same disease might be sneaking up on him from behind like an assassin. Ward was too young, wasn't he?

"No. Tell her you'll mail her the car unless she wants to pick it up," he said, not wanting to chance spooking the girl. That is, if she called.

Ward went to his office, which had remained pretty much the way his father had left it—cluttered but clean. He hadn't cleaned out but a few of his father's personal items, merely introducing a few of his own. Wardo hadn't had a computer in his office, preferring to write out personal correspondence by hand, or type business letters on his Selectric, using carbon paper. In his last years, he'd had his secretary type that which needed formalizing and make copies for files.

Ward, a generation later, had a desktop and a couple of laptops. A picture of his family stood on his desk that had been taken in Killarney,

Ireland. Dermott O'Caloughan, the owner of the Failte Hotel, had taken it the year before Barney died. Natasha had commented that she'd never visited any place as warm, or any place that had so many tourist shops whose inventory was comprised of so many things she didn't want to own. There was a second picture of Wardo, Mark, and himself taken during a charity tournament on the golf course at the Cabarrus Country Club. All three of the men smiled out from the framed snapshot like successful politicians who hadn't yet been caught at skullduggery.

For an hour Ward took care of necessary business. He was just about to walk to the warehouse to go over the incoming inventory, and to the studio to check the progress of designs on new products, when Leslie appeared at the open door, her long black hair tucked neatly behind her ears.

"Gene Duncan's secretary called to remind you that you're supposed to meet him for lunch at eleven-thirty at the Speedway Club. I don't have it on your planner."

"Today?" Ward asked. He didn't remember making the appointment. *Christ.* "Tell him I'll see him there."

As she turned to leave, Ward remembered something. "Leslie, are you still dating that private detective?"

"Yes," she said. "Todd Hartman."

"Is he good?"

Her cheeks flushed.

"Sorry, I meant is he a good detective?"

She giggled. "He doesn't brag, but his friends all say he's the best around. He has like two full-time investigators, a secretary, and lots of freelancers he uses. He does a lot of work for lawyers."

"Does he work for individuals?"

"Yes. Sometimes."

"And you'd recommend him. Even if you weren't dating?"

"My friend Erica hired Todd to check out a guy she was dating. The guy had just moved to town and he never let her pay for anything. He drove a Mercedes, dressed expensively, wore an expensive watch, was attentive, knew wines, took her to expensive restaurants, was handsome, always said and did the right things. She works, even though she has a large inheritance her aunt left her. When he found that out, he mentioned he was getting a thirty to forty percent return on some Chinese farm machinery deal a friend of his got him into. She never committed to it, but said she'd think it over. He never tried to push her. One day he left out a check where she'd see it, and it was for two hundred thousand dollars. He said it was a quarterly return on the Chinese deal, which he had a million dollars invested in. He said in four years he'd gotten back his million and everything from there out was profits. She wanted to make that kind of money and he said he'd ask if there was any room for another investor, but he doubted it.

"He told her a week later that he'd convinced his buddies to let her buy in. That wasn't a red flag for her. The red flag was from her lawyer, who wondered why he wasn't involved or married already, and told her that any deal that looked too good to be true was generally a scam. The lawyer hired Todd, and Todd found out that Mr. Perfect was using a false name. He discovered the lover's real identity by collecting his fingerprints. Mr. Wonderful was a con artist, with a wife. The Mercedes was leased and his rap sheet was two feet long. Todd set up a sting using Erica and a dummy bank check for half a million dollars and the cops arrested the guy.

Erica thought I'd like Todd so she set us up on a blind date. I'd recommend him."

"Well, I've got a little problem. You know the girl I said might call about the die-cast?"

"She hasn't yet."

Ward told her about the girl and the missing prototype. Leslie listened without interrupting, until Ward said, "Can you give me his phone number and maybe even tell him I'm a nice guy before I call him?"

"Of course." She scribbled down a phone number. "I know he'll be happy to help you out. I've told him about you. I mean what a nice guy you are."

Ward hoped Hartman could find the girl and get the model back, because he doubted the police would spend the investigative energy that would be necessary to locate a phantom girl with no contact information to retrieve what amounted to a toy, but he figured a private detective would at least make an effort for a fee.

"Sure thing," Leslie said. "I'm meeting him for lunch."

"That would be great. And thanks."

THIRTEEN

Ward had lunch at the Speedway Club two or three times a week because it was convenient and afforded him an opportunity to keep in touch with clients. Except for the occasional race-related traffic delay, it was just five minutes from his office. The food was good, they billed him so he had a record for the IRS, and he was on a first-name basis with most of the staff.

The hostess was seated at her ornate desk in the circular marble-floored foyer and greeted him with a warm, familiar smile.

"Mr. McCarty," she chirped pleasantly. "How's Dr. McCarty?"

"Hello, Crystal. Natasha is fine," he said. As he walked through the doors the odor of food hit him like a warm wave.

The dining room was beginning to fill up with club members and their guests. Gene Duncan was already seated at a table in the lower level at one of the enormous windows that were canted to damper the vibration from the roaring engines, overlooking the one-and-a-half-mile oval track.

Ward walked down the wide carpeted stairs and made a beeline for his friend, who was charming a middle-aged waitress from Harrisburg. She had three children and two grandchildren, and was sometimes remiss in having her hair dyed blond. Her uniform accented her large breasts and wide hips but she was light on her sensible black shoes.

Gene Duncan, the end product of a marriage between a Scot and a German (both lawyers—one a superior court judge), and Ward McCarty had been friends since they were in kindergarten. Gene was over six feet tall, weighed two hundred and sixty pounds, and wore his brown hair swept back over the tops of his ears. He had a casual air that seemed in stark contrast to the two-thousand-dollar suits he wore. He looked up at Ward and smiled easily.

"Sweet tea, Mr. McCarty?" the waitress asked Ward. She poured his glass to the brim before jetting off in search of empty glasses on the nearby tables.

"Sweeter the better," he said to her back.

"How was your trip out west?" Gene asked,

opening his briefcase and taking out a notepad, which he studied with furrowed brows.

Ward knew he'd asked without really caring, so he said, "My plane went down in the Grand Canyon and I had to survive for three days on cactus and rattlesnakes. Luckily the rest of the passengers on board were showgirls. Well, there was Wayne Newton, but his wife was along."

"Glad to hear it. Couple of things to go over," Gene said.

Ward looked out the window to his right and spotted a film crew gathered near turn one, probably making a commercial. Ward recognized the car as being Jeff Gordon's. Gordon, recognizable by the race suit, stood against the car. He was a fearless, extremely talented driver, and also a clean, classy, and intelligent man with a sense of humor, possessing the handsome boyish looks of a male model. He was everything brusque billionaire Bruton Smith, the track's owner, could want for NASCAR's image. Recently, Smith had threatened to move the track, lock, stock cars, and barrel, because he had started building a huge drag strip on the property and the Concord City Council had mentioned he'd need a building permit. Approval of the council was required since the constant noise of dragsters thundering down the quarter-mile asphalt might annoy homeowners near the raceway. Having NASCAR races twice a year for a few days and nights was one thing, but this new drag strip?

Bruton Smith was not one to ask permission from any council. Once he had cut down one hundred old protected oak trees to add spaces to one of his parking lots. He'd had them cleared late at night and paid the fine instead of seeking permission.

The drag strip fight had been public and, after Smith threatened to move, the city ended up waging a very public and humiliating ass-kissing from the politicians to save the seventy million dollars the races put into the local economy annually. The campaign included small airplanes pulling WE LOVE YOU BRUTON and PLEASE DON'T GO BRUTON banners, renaming a main street for him, offering tens of millions in infrastructure improvements to be paid for using tax dollars, and more. Natasha had said, only half in jest, that they should watch the "grovel-to-grovel" coverage of those city council meetings on cable TV.

Ward leaned back in his chair, waiting.

"Flash Dibble has fattened his offer."

"Why would he do that, or better still, why do you keep listening to them and bringing them to me?"

"Because everything is for sale."

"I am familiar with the adage, but RGI is the sole exception in the known universe."

"This whole NASCAR thing has been phenomenal for the past few years, but once the yuppies get bored with the smell of gas fumes and burned rubber, it will suffer the same fate as disco music. Jeff Gordon will rank right up there with the Bee Gees. As gas prices and ticket prices rise, profits will continue to go down for speedways. Smell the times, old buddy. Look, Flash says you can run the company just like now, if you want to, and he's offering a million five more as added incentive, plus the thirteen million he already offered for your stock, and he'll pay your uncle seven point five for his," Gene said. "That's twenty-two million dollars cash!"

"Before taxes," Ward said, smiling.

"So, it's still a frigging fortune. That's serious fuck-you money any way you look at it. You should seriously consider it. Fourteen and a half million dollars ain't a bad payday. You can retire at thirty-five. And I think he might agree to pay you a percentage of profits for maybe five years. I know . . ." Gene raised his hands, palms out. ". . . He could stack expenses and lower the profits, but we can make that a percentage of gross before expenses. Hell, you could draw your pictures till your fingers bleed and put them in your own gallery and only let your friends in to see them, or just buxom blondes."

The idea of selling his company and sitting around his house with nowhere to go filled Ward with anxiety. And the idea of selling to Flash Dibble—it would never happen. "And I don't want to throw money into the air and see how much of the floor I can cover. Or drive a Bentley. Or play golf." Leaning in, Ward said, "And what about the video game?"

"He doesn't know about that. We can negotiate that when the time comes. That's *if* it ever gets past the designing stage."

"I saw the beta in Vegas. Paul assures me it will be finished, bugs out, within the next six months. It is so cool."

"Christ, Ward. You just repay the money RGI put up for the development, and you'll have nothing to worry about."

"That game should be part of RGI, and our employees should be rewarded. I still intend to do the profit-sharing thing, and after it's released would be the time to institute that."

"Your father would spin in his grave," Gene said, looking down as he said it. The mention of grave brought the same unpleasantness into both their minds. "Like I said. Just think it over."

"What's to think over? You think Flash Dibble would share profits with our employees?"

"Aside from that. Talk to Natasha. Mark has been there from the start, and he'll sell if he can."

"You've run the new offer by Unk?" Ward asked, blindsided and suddenly annoyed. "When?"

"We spoke Sunday afternoon at the country club. You were still out of town, and I didn't think you'd mind. Do you?"

"I guess not," Ward lied.

"He'd be a fool not to consider it. Mark's not getting any younger, and his skin is going to get blue from the Viagra he's got to be taking to keep Bunny happy."

Normally the friendly dig might have made Ward chuckle. "Well, I don't intend to sell the company. Unk can't sell his stock to anyone but me. What else?"

"But—"

"What else?" Ward locked his hands tightly together and frowned. His old friend knew when that was exactly that.

Gene flipped a page and looked at the sheet like whatever was written there was, before that moment, unknown to him. "Lander Electric's insurance company's attorneys want a meeting," Gene said. "They want to settle. I think it's the smart move. Ward, you need to get this behind you. Natasha agrees."

"Natasha told you she'd sign a confidentiality agreement? Jesus, Gene, how many meetings are you having behind my back?"

"She called me, Ward."

"She said she'd sign?" he asked, not believing what he was hearing. She knew how strongly Ward felt about that. If Lander wanted to settle, they'd have to let the world know what they did.

"A trial would be hard on both of you."

"They put in a regular outlet instead of a GFI to cut maybe eight bucks and add it to their bottom line, and it killed my son," Ward said, feeling the familiar anger boiling up inside him. He punched the table with his trigger finger. "I want everybody they ever wire a home for to be watching over their shoulders and making sure their cost-cutting can't kill anyone else. Not negotiable. End of discussion."

"There's the expense of a trial and no guarantee that you'll win the suit. Look, let's just hear their offer. They're looking at a lot of bad publicity and they don't want to admit wrongdoing."

"A confidentiality agreement is a deal-breaker," Ward told him. He wasn't going to let that company cover up what their cost-cutting did to his son, to him, to Natasha, to people who loved Barney or would have in the years to come. "If you feel real strongly about it, I can find another lawyer to handle it and you can bill me for your time and your out-of-pocket to date."

Gene threw up his hands in real exasperation. "You're the boss, Mr. Bullhead," he said. "I'll tell them, but as I've said a hundred and two times, they can drag this out for decades."

"I plan to live a very long time," Ward said. "Now, I'd like to eat and get back to work."

"Okay, one condition."

"Name it."

Gene put the pad away and closed his briefcase. He leaned across the table and fixed Ward with his dark blue eyes. "You'll tell me all about those showgirls you were stranded in the Grand Canyon with."

Ward laughed out loud and felt a wave of relief sweep over him. Gene smiled; then his eyes focused behind Ward, and he said in a low voice, "Trey Dibble at twelve o'clock and closing."

The scent of Trey Dibble's cologne ran ahead of the man like a wind-driven, toxic cloud. Ward braced himself and stared at the white linen tablecloth, clinging to the bright blue cloth napkin.

"Gene Duncan," the confident voice boomed from behind Ward. "They'll let anybody eat here. You know what they call a hundred lawyers drowning in the ocean? A good start."

"I've never heard that one before, Trey," Gene said, trying his best to hold on to his smile.

"You know the difference between a lawyer and a turd?"

"No," Gene said.

"Neither does anybody else," Trey said, snickering.

"Another good one," Gene said.

"Just kidding, Gene." Trey Dibble moved to the side of the table within Ward's view to shake Gene's hand.

"You know I'm crazy about you," Trey said.

Trey looked down at Ward and smiled as though he was surprised to see him there. Since Ward's company had a long-term contract for Flash Dibble's race team memorabilia, Ward looked up and forced himself to smile. He didn't personally care for all of his clients, but he was always polite to them. DME, or Dibble Motorsport Enterprises, ran a lot of money through RGI for the products they needed to sell to fans to promote their racing team.

Bracing himself, Ward shook the clammy hand belonging to the most unpleasant human being he knew.

Trey Dibble was a poster boy for the spoiled only son of a man who had worked both tirelessly and brilliantly most of his life to build a billion-dollar empire. Flash employed a lot of people, and appreciated—even if he didn't show it—people who had the ability to help build his holdings. So, on one hand, Ward had a lot of respect for what that man had accomplished and the good he'd done. Trey, on the other hand, had a reputation for doing damage without any positive results.

Without lifts, Trey was five five, weighed a good two hundred pounds, wore his inch-long black hair heavily oiled, and had bushy sideburns and a thin mustache that gave him the look of a local-cable-channel evangelist. His shirt was opened to show off a gold chain the size of a ski rope that supported a gold medallion with the letters *TD* spelled in diamonds within a field of rubies. The face of the gold Rolex precisely mirrored the medallion's design, and several thick gold bracelets wrapped his other wrist like overfed snakes.

"Ward, how the hell are you?" he asked, with the sincerity of a snake-oil salesman.

"Fine," Ward said. "And you?"

"Good as a man can feel with his clothes on. Speaking of which, this beautiful young thing is Tami with an i Waterman. Not terribly long ago she was featured in an issue of none other than *Playboy* magazine."

A woman in her late thirties, with overlarge lips, tight facial skin, and a sculpted nose, stepped into Ward's view. She was chewing enthusiastically on a piece of gum.

"Waterman like the pen. It's a French name. She's not Jewish," he said, smiling.

"I'm a Sagittarius," she said in a high-pitched voice that brought to mind a cartoon chicken character.

Trey guffawed and slapped Ward on the shoulder. "She's not Jewish, she's a Sagittarius! Tami, honey, this is Ward McCarty. You've heard me talk about him."

Tami Waterman's tight gold pantsuit coated her contours like latex, showing off her narrow waist and muscular legs. Her enormous breasts were like twin racing blimps, running neck and neck, and she wore enough jewelry to decorate a Christmas tree. She offered her hand to Ward as though she expected him to kiss it. He took her hand and shook it once, wondering if her inch-long nails were glued on.

"He inherited that little toy company you're buying, right?" she gushed. "I love toys."

"We're still talking it over," Trey said with a straight face. "Ne-go-see-ate-ting. Ward here is holding out . . . for a bigger payoff."

Ward ignored that, tried hard to keep the smile from falling from his face to the floor.

"Not toys. NASCAR memorabilia," Gene told her. "Everything the race fan desires."

"You don't sell those little toy cars?"

"They do," Trey said. "And a lot of other things."

Using her tongue, Tami moved her gum to one side. "Well, did you ever think about making calendars featuring drivers with their shirts off, maybe in BVDs. Female fans would buy them by the thousands, I bet. And what about a line of fragrances or charm bracelets with itsy-bitsy cars on—"

"Whoa, Tami!" Trey interrupted. "Don't give away your money-making ideas for free." He narrowed his eyes. "Man, I tell you, Ward. She has got a million of them."

Tami's smile wavered, and she looked at Trey before meeting Ward's eyes again. "You wouldn't steal my ideas, would you?"

"Of course not," Gene assured her. "New product ideas have never been a problem for Ward."

"Gene here tell you the good news?" Trey asked, changing the subject.

Ward turned his eyes to Gene, and despite

their friendship, wondered if this meeting was a chance encounter after all. *Try to read a lawyer's eyes sometime.*

"He was just telling me about your father's latest offer," Ward told him.

"Trey running a toy company," Tami said. "Can you just imagine it? His toys are mostly big expensive ones. Have you seen his new Viper? Oh, my god! Cherry red with those little sparkle flakes and heavenly yellow leather interior. And my lord, is it ever fast."

"I bought it because it matches her lipstick and hair," Trey said.

Ward couldn't think of anything at all to say that wouldn't have been insulting.

"Well, are we close to a deal yet?" Trey asked.

"We were just discussing it," Gene said.

"Actually," Ward said, "I've decided that although your father's offer is generous, I'm not interested in selling RGI at the present."

Trey's smile remained, but something in his eyes was now decidedly reptilian. "That so? We'll leave the door open awhile yet. I'm sure you'll come to see that selling to us is in everybody's best interest."

Ward felt his smile evaporate. "The truth is, I

don't imagine I can come around to see anything of the sort." He was sure Trey was unac-
customed to having people turn down offers, and
the fact that what Trey had just said sounded like
a threat made his blood boil. He wasn't afraid of
this malevolent slob on any level, and he would
never defile his father's company by turning it or
its employees over to this worthless sack of shit.
He wanted him to know it.

"Well, I'll let you two get back to your lunch
meeting," Trey said. "I expect this lawyer's
charging you an hour to watch him eat. I need to
work the room."

"You have to try the crab legs," Tami said, rubbing her stomach and rolling her eyes. "I ate
about twenty of them. I'll have to work out for
a week to get rid of the calories."

"She eats like a pig," Trey said. "How she
keeps her dancer's figure is a mystery to everybody."

Trey and Tami moved on to another table
to speak to the manager of the track. He
was sitting at a table with Dale Earnhardt, Jr.,
and three men in suits Ward didn't know.
Earnhardt, often called the best-loved driver in

the sport, had recently signed with a new team and would have a new number. Ward couldn't hear the conversation that Trey and Tami had hijacked, but Earnhardt's frozen smile was freakish in its insincerity, and Ward wondered if the young man might suddenly bolt for the door.

"I didn't know Trey would be here," Gene said, sincerely.

"The idea of that prick ordering our designers to work on Tami's product lines makes me want to throw a chair through this window."

Gene shrugged. "Twenty-two million dollars. Plus a percentage." He winked. "It's very appealing."

"Not if it was twenty-two billion. I'd live under a bridge first."

When Ward went to the buffet to fill his plate, he didn't so much as look at the crab legs, going straight for the beef tips.

FOURTEEN

When Ward returned to the office an hour later, Leslie was in her office talking with a man Ward recognized from the picture she had on her desk. Todd Hartman had short red hair. He sat bolt upright, with an athletic build featuring wide shoulders, narrow hips, and eyes that were the same pale blue-gray as a Siberian husky's. He was a couple of inches taller than Ward, and looked to be in his early thirties. He was seated beside Leslie's desk with an aluminum briefcase at his feet.

"Mr. McCarty, this is my friend, Todd Hartman."

Todd stood and shook Ward's hand with a firm assuredness.

"Mr. Hartman, it's a pleasure to meet you. I didn't expect you to come right over."

"Call me Todd. We had lunch earlier and Leslie said you needed some help recovering something, and I've got forty-five minutes before I'm due back in the office, so I figured if you came back in time and had a few minutes we could see how I might help you."

"Please come to my office and we can talk," Ward said.

He led Todd into his office and they sat opposite each other at the conference table. Todd placed his aluminum briefcase on the floor beside him.

"Leslie says you want to recover a model car that was stolen."

"That's pretty much it."

"Have you called the police?"

"No. I don't think law enforcement would be interested."

"What's the value?"

"I've never thought about it. I suppose to a serious collector, it's worth a thousand or more, but its sentimental value is immeasurable."

"Tell me about the theft first," Hartman said. "As much as you know about the circumstances surrounding the loss."

Ward showed Todd a picture of the car in its showcase his father had taken years before. He told Todd about the strange girl, his trip to the plane's lavatory, which left her alone with his briefcase, and opening the briefcase that morning to discover that the car was missing.

"Is this something you want to spend your time on?" Ward asked.

"Of course I want to help, and I think I can. Are you sure you want to invest in the recovery?"

"I am. So I guess we should discuss your fee."

"My base rate is seven a day plus expenses. I bill a buck a mile, and any additional personnel will be billed at forty dollars an hour. I usually ask for a two-day, nonrefundable retainer to cover my start-up costs, payable upon signing."

Ward nodded and thought about the expense for a few seconds.

"For friends, family, and Leslie's boss, the rate is three seventy-five a day plus straight expenses, and I'll forgo the retainer. This appears to be a simple recovery job and I doubt it'll take more than a day or two at the most. If I don't have it back by then I'll be surprised."

"I appreciate your generous offer, but I'll pay you your regular fee," Ward said. "And I insist on paying the standard retainer. If you were doing me a favor, I'd feel like I was imposing if I made suggestions, or wanted to be critical. Let's forget that you and Leslie are friends."

"That's fine," Todd said. "I don't want my personal relationship with Leslie to be awkward on a business level. I want to assure you that I don't discuss clients or my cases with anyone. Leslie knows that."

The fact was that Ward's father had often told him that if you hired someone to do a job at less than their normal rate, it was just human nature that you usually received a discounted effort. And Ward could certainly afford to pay the investigator his full fee.

"Then here's my standard contract." When Hartman opened his briefcase to remove a duplicating form and ballpoint pen, Ward saw the handgun in a holster nesting in the briefcase. It was a semiautomatic Colt 1911. Ward's father had had a similar weapon, although that one had been a standard government issue. Ward didn't know much about handguns, but Todd's gun was blue with stag grips and stainless accents. Because Natasha had hated the idea of having a firearm in the house with their child, Ward had given Wardo's gun to his uncle Mark, and she'd agreed to the enhanced alarm system as adequate protection from outside threats to the family.

"Your identity will be privileged information. The contract states that you can't be held legally liable for anything I do while working on your behalf. It also addresses other conditions and concerns to our mutual benefit," Todd told him.

"Like what might you do that I won't be held liable for?" Ward's mind flashed running gunfights, broken bones, breaking and entering, high-speed car crashes. This guy looked like someone who could do a lot of damage if he were so inclined.

"I always suggest clients read this, and even have a lawyer go over it before they commit. I also offer a list of satisfied clients so they can check me out, and it's sometimes helpful to talk to other investigators so they can compare rates before making an informed decision."

"Leslie is a good enough recommendation for me."

"Hopefully she's biased." Todd smiled disarmingly. "I can't guarantee a successful outcome, but I will do everything in my power to get the job done expeditiously, and I won't waste my time or your money."

"Then I won't waste your time reading it. We have to trust each other." Ward signed the contract using Todd's pen. "I'd like to get this moving."

"Then, if you could do me a favor, I'd like to give this my undivided attention. I'll turn over my caseload to my other investigators. They are as competent as any. I'm going to have Leslie on my back until this is resolved."

Ward smiled back and nodded. "Thank you," he said to Todd.

Without looking at Ward's signature, Hartman peeled off a copy for Ward to keep. Ward picked up his checkbook from his desk and wrote Hartman a check for fifteen hundred dollars.

"Tell me everything you can remember about the young woman."

"I don't really know any more about her than I've told you. I don't know her name, but I think I saw her in a dark-green or maybe black Porsche Cabriolet with a woman driving."

"That could be a helpful detail." Hartman placed the check into his briefcase and closed it. "I need your contact numbers. Home, cell."

"Where do you start?" Ward asked, handing Todd a card with his numbers on it.

"Talking to some people I know and tickling the keys on my computer," Todd said, putting Ward's card in his pocket. "Often as not this all hinges on contacts and following tracks left on servers as they go through life. You'd be amazed what you can discover about anybody in a few minutes with very little information." Hartman placed his own business card on the conference table and closed his briefcase, and Ward showed him to the door.

FIFTEEN

Since the legal system had failed to punish drunk driver and murderer Howard Lindley, Watcher had decided to handle the matter personally. Killing the man, or making him disappear, presented a problem since Watcher would be the sole suspect with motive and he was not a man who had any desire to live out his life in a cage. So Watcher had to make sure the death looked like an accident. With time on his side, Watcher monitored Lindley and waited until the timing was perfect before making a move. The Army had trained Watcher to be not only a killer but a thinking professional.

On a cool Friday night, after a football game, Watcher trailed Lindley and three of his buddies to a liquor store. After they bought two quarts of vodka the boys went to a cabin on Lake Norman that belonged to Lindley's father. Watcher knew everything he could find out about the Lindleys, but far more about their son, who was a killer and Watcher's target.

At nine o'clock the boys arrived at the large cabin and immediately started in on the vodka. At ten-thirty, five college-age girls arrived and joined the festivities. As the evening progressed, and the vodka bottles lost volume, Watcher studied the kids from the dark wooded lawn outside the house. As Watcher stood there he saw the girl Howard was trying to put the make on rebuff his advances. Howard, being the spoiled brat he was, slapped her, and one of his friends took her side, whereupon Howard and the boy wrestled around in the living room and threw a few drunken punches. Losing the bout, Lindley gave in and his friend released him. After standing, Lindley picked up a baseball bat from the

corner of the room and brandished it to intimidate his friends, saying he'd bash their brains in.
At that point the girls decided to call it a night,
and despite pleas from the other boys, they left
in a Honda sedan filled with cigarette smoke and
loud music. Watcher smiled grimly as an idea ce-
mented.

Howard and his friends rapidly adjusted
to the loss of female companionship and sang
along with their too-loud rap music until after three in the morning, when a man in a
robe came rushing out of the next house and
across the lawn to pound heavily on the front
door.

Howard answered the door with the baseball
bat in his hand. The man demanded that the
boys cut off their music and get to sleep before
he called the cops and lawyer Lindley. Howard
kept the weapon at his side but told the neighbor there was no sense waking his father. After
the man left, the boys, deprived of their music
and out of vodka, decided to go to bed.

By four, the boys were all passed out in their
beds. The only light was from a television set in
the living room. Watcher waited half an hour before going to his vehicle and getting a bottle he

kept in his work satchel. After putting on latex gloves, he entered the house, took a washcloth from the bathroom, and doused it with chloroform. Moving to Lindley's bed, Watcher placed the cloth over the drunk kid's face and held it tight until he stopped resisting, which took minimal effort. That done, Watcher put the cloth in his coat pocket, took a look at the unconscious young killer, and stripped off his own clothes. He took Howard's clothes—piled on the floor—and put them on. Howard wore ridiculous, loose-fitting clothing, so they fit the much larger man reasonably well. Sitting on the side of the bed, he slipped on Howard's flip-flops to cover the footprint angle. Taking up the aluminum baseball bat, he went from bedroom to bedroom making an unbelievable mess of the other young men's heads. The boys were so drunk they didn't awaken at the hollow wet smacking sounds Watcher made.

When Watcher returned to Howard's room, he flipped on the lights and, looking in the mirror, admired the amount of gore covering Howard's clothes. The wet shoe patterns stood out on the hardwood. He wiped blood on Howard's hands and he put the bat in them so the kid's bloody fingerprints were clearly printed on the handle like words on the pages of a Bible.

In the bathroom, Watcher stripped off and dropped the saturated clothes onto the floor, covering the bat. Watcher ran a bath, got in, and let the water grow pink with the blood of dead boys. He dried off, and laid out the towel before stepping onto it. After dressing he placed the towel in a plastic Wal-Mart bag he'd brought along in the back pocket of his jeans.

The last thing he did was carry the naked Howard Lindley into the bathroom and place him in the tub, washing him and using a plastic glass to rinse his hair. Lindley remained unconscious the entire time.

His work done, Watcher slipped from the cabin, and, after removing his surveillance equipment from young Lindley's Tahoe, he returned to the lake house, raised the windows in the den overlooking the neighbor's house, and turned on the stereo full blast. He slipped out the back door and crossed yards stealthily until he came to his truck.

Even now, fifteen months later, Watcher found himself smiling at the totally impromptu plan, spurred by the sight of the bat Lindley had been using to threaten his friends.

He gave little thought to the dead boys in the cabin.

They should have chosen their friends better.

SIXTEEN

When Ward got home at five-thirty, there was a message on the answering machine from Natasha. "I won't be home before eight, so I guess you better fend for yourself for dinner." He replayed the message twice, listening closely. Each time her clinical delivery left him cold. These days she left messages, even though she knew he always carried his cell phone.

Ward took a long cool shower, changed into a T-shirt and shorts, and turned on the television to the local news.

Ward's cell phone rang at a few minutes past seven. The caller ID showed a number he wasn't familiar with.

"Ward McCarty," he said.

"Mr. McCarty, it's Todd Hartman. I hope this isn't a bad time."

"No, it's a good time."

"Just wanted to let you know I've tracked the young girl down."

"That was fast," Ward said.

"Alice Palmer. That's her name. She's eighteen. Five five, ninety pounds, blond hair, green eyes. Her license picture fits your description. Attends UNCC, math major, with a petty rap sheet that points to a troubled, not a criminal, young woman. She lives with her mother in a three-quarter-million-dollar home in Dillworth. Her mother, Delores Palmer, sells high-dollar residential real estate and she makes mid–six figures. Drives the Porsche you saw to impress prospective clients, and has a large BMW to ferry clients around in. Alice travels to Vegas to see her father a few times a year. She probably doesn't know the monetary value of the car. This was probably for attention from someone. Maybe the parents."

"What do you do next?"

"I'll catch her in the A.M. on her way to classes on campus. Lots of people around so it's a safe atmosphere for her. I'll talk to her and I'll know where we are."

"Great work," Ward said.

"Nothing to it. Just a short conversation with a friendly aviation employee I have on my Christmas list, followed by a computer search. I'll call after the meeting to let you know what happens."

Ward hung up and his eyes came to rest on the calendar on the counter. He saw that Natasha had marked the anniversary of Barney's death with a red circle. He wondered why she'd have to mark the date to remember that day. While she hadn't mentioned anything to Ward, he couldn't help wondering what she had planned to do on the anniversary.

SEVENTEEN

When headlights illuminated the backyard it was eight-twenty. Ward was in his kitchen and had poured a Scotch to help obscure the memory of his afternoon visit with his mother, who hadn't spoken to him for the hour he'd been there. The disease had about run its course, reducing her to a slow-breathing mannequin lying in a bed staring at the ceiling.

Standing at the sink, he noticed the glasses still there from the night before, and Natasha's orange juice glass from her morning jolt. Thinking he should put them in the dishwasher, he was struck by the fact that he'd put his expensive Riedel glass, designed specifically to allow for the appreciation of fine Scotches, rim down in the sink. He never did such a thing. No, he didn't recall putting that glass in the sink the night before, but he always set glasses base down, especially those, to prevent chipping the delicate rims. He wondered if Natasha had done it without thinking, but that was not like her. If she touched it, she would have only done so to put it into the dishwasher.

He heard Natasha's car door slam shut out in the garage, followed by the sound of the garage door's motor engaging. When Natasha came in, Ward was drying the clean glasses with a towel. He opened the refrigerator, took out a bottle of Pinot Grigio, pulled out the cork, and poured some into her glass.

"How was your day?" he asked her.

"Not real good," she answered, fingering her

way through a stack of unopened mail he'd left on the counter.

"Generally or specifically?" he asked.

"I had a session with Dr. Richardson this afternoon."

He handed her the glass of chilled wine. "And did the shrink make you feel better?"

"No. But I appreciate your genuine concern."

"I didn't mean anything, but if he doesn't make you feel any better, why do you keep going to him twice a week?"

"You can take one of the sessions."

"Did he tell you again that I'm in denial?"

She glared at him reflexively for a second before looking away.

"Have you eaten?" he asked, changing the subject.

She shook her head.

"Good," he told her, handing her the glass. "I'll whip us up a little something."

She frowned. "Like what? Peanut butter on rye?"

"How about pasta with garlic butter and a delightful Caesar salad?" Ward had already checked the fridge when he had been trying to decide if he had the energy to make himself dinner.

"Sure," she said, smiling quizzically. "You make the salad while I boil the water."

"You don't trust me to boil water?" he asked. He gave her a reluctant smirk. "God, you have an impeccable memory, Natasha."

"How about because you make a great salad," she replied, a smile gracing her face for the first time in days.

Twenty minutes later, Natasha and Ward were seated at their dining table with the lights dimmed. Although he'd brought the bottle to the table, her wine was untouched.

"How was your day?" she asked, taking a mouthful of her salad and chewing slowly.

"I had lunch with Gene," he told her.

"Did you?" She looked down at her plate as she rolled linguini onto her fork delicately.

Ward took a sip of his Scotch, savoring it before swallowing. He wasn't hungry. "He told me you're willing to settle with Lander. He seemed to think you'd sign a nondisclosure agreement."

Natasha set her fork down. "I don't want this dragging out for years over that one point."

"I thought we agreed on that point."

She lifted her glass of wine and stared at it. "Barney's gone. Nothing will bring him back, but we have to go on. I have to go on."

"He's not *gone* anywhere," Ward said quickly. "He's dead."

Natasha's eyes filled with tears. "You imagine I don't know he's dead. He was killed by the actions of some idiot and I'm mad as hell about it. Beyond mad. I just want to stop feeling so mad, so damned empty, or whatever it is I'm feeling all the time. Maybe if this suit was over we could get on with our lives."

Natasha looked out through the windows. "I can't keep hating faceless electricians."

"Natasha," Ward heard himself saying. "I'm dead set against settling. This is not something we're doing to be vindictive. This suit is supposed to be for Barney, not us. So they'll remember. So some good can come from this. The money from this suit is going to help children who need helping. Kids who will have a chance to live longer lives because of Barney." *Instead of Barney living longer.*

Natasha said, "I know all of that. Can we please change the subject?"

Ward finished his Scotch and set his glass down. Natasha took a sip of her wine.

"Flash Dibble raised his offer for the company," Ward said.

"The amount hardly matters, does it?" she said.

"The idea of selling the company to the Dibbles makes my skin crawl," he said honestly. "I don't know how much clearer I can make that to Gene. Trey was there and I told him to his face that he'd never get his hands on the company. I think even Gene understands, but I doubt it."

"Gene's a lawyer," she said.

"He's my best friend."

"Yes, he is. But he is seeing the fees attached to a twenty-million-dollar transaction he'll handle."

"That's true enough. Can't blame him there."

Natasha took another sip. "What does your uncle want to do?"

"We haven't discussed it lately, but Gene told me he'd sell. Unk stands to make seven million dollars. I'm sure Bunny knows."

"Well, couldn't you buy Unk out?"

Ward hadn't thought about that, but he imagined he could get a loan to buy Unk's stock. "I suppose I could."

Natasha put it into words. "It wouldn't be the same company without him. No offense, but he is the people person. He has the close relationships with the clients."

Ward tried to imagine the company without his uncle, and couldn't, because he knew that his uncle was such an integral part of the business that his absence was unimaginable. It would take a team to replace him, and Mark was RGI in the minds of most of their client base.

"I'd need at least two people to take his place. We have other salesmen, but he's the closer. He makes sure the contracts are fair to us, and to the customers."

"Gene could help you with the contracts," Natasha said. "He looks them over and passes on them anyway. And I'm sure Unk would still help you out. You could pay him, pay for his entertaining the clients."

"I hired the guy who's been dating Leslie."

"For what? I thought he was a private investigator."

"I hired him to be a private investigator."

Natasha's eyes grew large with disbelief. "Why would you hire a private detective?"

Ward told her the story about the stolen prototype, and how Todd had already located the girl who took it.

"Why did you take it with you?" she asked. Precisely the question he didn't want her to ask, because she knew the answer. *It was Barney's favorite toy.*

He shrugged. "Just an impulse. I shouldn't have. Maybe the same reason you took Barney's baseball out of his room and put it in the bowl in the den."

"What are you talking about? I found that ball where you put it."

Ward couldn't believe what he was hearing. "Where I put it?"

"Under the other pillow in my bed. The one you used to lay your head on. Remember that pillow?"

"I'm pretty sure I would have noticed taking the ball out of Barney's room. Why the hell would I put it under your pillow?"

"*Your* pillow," she said angrily. "Just like you didn't take Barney's watch from my jewelry box, or any of the other things you don't want to or can't remember. I'm sick of these games, or whatever they are." She looked at him with genuine concern. "Maybe you should see someone to make sure it isn't . . ." She didn't say it.

"It is not early Alzheimer's," he said defensively, but he'd sure as hell wondered the same thing over the past three months.

"I never said it was. You're way too young. You're just under a lot of pressure. We both are. But it worries the hell out of me, and it should worry you. I have no idea what it is, but it's sure something. Maybe it's your nightly Scotch consumption."

"Maybe it's not all me," Ward said.

"Ward, you have to see a professional. If not Richardson, then someone else. Find out what this memory loss is. Deal with your grief. The sleeping late is probably because you don't sleep at night."

"Don't sleep! I sleep like a dead man. Is this going to be the grief counselor discussion?" he said. "Someone who can help me forget about Barney? I don't want to forget about him like you seem willing to do." He immediately regretted saying it.

"I'm not sure what I want," she replied sadly.

"But I can't keep going like this. I just can't. It's killing me, Ward."

"Natasha, do you still love me?" He wished he hadn't asked the question, but there it was, hanging like a cloud in the air between them.

"What kind of question is that?" she asked, looking at him angrily.

He shrugged. "One that has been on my mind lately."

"You honestly have to ask me that?"

"I saw the letter from your doctor friend in Seattle."

She didn't accuse him of snooping, nor did she say it was an old letter that was of no consequence. What she said was, "I was seriously considering his offer, but just as an alternative. I'll tell you the truth. I don't honestly know how I feel about anything or anybody at this point. I have feelings for you, but you're a different person. I never know how you are going to react to anything. You forget things and you do things you say you didn't do, things only you could have done. Maybe you're walking in your sleep. That might explain things. Who else could be moving things around?"

"You blame me for Barney," he said.

Natasha rolled her eyes. "The only person who blames you is you. It was a horrible accident. That's what *accident* means. If one of us blames the other, it isn't me."

"But you could have saved him," he said, an anger growing. "Don't tell me you haven't thought a million times that if you'd just been here instead of me, he'd be alive. You would have resuscitated him. Admit it. You think I killed him."

"Your feelings of guilt are self-induced. You're projecting what you feel inside onto me."

"I can't talk about this," he said, feeling nauseated.

"Then what else can we talk about?" she asked, throwing her napkin on the table. "You want the truth? My son is dead and now I feel like you want me to get into his grave with you. Maybe you want to die, but I don't. I won't."

Natasha stood and rubbed her eyes with the heels of her hands. "Right now, I just want to take a hot bath and go to sleep." She started to leave, her eyes filled with fury, perhaps disgust, but definitely tears.

"Don't forget your Ambien." He knew better than to say that, but he'd said it anyway.

"Go to hell," she said, storming from the room.

After she slammed her bedroom door, he stared at her plate, her nearly full glass, and for a second Ward had the strangest feeling that Barney was watching him. He stared out through the dark window and he could almost see his son standing there, staring at him. His look would be asking, *Why are you being mean to my mama?*

I don't know, Barney, Ward thought. He was sure Natasha had put the ball under the pillow. Why would anyone else do such an absurd thing? It wasn't the first time in recent weeks; either she'd moved things around and accused him or he had done so and didn't remember. Sure, he had felt oddly detached from the real world, but not that disconnected. If one of them was losing his mind, he didn't think it was only him.

Ward walked down the hall and stood frozen outside Natasha's door. He wanted to go to her. He wanted to hold her, to be in her arms again the way it was before. He raised his hand, but he couldn't force himself to knock. He imagined her lying alone in their bed. He wanted to comfort her, to make love to her, to make her feel something for him, but somehow he couldn't make the leap.

He thought about the last time they'd made love, seven months before, and how mechanical and unsatisfying it had been. Love with a stranger, but who had been the stranger? Filled with the fog of uncertainty and perhaps insecurity, he just could not make himself open the bedroom door.

He moved silently into the guest bedroom and, without taking off his clothes, lay awake in the dark for what seemed like hours after getting into bed. Something he couldn't understand, or didn't want to admit, was keeping him from reaching out and trying to make things right.

Ward couldn't imagine life without Natasha, but forgetful or not, he wasn't going to pay some pompous, two-hundred-dollar-an-hour asshole to make him let go of Barney.

EIGHTEEN

After leaving Ward at the dinner table, Natasha took a long warm shower, brushed her teeth, and toweled off her hair.

She was still upset—more upset than angry—and mostly because she'd blown an opportunity to really talk with Ward and resolve their problems. Her psychiatrist had suggested that she give Ward an ultimatum of sorts, force him to understand what he was about to throw away. Barney was dead, and she'd accepted that. She knew Ward knew it as well, but he couldn't put it aside and move on with what was left of his life—of their life together.

She often wondered how she, Barney's mother, was trying so hard to come to terms with Barney's loss and her husband wasn't. She had carried him in her womb, had given birth to him, nursed him, and loved him beyond rationality or description. Yes, Ward had seen him die, had held his cooling body as he waited in immeasurable anguish and pain for the ambulance to arrive. Yes, Ward alone had suffered that, but she certainly felt the same horror and grief even so.

Due to the demands of her career, Ward had spent more time with Barney than she had, and in the last years had been closer. She couldn't compete with the father/son contact and shared interests that became more and more important to them both. As a woman she'd been the odd one out, and she'd accepted that—had welcomed watching their bond strengthen, even at the expense of her own. She knew she loved Barney every bit as much and missed him every bit as deeply. How could it be otherwise?

Ward appeared to be in more pain, and it most bothered her that there was a wall between them that kept them from sharing the pain, the grief, from talking about their lives, and how they would go forward together. She wanted nothing more than to be in Ward's arms, to feel him against her, his warmth to fight away the cold, his strengths to shore her weaknesses, to lessen her fears, maybe even somehow mute their emptiness.

Natasha climbed into bed and turned off the lamp. She reached for the familiar stuffed bear, and after not finding it where she'd left it, ran her hands top to bottom and side to side over the bed, seeking it. Turning on the lamp she got on all fours and, from the bed, looked around the floor. Panicked, Natasha slid off the bed to peer under it, but the bear was not there.

She climbed back into bed, cut the light off, and tried to decide what to do. She didn't want to confront Ward and demand the toy's return. That was impossible after she'd made the point about him taking the little blue car to Las Vegas to be close to something Barney had treasured above all of his other possessions, even the bear.

At Ward's insistence, she had recorded the bear's short message for her child's ears alone. She had imagined that anytime he needed to be comforted by his mother, and she wasn't there, he would have her assurance that her love was constant and he was safe.

Ward had obviously taken it, and if he had, it was maybe because he had needed it as an anchor, since his own line to his dead child—the metal car—had been stolen from him. If he needed Buildy more than she did at the moment, she only prayed that if he pressed the bear's hand, her message would comfort him.

Through everything, Natasha had fought to

believe in God, and to believe that He had their son in His arms and loved him—as she had been taught since childhood—more than his parents possibly could. Hugging a pillow to her, she prayed to God to keep Barney in His arms so that he was never afraid, and that God would make sure the boy knew how deeply his parents loved him.

NINETEEN

From his hide overlooking the house, Watcher observed the couple through his binoculars as they ate dinner. The romantic tint to the evening was an unpleasant development, but his spirits soared when the meal was ended by an argument. Dr. McCarty stood up, had a few heated words to say—no doubt about what a limp-dick idiot her hubby was—and left the room. Seconds later her bedroom light came on. Ward remained seated at the table alone after she was gone. The man watched through the binoculars as Ward stared out through the window into the darkness—a beetle in a jar. Watcher knew McCarty couldn't see him, but he found himself holding his breath as their eyes met.

Watcher waited until Ward was in the kitchen cleaning up like a housewife before he put down the binoculars. He pulled out his survival knife and the diamond stone and started sharpening the blade slowly and deliberately. The tip was the only part of the knife he had used in a long time, and it was the tip he concentrated on sharpening while he waited in the hole he'd dug into the earth.

He looked at the blade in the moonlight, tested the edge with the sole of his thumb. He felt the notches he'd filed into the top of the blade near the hilt years earlier. Each represented a man killed in a war in a country whose landscape looked like the surface of Mars. He had liked doing it, more than that; Watcher had felt like he'd been born to end the lives of his enemies.

The luminous hands on his watch dial told Watcher it was nine-forty. He gathered his binoculars, notebook, and camera, and packed them all away in the rucksack. That done, he lifted the hinged roof and slipped out of the hide, lowering the lid until it was flush with the ground. Slowly, he walked through the woods with the pack over his shoulder.

Because tomorrow was going to be a very busy day, he would sleep tonight. In the morning, he would go into the house to collect the tape and he'd find out exactly what it was they had been arguing about. Their marriage was at the breaking point, and that gave Watcher a decidedly warm feeling. If things were allowed to run their natural course, the once perfect couple would break up and go their separate ways. Time was too short for that to happen.

TWENTY

After Dr. McCarty left the house at five A.M. on Tuesday morning, Watcher went into the garage and removed the GPS from under Ward's BMW and dropped it into his rucksack along with the stuffed bear. Inside the house he collected his recorder, since he wasn't going to need video going forward from here. He moved silently through the house collecting the other cameras and microphones that were tied into the recorder, leaving only the ones that transmitted so he could access them remotely.

He looked at the thrown-back covers and he leaned down so his face was inches above the sheets. Watcher drank in the scent of the doctor. Smiling, he made up the bed, pulling the sheets and spread tight enough to bounce a quarter on, and all the while wondering what it was going to be like to get a good look at her internal organs.

He looked at the curtains and couldn't see the microphone that was pinned into the top seam. There had been no need to visually record people sleeping.

He eased Dr. McCarty's door closed and crossed to the bedroom where Ward slept. He pressed his ear to the wood, and was rewarded with the sound of McCarty's light snoring. He pressed down the lever carefully, eased the door open. Watcher moved to the foot of the bed, studying the sleeping man's relaxed face. The man was still wearing the clothes he'd been wearing the evening before. Watcher put his hand to the hilt of the survival knife, and suppressed the desire to do something like slit the shirt off Ward's body. Watcher tensed when

Ward suddenly rolled over onto his side, but he doubted he'd awaken yet. The Scotch should be good for another few hours.

It was odd, standing there studying a man sleeping like he didn't have a care in the world. And it was exhilarating to know you would be carving him up in forty hours, give or take. Deciding he should not do anything more, he left the room, closing the door behind him.

He went into the child's bedroom, opened the dresser, and placed a special object he'd fashioned under the child's folded underwear.

Outside, the heat hit him like a blast from an open oven door. Watcher made a beeline up through the woods, passing his hide. He kept going until he arrived at the back door of the small house in the subdivision that bordered the McCarty acres. He went to the guest bedroom, his media room, and listened to the audio of the dinner conversation he'd captured. He especially enjoyed the part about the baseball. Being in denial, not seeing themselves as evil people, they dismissed the idea that someone from the outside could violate their precious and expensive security system. The McCarty home was a house divided, and it was going to get much worse.

He looked at the stuffed bear, picked it up, and pressed the hand to hear the message a mother had put there for a child who could never hear it again. He laughed and, holding the animal by its arms, made the bear perform a dance of death.

TWENTY-ONE

At 7:43 A.M. Alice Palmer parked her battered Toyota in the student lot and walked away without locking it. Investigator Todd Hartman moved at an angle across a grassy knoll to intercept her on the walkway leading to the nearby campus buildings. Even if Todd hadn't seen her driver's license and student ID pictures on-line, he would have recognized her from Ward McCarty's description, accurate right down to her rainbow nails.

Head down and wearing a baggy tie-dyed T-shirt, cutoff denim shorts, and yellow flip-flops, she approached in a thin line of students trickling from the parking lot.

When she was ten feet away, Todd stepped into her path.

"Alice Palmer," he said, turning on his warmest smile.

Blocked by the imposing stranger, she stopped and stared up at him. When she grimaced, her braces glittered.

"My name is Todd Hartman. I'm an investigator."

"Good for you," she said, her eyes suddenly suspicious, "I got a class. See ya." But she didn't try to go around him.

"We need to talk for just a minute," Todd said.

She looked down. "About what? You think I did something, Officer?"

"I'm a private investigator and my client has hired me to retrieve something for him he believes might be in your possession."

"Who?" Her eyes looked right then left nervously to take in the students walking past.

"There's something he may have left on a plane and he really hopes you were kind enough to pick up for him. You sat beside him Sunday on the flight from Las Vegas."

Todd saw it register in her little kleptomaniac mind, and, almost as quickly, she was weighing the various routes of escape open to her. He had given her plenty of wiggle room, and a way to save face. She wouldn't have to admit any wrongdoing.

"I didn't take his little toy car," she said, cutting her eyes to the right.

"I didn't say it was a little toy car, Alice."

"You sure did. So, I hope he finds it," she said, skirting him.

"There's a reward," Todd said to her back. "A rather substantial one, I suspect."

She stopped and turned. "How substantial?"

"That model car meant a lot to his son. This is purely a sentimental item for him."

"Well, he said he didn't have kids. Is he like a liar?"

"His son is dead. If you can help him, he would really appreciate it." Todd took a card from his shirt pocket and held it out to her. "Maybe it fell into your bag and you didn't even realize it."

"I'll check and if it somehow did, I'll call you. And you'll . . ."

"Pay you a cash reward of five hundred dollars. Everybody makes out. No questions asked, no police involvement."

"Cool," she said cheerfully, as she took the card. "You know, he said he'd give me a free toy car."

"He'll be happy to do that. He asked me to talk to you because he just wants his son's car back."

A slight smile blossomed in her eyes and she combed her hair back with short fingers. "Are you sure he didn't send you because he was like attracted to me? He was, you know." She smiled at Todd, and walked away with a spring in her step that hadn't been there before.

Todd watched her, thinking.

Something about the odd-looking girl made him uneasy. History told him that big trouble often sprang from small boxes.

TWENTY-TWO

It took a concerted effort for Ward to open his eyes. Lying on the bed in his clothes, his body felt heavy. He could tell he'd overslept by the angle of the sun's rays stretched across the floor. He stood and went into the bathroom to shower, and after, as he shaved, he studied his face in the mirror. The still-young man staring back at Ward had the dull gaze of a man who'd had too much to drink, and the body seemed to have softer edges than he remembered. How many Scotches had he consumed the night before? As best he could recall he'd had no more than two drinks. He didn't remember feeling tipsy, nor did he have any memory of going to bed in his clothes.

Up until a year ago, Ward had been in pretty good physical condition. He had done daily laps in their pool year-round, and he and Natasha rode their bikes several miles through the countryside. While his biceps were still solid enough and his leg muscles well defined, Ward was going to seed, and he resolved to start riding his bike again.

In the kitchen, Ward looked at Todd's business card. The address was the Bank of America Tower, pretty expensive real estate. The card contained a landline, a fax number, and a cellular line. Ward slipped it into his wallet next to a picture of Barney and Natasha.

Ward looked out at the covered swimming pool and felt a rush of sadness. The fading blue cover had remained in place since just after the accident. A year before, he and Barney had been swimming in the pool when the phone rang. Ward had been expecting a call. His uncle had business to discuss. Ward left Barney alone for a minute. He rushed into the kitchen and grabbed the phone before voice mail picked up. As he spoke with his uncle, the lights blinked for a split second. A flicker. A damaged spot in the insulation on a wire connecting the pool's pump and the lights had become saturated by the sprinkler system, and when the barefoot and wet child got out of the pool he stepped on a hot spot and was electrocuted, his heart stopping forever. When Barney fell, he broke the connection. Had that not been the case, Ward would have also been electrocuted when he'd knelt and grabbed his son up into his arms. The child had a gash in his head from the fall, which never bled because his heart had stopped.

When Ward turned, his eyes found the defibrillator case on the refrigerator. He'd bought the apparatus after Barney's death. Maybe if he'd had it then, he could have brought his son back. Its presence was a perfect example of closing the barn door after the horses were running free in the meadow.

Ward wiped a tear from his eye. He unplugged his cell phone from the charger, slipped it into his pocket, and took his keys and briefcase before leaving the house. The BMW's big eight-cylinder purred, and as he pressed down on the accelerator, he could hear the tires against the asphalt humming as he gained speed. He tuned in to that sound and tuned everything else out.

When his cell phone rang a few minutes into the trip, Ward glanced at the name and saw that his uncle was calling.

"Yes, Unk," he answered.

"Ward, where the hell are you?" Mark yelled into the phone. "I've been calling you for an hour."

"I overslept. I'm leaving the house. What's up?"

"We've got big trouble here."

"As in?"

"Computer virus. It's a disaster."

"Give me fifteen minutes."

TWENTY-THREE

Natasha closed the door to her office and sat heavily in her chair. She picked up the phone with steady hands and called Dr. Edmonds's receptionist to make an appointment on that Friday for a consultation. Normally it would have taken weeks to get in to see the specialist, but with physician's credentials, exceptions were ordinary. She hung up the phone and turned to her computer to check her e-mails.

There was a light rapping on her door and she turned around to see Dr. Walls. "Natasha, could I have a word?"

"Sure, George," she said with a smile. "Come in."

"I want to discuss your tremors."

"I just made an appointment with Dr. Edmonds. It really isn't a big deal. In fact it's getting better, but I wanted to be sure."

"I've spoken with the partners, and we agree that you should let us cover your surgeries until you've seen Dr. Edmonds. Before you protest, let me say that we know you are under a lot of pressure, and we're sure you'll be good as new in short order. I hope you don't see this as meddling, but I think you'll agree that there's a lot at stake here for all of us. You are an exceptional physician, and we all care a great deal about you." He tapped his hands on her desk to punctuate his last point, and to give it finality.

"I understand fully," she heard herself saying, "and I appreciate your concern." She felt assailed professionally, but she knew she had no business operating in her present condition. She wanted to know what was wrong with her.

"We'll just take the precaution and cover your surgeries until then," George said, smiling. "And if you'd like to take a few days, we will gladly cover your other appointments."

"Of course," she said. "And thank you. But covering my nonsurgical appointments won't be necessary."

"If your hands were to shake while you were seeing a patient . . ." He paused. "Well, word might get around. I think it is for the best. Just get some well-deserved rest and don't worry about anything."

George left the room and Natasha felt embarrassed and even, to some degree, grateful. She looked at her hands and they began to tremble ever so slightly.

Opening her laptop, she went into her e-mail and ran down the list of waiting correspondence. One was from Ward, titled "You have to see this." She clicked on it and sat stunned as the screen began filling with a changing montage of horrible images she couldn't believe she was seeing.

"Oh, my dear god," she said. Her heart pounded and she slammed her eyes closed, fighting to control her breathing. "My god. He's completely lost his mind."

TWENTY-FOUR

Ward rushed into the RGI building. As he passed by the receptionist, he saw that her phone lines were all lit up, and he could hear a loud angry voice leaking from her headset.

"Mr. McCarty," she said, covering the mouthpiece. "Mr. Wilson is waiting for you up in the conference room."

Ward took the steps three at a time, rushed to the door, and entered the crowded conference room. His uncle was talking to their head computer technician, Paul Wolfe. A pair of Wolfe's assistants were staring at the screens of laptops open on the table. Over the men's shoulders Ward saw pop-ups opening and stacking in rapid sequence on the screen, each flying up and covering the last in the space of a second or two. It took Ward a minute to realize what he was looking at, but by that point he already felt ill. Naked bodies flashed rapidly, one after the other.

"What's this? What the hell's going on?" he demanded.

"Kiddie porn," Mark said.

"Somebody had that on one of our computers?" Ward asked, furious at the thought. "Who?"

"We don't know, but our servers are inundated with pictures of kids engaged in sex acts with other kids, kids with adults. Jesus, there's even animals in the mix."

Paul Wolfe said, "Ward, this crap went out from our server. That's all I can tell at the moment. Viruses are sort of out of my line of expertise, but it's a replicating virus. We're offline and trying to figure out how to shut it down. I've got some calls in for help."

"Jesus Christ," Ward said. "What do you mean replicating? What the hell does that mean?"

"It makes copies of itself."

"I know what replicating means!" Ward snapped.

"I'm sorry. It gets sent in and sends itself back out to the e-mail addresses in the infected computer," Wolfe said, red-faced.

"So this got sent out to which of our e-mail addresses?"

"All of them, from every computer in the house. The phones are ringing off the hook," Mark said. "I've never seen anything this big or this bad. There's a massive freak-out going on that started with our clients and friends and families. The media is already calling us about it."

"And our company's signature is on the outgoing e-mails. We closed off the system to the outside immediately," Wolfe said. "It opens infected computers to outside servers and downloads compressed files, and those files replicate over and over so our server's memory keeps filling up, and as it does so it overwrites what's stored there. We back up everything nightly, so we won't lose anything we had before the invasion. I think it'll stop when it finishes filling the available memory, but who knows."

"Call the police," Ward said, feeling as though someone had dropped a waterbed on him.

"I called the cops right before you got here," Mark told him. "This is illegal as hell. This will ruin us. I've called our PR firm so we can get in front of this."

"I'll call . . ." Ward didn't even finish the thought. He just dialed Gene's number.

"Hello," Gene answered.

"Gene, it's Ward. Get out here right now." Ward couldn't control the anxiety, the fear, in his voice.

"I'm going into a meeting," Gene replied. "What's up?"

"Have you looked at your e-mails from us this morning?"

"Tell him not to," Paul Wolfe said.

"Just a second," Gene said. "I'm looking. Okay, here's one from you. 'You have to see this.' Okay . . ."

"No, don't open it!" Ward yelled. "A virus has gone out to everybody in our address books and it's filling our servers with child porn. You open that and it will send it to all your e-mail contacts."

Paul added, "Tell him to shut down his system. Or delete everything from us without opening anything. Any e-mail that is headed 'You have to see this' is going to contain the virus."

Ward told Gene what Wolfe had said. "I need you here now," Ward said. "Unk's already called the cops."

"Relax, I'm on my way," Gene said. "Don't answer any questions from the cops or anybody else until I get there."

"I think this crap could be all over the country, hell, the world, in a matter of hours," Paul Wolfe said, rubbing his eyes.

"Hurry," Ward said to Gene. He hung up and noticed a teary-eyed Leslie Wilde sitting at the end of the table with a crushed tissue in her hand. "Leslie, are you okay?"

She looked up at him and shook her head vigorously. "I'm sorry," she said, sobbing freely, "Mr. McCarty. I just turned on my terminal and it went crazy showing those images. I shut down the computer, but it was too late. I didn't mean . . . It's horrible. Those awful pictures . . ."

"It isn't your fault," Ward told her, sure that

was the case. "We'll fix this," he said to no one in particular, praying that it was even possible to fix. Thinking about their clients seeing these images made his heart sink.

"Mr. McCarty," the receptionist's voice said over the intercom. "There are two FBI agents here to see you."

Mark ran his fingers over his hair. "We're the victims here," he told everybody in the room and nobody in particular. "Figure out a way to stop it immediately. Get it back or something. Remember, people, we don't make any statements until Gene gets here."

Ward told the receptionist to direct the agents up to the conference room.

TWENTY-FIVE

The FBI agents looked to Ward like a pair of young stockbrokers dressed to call on a wealthy client. They introduced themselves as Bill Firman and John Mayes, though Ward quickly forgot which was which.

Despite what he had told the assembled seconds before the agents entered, Mark immediately started to explain to the pair what had happened, but as soon as they looked at the computer screen over the techs' shoulders, Agent Firman said, "Sir, close the computer and move away from it." To Mark he said, "Tell your employees to turn off their monitors. We'll have our techs here as soon as possible to take over."

"Agent Firman, we can't operate without our computers," Mark protested.

"I understand that," Firman told Mark. "But someone here sent a virus of child pornography over the Internet. Whether or not you did it on purpose, it's a federal crime, so we'll need to interview any employee with access to your computers, see if we can figure out exactly who is responsible."

"Our attorney is on his way," Ward said. "You can work it out with him. Until he gets here to sort this out, he's advised us not to answer any questions."

"Well," Agent Firman said, "that's your right, Mr. . . . ?"

"McCarty. Ward McCarty."

"Ward is our CEO," Mark said.

"Well, Mr. McCarty, until we get this sorted out, we're closing down your computers. No employee is to remove anything from the premises, or leave the building, until we say so."

"You can't do that," Ward said. "We called you."

"Actually, Mr. McCarty," the agent said, taking a folded piece of paper from his suit pocket. "Certain recipients of your illegal pornography called us. I have a warrant on the way," he said. "Your computers are closed down until we say differently. Are you still online?"

Paul shook his head. "We closed off the servers to the outside as soon as we saw what was happening."

Agent Mayes said, "Just make sure all of the computers are turned off. Yours, too; it's illegal for you to look at that."

"You can't be serious," Mark said.

"You can't think we did this on purpose?" Ward asked, incredulous.

"Of course not," Firman answered.

Ward's cell phone rang and he recognized Natasha's number. When he opened the phone, everybody in the room could hear the sound of his irate wife letting him have it with both barrels. Ward shuddered at the thought of the people on her e-mail list.

TWENTY-SIX

Gene Duncan's arrival made Ward feel better, but not for long. A contingent of no fewer than twenty FBI agents and other personnel arrived minutes before his attorney, moving through the building in ones and twos searching the offices. FBI computer techs, armed with laptops and other electronic equipment, hooked up to the RGI servers and sat typing as they stared intently at illuminated screens.

In the three hours since the virus's release, media vehicles had made their parking lot look like the streets outside the L.A. courthouse during the O. J. Simpson trial. The television viewing public was fast becoming aware that the virus had originated from a system serving a NASCAR-related business right smack on the buckle of the Bible Belt. The pundits descended.

As unnatural disasters went, this one was way off the charts, so RGI's name was fast becoming a household word, and not in a good way. Ward's suspicion was that someone was out to destroy his company, and this was probably going to accomplish just that. It was noon before it was Ward's turn with the interviewing agents, and Gene Duncan was at his side. The agents who'd arrived with the initial warrant, Mayes and Firman, were in charge. They interviewed Mark, Leslie, and the company's techs before they got around to Ward.

Agent Firman, whose expression was as unreadable to Ward as Chinese characters painted on a wall, was doing the talking.

Firman said, "Mr. McCarty, what we've established so far is that the virus originated here in this building."

"You think someone here did this?" Ward asked incredulously.

"Obviously someone did this to damage the company," Gene railed.

Firman asked, "Do you have any enemies, Mr. McCarty?"

"Flash Dibble has been trying to buy this company for six months," Ward said. "I have refused to sell it. Maybe he figured if he couldn't have it, he'd destroy it to lower the price, or start another company using our pissed-off clients as his base. Yesterday I told his son I'd never sell to them. He threatened me."

"Flash Dibble's son is trying to destroy your company? Okay, it's a theory," Firman said, writing. "Our techs tell me that the images seem to be mostly Russian pornography. Is your Mr. Dibble a Russian mobster?"

"It makes as much sense as anything else," Gene said. "The threat was veiled, but it sure sounded like a threat to me. Couldn't anyone with the knowledge create the virus? That is something that could be purchased. What *about* Trey Dibble? Who else would want to destroy a company that he can't buy? He's a malicious brat."

"Destroying it would certainly be a lot cheaper than paying twenty-two million," Ward said.

Firman reached into a sack and removed a glassine envelope with a padded envelope in it. Ward could read his own name on the front, above his home address, complete with canceled stamps. The return address wasn't one he was familiar with.

"We found this in your desk," Firman said.

"I've never seen it before," Ward said.

"My techs tell me that the CD inside this envelope was the source of the virus. Our techs have tracked the virus's point of origin to one desktop computer here, Mr. McCarty. Yours."

Ward felt as though he'd been hit in the chest with a sledgehammer. "That's impossible," he protested, feeling suddenly nauseated.

"When someone put this disk in your computer, it infected your servers, and spread and sent e-mails containing the virus to the addresses in all of the computers in the building."

"You can't think I did it?" Ward asked, stunned. "I didn't use my computer yesterday except to check e-mails, and I haven't put any CDs into it in ages."

"Based on what we know, it's possible you did," Firman said. "I don't say so, the evidence does. I'm sure whoever did it didn't do it on purpose. If you did it, you obviously didn't know when you looked at it that it contained a Trojan horse that waited some amount of time before it came to life. I *strongly* suspect you, or someone not yet identified, just wanted to look at the porn, but whomever you, or someone else, got it from played a dirty little trick on you, or them. I strongly suspect that you, or someone else yet to be identified, is a pervert who's going to spend some quality time in a federal prison."

Ward said evenly, "I've never seen that envelope before."

Gene said, "So even if Ward received the envelope—and who knows what was originally inside it—and inserted it into his computer, you can't prove he knew its contents. And he says he's never seen it before, so you have to prove that isn't the case. Anybody could have put the CD inside the envelope. You have no case against Mr. McCarty."

"If he's never seen either, then your client's prints won't be on the envelope or the disk," Firman said. "And naturally it doesn't have a label saying what it is. That would be a first. There will be more evidence, I suspect, and then we'll have more to go on."

"Okay, Agent Firman. If it's true, and he knew, for argument's sake," Gene said, "and it certainly isn't, why would he be stupid enough to keep that CD in his office?"

"I don't know, Mr. Duncan. I'll check with the Behavioral Science Unit. Maybe—theoretically speaking, of course—he thinks his office is safe. According to his computer logs, he's visited questionable pornography sites for the past year."

"I've never visited any pornography sites," Ward said.

Gene put his hand on Ward's forearm. "Are you placing my client under arrest?" he asked the agent.

"Not yet," Firman said. "But we'll need to take Mr. McCarty's fingerprints for exclusionary purposes."

"No problem," Ward said, quickly.

"A polygraph would help to clear him," Agent Mayes added.

"I'd be happy to," Ward said.

"My client will not be taking any polygraph," Gene said.

"Why not, if he isn't guilty?" Firman asked.

"Because it isn't admissible," Gene said. "And we all know there's good reason for that."

"You aren't a criminal attorney, are you, Mr. Duncan?" Agent Firman drawled.

Ward said, "I have absolutely nothing to hide."

"Oh, Mr. McCarty," Firman said, smiling for the first time since he'd come into the building. "It's pretty obvious that your lawyer doesn't believe that's the case."

TWENTY-SEVEN

Watcher parked his truck outside a textile mill in Charlotte's south side that had been converted into lofts. He walked to a red door with the gold number 12 on it and rang the bell. He scanned the parking lot and was glad to see that it was deserted.

The peephole went dark and a second later the door opened. The young man who squinted out at Watcher was thin, stooped, and bald on the top of his head. The remaining halo of hair surrounding his pate was long and gathered into a thin ponytail. He wore a soul patch between his narrow lower lip and the weak chin beneath. The thick lenses held in heavy black frames enlarged his bloodshot blue eyes. He wore a soiled undershirt, and the boxer shorts he wore looked like they were going to fall off as soon as he exhaled. Obviously he'd been awake for a very long time.

"Hi, Bert," Watcher said.

"Hey, man," Bert said. "Come in. You know what the frigging sun does to vampires."

After Watcher went in, Bert looked out and scanned the parking lot before he closed the door. Except for the bathroom, Bert's condo was one open space with eighteen-foot ceilings. The lower seven feet of the floor-to-ceiling windows, built to provide both light and ventilation to the workers in the cavernous weaving room, were covered by stained bedsheets. On a mezzanine, accessible by narrow stairs, an unmade bed was surrounded by piles of clothes and other flotsam from Bert's solitary lifestyle. The space smelled like a locker room after a football game.

The TV was on and Watcher was treated to a live report of the havoc wrought by the pornography virus. Watcher and Bert took a moment to watch and admire. Bert laughed out loud when a mother being interviewed started sobbing as she described the trauma to her young daughter the e-mail had caused. The report went from the woman to a minister who called

for the arrest of the guilty party who'd perpe-
trated the unspeakable assault on human de-
cency. The red-faced, gravel-voiced parson
called further for the government to control the
smut that was destroying the innocence of children and thousands of wholesome God-fearing
families. "This is a war with Satan himself," the
sanctimonious minister bellowed. Before his
segment ended, he managed to name his min-
istry and his dot-com address so Christians could
send their dollars to help fund his antipornogra-
phy campaign.

"Man, oh, man, I've never been a general in
Satan's army before," Bert said, barely able to
contain his glee.

The damning evidence was purposefully cir-
cumstantial in nature. Watcher still knew that
it was possible, though unlikely, that Ward
would be arrested. Public outcry was too
great. The authorities were under too much
pressure. Watcher imagined the pressure on the
McCartys and smiled back grimly at Bert.

A table made from a sheet of heavy plywood
and set on sawhorses dominated the living
room/kitchen. Five computer terminals lined the
table. An expensive armchair on rollers was

pushed up to one like a captain's chair. The screen of one computer held hundreds of lines of program coding, as undecipherable to Watcher as sheet music. The young man opened the refrigerator and took out a chilled bottle of beer. Except for a six-pack of Budweiser, a pizza box, and ketchup, the unit's interior was empty.

"Want one?" he asked.

"Too early for me," Watcher said. "I brought you something," he said, putting a glass vial on the table. He had taken it from his jacket pocket, using his fingertips on the edges to avoid leaving prints.

"What's this?"

"A reward for your amazing work."

Bert lifted the vial and opened it, peering in at the white powder.

"Meth? I have plenty of meth. I like meth. You want some?"

"It's Peruvian flake, Bert. Ninety-eight percent pure, so be careful."

"No shit?" Bert poured the powder on a plastic CD case. "Cool. I haven't had any coke in months. So, we're rock stars, man! We made a humongous splash with the naughty porno thing." He laughed and held his clammy hand up for a high-five slap.

Watcher slapped the young man's open hand and smiled.

"You keep any of the kiddie pictures to look at later?" Watcher asked.

"Well, I've got the virus copies like you said to keep for you, the code and all that, but I'm not stupid enough to keep it around longer than necessary, even if it's a thing of beauty, virusly speaking. Not the porn, though. That's really creepy stuff, man."

Watcher took a number-ten envelope from his pocket, again by the edges, and handed it to the programmer. "Five thousand dollars," Watcher said.

"You already paid me," Bert said. "Why the bump? Oh, because I'm such a rock star and because it was so effective for your guy?"

"Yep. It's a bonus. You earned it, man," Watcher said, handing Bert a business card without his prints on it, but those of its owner. "Cut it with this."

"Cool," Bert said. He took the business card from Watcher—putting his own prints on it in the process—chopped at the pile of cocaine, and deftly split it into wide two-inch-long rails. Rolling up one of the bills from the stack inside the envelope, he bent down and snorted each rail, one, then the other. He straightened, pinched his nose like a child about to jump into a swimming pool, and sucked in air abruptly as he released his nostrils.

"Far out!" he said, spinning his chair in circles, using his filthy bare feet for propulsion. "We've been all that's on the jazzing news." He stopped spinning, sighed. "Wish I could use this in my portfolio. I mean, I wouldn't, because I'd end up in jail . . . again. But I sure wish I could just tell some of my hacker buds. They'd go ape shit, man!"

"Are you sure the FBI can't trace this job to you?"

"No way, man. No frigging way. I put in so much bullshit code around the meat—excuse my pun—that they will never work through all of it. Then I piled the covering shit on shit, so deep that I'm never going to have anybody within ten miles of me. You hired the best, man. The absolute best."

Watcher shrugged. He knew Bert's confidence was horseshit. The cops knew all about people like Bert, and given time they'd brace him and he'd end up rolling over like a dachshund puppy approached by a pack of ravenous wolves.

When Bert bent over the table to put the envelope into a wire bin, Watcher slipped the stiletto from his pocket, pressed the button releasing the long, thin blade, pressed the tip against the base of Bert's skull, and pulled back on his ponytail, shoving the blade in to the hilt. Watcher pulled it out, closed the weapon, and, after wiping off his prints, dropped it into a plastic bag, which he then put into his pants pocket.

He looked at the disposable cell phone on the table that he'd given Bert. Using his fingertips, Watcher took the envelope of cash and put it under the computer's keyboard. Satisfied, he took one of Bert's business cards and pocketed it for later use. Now, he thought, the circular evidence trail was exactly half laid.

TWENTY-EIGHT

While Ward was relieved that he wasn't leaving his building in handcuffs, Gene Duncan had told him that being arrested by the FBI in the near future was possible. Just being accused of anything related to child pornography would leave a permanent stain. As he walked out of the building with Gene and Mark, Ward saw that all of the cameras in the parking lot turned on the trio. Ward realized the mistake they'd made in agreeing to join Gene when he made a statement. The cameras were pasting human faces to the scandal.

Ward fought the urge to turn and bolt for the building. He walked out in front to stand behind Gene, facing the waiting cameras like a politician. Firman and his partner, Mayes, left the building after them. They strolled to a stone gray sedan and drove off, watching Ward the whole time.

"All we can tell you at this point," Gene was saying when Ward focused on him, "is that RGI called in the FBI as soon as they were aware of what had happened. It appears obvious that someone intentionally infected RGI's computers with this despicable virus, and we are hopeful that the FBI will find the culprit or culprits and bring them to justice. Raceway's owners and all of its employees are cooperating with the FBI and hope to see this resolved in the very near future. My clients, I am certain, will be exonerated. Thank you."

Ward felt certain that not one of the people in the lot or out there in the free world would believe for a second that he was innocent.

After Gene's statement, the three men went to their respective cars and drove away. Ward drove straight home, with Gene following him. Twenty minutes later, they had to slow to pass through a sheriff's department roadblock at the entrance of his driveway. He couldn't believe the number of cars and trucks parked on the side of the road, the milling curious, and the reporters shouting questions at his car as he rolled by. Even though he knew the FBI was planning to search his house, Ward hadn't expected them to be at it so soon.

Gene and Ward parked in the grass beside the Crown Victoria driven by Firman and Mayes. Ward walked with Gene to the open front door.

Natasha stood in the foyer, crying. Her trembling right hand held the FBI search warrant, which she handed to Gene.

"They're searching Barney's room," she told them between her sobs. There were no words for what Ward was feeling as Gene took the warrant and started reading it. Ward tried to put his arms around his wife to comfort her, but she pulled away, crossed her arms, and went outside into the sweltering heat. Firman and Mayes both walked in and out of view, directing traffic. A tech wearing surgical gloves who was carrying Ward's personal laptop computer walked around him, heading out to the closest van.

An hour later, while Ward sat on the couch in black-cloud thought, the last of the FBI search party left the house, leaving a mess behind. Gene had a list of everything they had taken, and, seated beside Ward, studied it carefully. Ward got up and went to the door leading into the dining room where Natasha sat at the table in silence, sipping a glass of orange juice.

"I'll clean up," Ward told her.

"I work with children," she said. "Can you imagine what my patients' parents think?"

"Someone did this to us," he said angrily.

Ward wasn't so much angry as he felt like he wanted to lie down on the floor and die in place so this would end.

She looked up at him, and in all the years he'd known her, and except for the ordeal they'd gone through with Barney's death and its aftermath, he'd never seen her so utterly devastated.

"Who? Why?" she asked.

"He's right," Gene said.

"Can you prove it?" she asked.

"We will," Gene said positively.

She shook her head slowly.

Ward wanted to believe him but wasn't any more convinced than his wife seemed to be.

"You can't believe I had anything to do with this?" Ward asked her.

"How does what I think matter here?" she demanded. "My husband's company sent child pornography out to the world. The press has already told everyone he's a pedophile. The FBI questioned me like I was a criminal, destroyed our home, and carted off our computers. My office phone hasn't stopped ringing all morning because our computers sent the trash out to hundreds of people, my patients chief among them. The majority of my new patients have asked for a transfer to one of my partners. I'm out of business, probably for good here. My partners have suggested that I stay out of the office until this is resolved. Do I believe my husband is guilty? What the hell does that matter?"

"It matters to me," Ward told her. And he had never spoken truer words. "If you don't believe me, who will?" He tried to look at her eyes but couldn't, so he looked down.

"Your hands . . ." he said, noticing that her fingers were trembling.

He knew he would never forget the look she gave him, and what was left of his heart broke into pieces. And he felt an odd lightness just before the room vanished.

TWENTY-NINE

Ward opened his eyes to find himself lying on the floor in his son's bedroom. He looked up at Barney, who was seated on his bed, staring down at Ward. He dangled his legs back and forth. "It'll be all right, Daddy."

Ward knew this event wasn't real, but he hoped somehow he wasn't dreaming, but that he was dead, too, and this meeting could last forever.

Suddenly the windows darkened, as though fast-moving, rain-heavy clouds had blocked the sun, and Ward felt a sense of growing danger.

"You and Mama have to be together," Barney said, looking at the windows. His legs stopped swinging.

Ward jerked awake on the couch to the sight of Natasha looking down at him, the odor of ammonia burning his nose.

"Ward?" Natasha said. "He's awake, Gene."

Ward slowly sat upright and saw the ampoule in his wife's hand.

"What happened?" he asked.

"You fainted," she told him.

"You okay, buddy?" Gene asked. He had a cell phone in his hand.

"I'm fine," Ward said, putting his hand to the back of his head. "My head hurts."

"You hit it on the floor," Natasha said, studying her husband's pupils for signs of a concussion. "Just rest there for a few minutes."

"Never mind," Gene said into his phone. "I

won't need EMS. Yes, he's with a physician and she says he's fine." He closed the phone.

"I couldn't catch you in time. Sorry," Gene said sincerely.

"It's okay."

"As soon as you feel steady enough, you need to go lie down on your bed," Natasha said, in her professional voice.

"I have to run," Gene said. "I have a meeting with Tom Wiggins, who looks to be your other lawyer."

Ward had met Wiggins at a formal dinner at the hospital to raise money for the children's oncology wing of the medical center. He was a mild-mannered man in his mid-sixties, and a top-notch criminal attorney from Charlotte who was the attorney of choice for the wealthy—whom everybody usually figured were guilty. He was known to the legal establishment, and much of the public, as "Reasonable Doubt Wiggins."

"I think he's going to be our best shot at getting this crap handled. Any problem with that?" Gene asked.

The bell rang, and Natasha went to the door. When she came back Leslie Wilde was with her.

Leslie came over to where Ward was lying on the couch and peered down at her boss.

"Are you okay?" she asked. Her look of concern was comforting to Ward.

"Yeah," he said. "I just passed out."

After pausing to place his hand on Natasha's shoulder in a show of support, Gene left for the front door.

Leslie said, "I told the FBI that I started Mr. McCarty's computer, because mine was on the fritz. It's my fault it happened."

"It wasn't your fault," Ward said.

"They asked me if I'd put any disks into your computer and I said I had, that my computer was on the blink last week and I used yours a lot when you weren't in your office. I told them that I found some unmarked disks on my desk and that I looked at them to see what they were, but none of them had porn on them."

"Is that the truth?" Natasha asked her.

She looked at Natasha and shrugged. "The FBI agents are jerks. The truth is that I came in early because I had something to do for Mr. Brooks in accounting, and when I brought my computer up, it started displaying the porn. I didn't call anybody for like ten minutes. If I'd called Paul Wolfe sooner, maybe he could have stopped it. I'm sorry. I have used Mr. McCarty's computer, which is the truth, but I've never put any disks into it that I can recall. So this is sort of my fault. And I know Mr. McCarty didn't do what they said."

Ward told her, "You shouldn't have put yourself in such a position. I don't want you to lie to anybody. I appreciate your loyalty, but this is bad enough without you being pulled into it."

The doorbell rang.

"That's probably Todd. I called him after the FBI left the office," Leslie said. "I hope you don't mind."

"Of course I don't mind," Ward said. "Maybe he can offer some suggestions."

Natasha shook her head. "I feel like the maid in a sitcom, except there's nothing amusing about this," she said, leaving to answer the door.

When she came back, Todd Hartman was with her. He put his hand out and gently squeezed Leslie's before letting it drop, turning his eyes toward Ward.

"Leslie told me what happened," he said. "Maybe I can help."

"Mr. Hartman," Natasha said, "can I get you something?"

"Nothing for me, Dr. McCarty," he said. "Thanks anyway."

"Todd," Ward said. "This is all totally insane."

"It's all over the radio," Todd said. "I made some calls and found out from a friend in the sheriff's department that the deputies were going to be pulled off their guard detail here after the FBI finished their search," Hartman said. "So I took the liberty of putting two of the security guys I use at the end of your driveway to make sure you aren't bothered. I hope you don't mind."

"I had to take the phone off the hook," Natasha said, frowning. "There was a constant stream of calls. Angry strangers saying hateful things."

"If you'd rather use someone else, my guys can stay until you make other arrangements. But my guys are good at their jobs and no more expensive than any guards would be."

"Do we really need them?" Natasha asked.

"This is a big story," Todd said. "The media will be under pressure to get in here to it. The guys I use are professionals. Ex-military, mostly. They'll keep the press from bothering you."

"That's great," Ward said, relieved. "Glad you were on top of it."

Todd said, "I don't know what else I can do, but if your lawyer needs any work done on this, I'll make myself available."

"If you'll excuse me," Natasha said, "I'm going to straighten up some."

"I'll give you a hand, Dr. McCarty," Leslie offered.

"That would be nice, Leslie," Natasha said. "If you don't have anything else you need to do. This is a little overwhelming."

Leslie said, "I'd like to help in any way I can, and I'm sort of a neat freak."

"And both of you call me Natasha, and call Ward Ward."

After the women went off toward the bedrooms, Todd sat down. "By the way, I spoke to Alice Palmer."

"Who?"

"The car thief from the plane," he said. "I guess that isn't the priority it was yesterday."

"It's less pressing."

Ward flashed an image of Barney and what he'd said in the dream. "I still want it back," he said. "Let's say it's a secondary priority. The virus is number one."

"I assume this whole virus thing is a setup of some kind."

"It has to be. Before today I've never even seen any child porn."

"Disgruntled former or present employee?"

"We don't have any disgruntled employees that I know of. We have very little turnover because my father and my uncle Mark believed in taking care of the employees and so do I. More likely it's related to the fact that someone wants to buy RGI and I won't sell to them. The Dibbles."

"Flash and Trey?"

Ward nodded. "It's hard to imagine why anyone would pull this kind of crap for grins. I haven't had any enemies of any kind since fourth grade when Warren Pepper beat me up after school because I pitched a fastball into his ribs."

"If you want to tell me about it, I'm already working for you."

Todd opened his briefcase and pulled out his

notebook and pen, and for the first time since Unk's call that morning, Ward McCarty felt some small measure of relief.

THIRTY

Ward stood in the doorway to Barney's room disbelieving his eyes. The dresser drawers had been dumped out onto the floor and leaned haphazardly against the wall. His son's toys were piled on the twin beds; the sheets and pillows had been balled and cast into a corner. Looking at the model cars he was sickened at the thought of the scratches that would be left from their rough handling. The searchers' actions had defiled Barney's bedroom. Natasha sat on Barney's bed looking crestfallen, a model car in her hands. Ward could hear Leslie in their bedroom straightening up the FBI's mess. She looked up and saw Ward looking in.

"How could anybody leave a child's room like this?" she asked sadly. "Where do we start?"

"Maybe we shouldn't put it back like it was,"

Ward said, surprising himself as much as what he'd said seemed to surprise her.

"What do you mean? We have to clean it up," she said.

He thought about what Barney had said to him when he'd been unconscious earlier. "Barney will never be here again. I guess it's time to face that."

Ward stepped into the room and sat on the other bed and stared at his wife.

She said, "Ward, I don't think you are responsible for the virus. I was just so angry that it happened I said things I didn't mean. Call it . . . displaced frustration. When I said you weren't the man I married last night, I was serious, but whatever else happens between us, I know that inside you are still that man."

"I want to be him again," Ward told her.

She looked at her hands, balled tight in her lap. "There's something else I haven't told you. Lately my hands have been shaking. It's probably nothing, but I'm going to see a neurologist and find out what's causing it. My colleagues have had to take over my surgery and I'm sidelined until I get it figured out. I'm sure it's just stress."

Ward took her hands in his and held them. They trembled gently in his.

"See?"

"Why didn't you say something? Dear God, I . . ."

"It's all right, Ward. At the moment there's no point in wasting time worrying over that. If Dr. Edmonds tells me there's something to worry about, we can worry about it then." She frowned. "I think there's some boxes we can put Barney's things into in the storage room."

"When did it start?"

"Two or three weeks ago. Been getting worse."

Ward said, "We can decide what to do with his things when we feel up to it. One step at a time."

"Even the cars?" she asked.

"Even the cars."

Ward knew that he had to do it before he had time to think about it, or he might change his mind.

Natasha bent over and picked up, from among Barney's clothes, a small black box about five inches long. When Natasha opened it, she gasped loudly, and dropped it to the floor and backed away as though it were a rattlesnake.

Ward knelt down and looked at the replica of a casket complete with gold handles fashioned from wire. Lying inside the casket was an effigy—a Star Wars action figure of ten-year-old Anakin Skywalker—with bold black lines crossing out each of its little blue eyes.

THIRTY-ONE

Ward's finances wouldn't allow him unlimited help from investigators and attorneys. His house was mortgaged. He didn't have a fortune in the bank. No gold bars, jewels socked away in a vault, or valuable paintings. He kept between ten and twenty-five thousand dollars in his bank accounts; at any given time he had maybe two hundred thousand in other stocks and bonds he could liquidate. The company had plenty of money in its various accounts, but corporate funds weren't his to spend as if those were his personal funds. The McCartys were comfortable, not wealthy. Ward thought about that when he thought about what it would cost to get his life back.

The FBI had left the storage room a wreck, but Ward quickly stepped over the debris scattered on the floor and found three boxes stored flat behind the shelves. He located a roll of clear tape and enough bubble wrap to pad the model cars.

Packing Barney's things was difficult for them both. Leslie sensed this, working in the other parts of the house, finishing up before the boxes were packed, taped up, and labeled. Ward put the small coffin in a shopping bag and that in the back of the pantry.

"Leslie lied to the FBI for you. How did you inspire such loyalty in an employee?"

"She's good people," Ward said. "I do wish she hadn't done it, though."

Natasha said, "She obviously admires you. This will all be straightened out and the fib lost in the shuffle. I'm not sorry she lied for you."

"Would you lie for me?"

Natasha frowned at him and began taping closed the last box. "I suppose I would."

Ward, Leslie, and Natasha finished straightening the rooms before they went to the kitchen, where Natasha cooked eggs, bacon, and toast. They ate a late breakfast for lunch. Ward had known Leslie Wilde for almost three years, but, as the trio talked and laughed, it was as if he was actually meeting her for the first time that evening. She and Todd seemed to have a comfortable relationship. He decided that, as soon as he could get back to work, he was going to give her a substantial raise.

THIRTY-TWO

Watcher held the knife up and ran his eyes over the curve of the gleaming blade. On a cold October night in Afghanistan, he had killed three men with this knife in the space of thirty seconds, give or take. They became notches on the hilt.

He thought about another day when he'd used the same knife.

Watcher crouched among trees, silent, listening. In the late afternoon light, he could see the lake, fractioned by the trees, and he heard the drone of speedboats. He had been sitting with his back against a pine tree when he saw the boy leave the tent and step out near the still-smoldering campfire. The boy picked up a stick, squatted, and began prodding curiously at the coals. The child was a beautiful creature—a tow-headed boy of three, and Watcher smiled as a shaft of sunlight illuminated the buttons of the boy's spine. Inside the tent a woman lay sleeping. Watcher was close enough that he could just hear the child's stick punching through the crusty bed of ash.

The boy wore a wrinkled red swimsuit and sandals. After a few minutes of poking, the child grew bored, and started to wander aimlessly around the campsite. Watcher stood and crept silently within fifteen feet of the boy.

The child turned his head and saw something that caught his attention. He approached curiously the rotting trunk of a fallen tree. The boy's excited laughter floated to his stalker. Holding the stick like a sword, the child began stabbing at something in the leaves beside the tree.

Watcher moved swiftly, using the boy's laughter to cover his footsteps, and he swept his way quickly around behind the child. Three paces behind the boy, Watcher reached down, un-

snapped the knife from its sheath, and drew out
the curved blade. In one fluid motion, he flipped
the knife in the air, caught the blade with his fingers, and threw the knife hard.

The child squealed as the knife hit home.

Watcher grabbed the boy's arm and pulled
him aside, looking down to see his knife pinning
down a three-foot-long snake, its sleek body covered over with a light and dark copper-colored
pattern. The inch-wide triangular head rose and
the snake tried in vain to strike. Small sharp fangs
curved from the roof of the reptile's open mouth.

" 'Nake!" the boy shouted, laughing. " 'Nake!"
He raised the stick and swatted at the reptile,
striking its thick body behind where the blade
had it pinned to the exposed root of the tree.

The snake writhed futilely until Watcher
stepped on its head and withdrew the Randall.
Watcher pressed down hard, feeling the small
skull give as he moved his boot as though grind-
ing out a cigarette. He reached down in a swift
movement and severed the flattened head from
the copperhead's body. After wiping the snake's
blood and dirt off onto his black jeans, Watcher
slid the knife back into its leather sheath and
snapped the strap.

He reached down, picked up the severed head, and cast it off into the woods.

Turning, he lifted the startled child into the air, raising him as high as his arms allowed. When he lowered the boy he kissed him on his warm soft cheek and hugged him to his chest.

"Snakes will bite you, and you can die," Watcher explained. "You *never* mess with snakes."

"Bad 'nake," the boy said, throwing his small arms around Watcher's neck and squeezing as hard as he could.

"You have to be careful," Watcher said. "The world is full of danger, and I won't always be here to protect you."

THIRTY-THREE

Alice Palmer reached under her bed and took out the model car so her boyfriend, Earl Tucker, could see it. He took it in his hands and turned it in the sunlight streaming in through the window to get a better look.

Her mother hated Earl, and that alone made him appealing to Alice. She told Alice that Earl lacked class, had no sense of propriety, and had been shorted crucial social filters necessary for any interaction more involved than buying cigarettes in a convenience store. She further said he looked like a shiftless, genetically crippled cartoon hick. She said that the biggest decision he'd made in life was not only that being an illiterate black man was glamorous, but that he actually was one.

At nineteen, Earl was six feet four inches tall and had never in his life weighed more than one hundred and fifty pounds. He smoked Newport cigarettes, and did whatever drugs he could get his hands on. He had closely cropped hair, acne, a pronounced overbite, and large ears you could see light through. When he talked he motioned with his hands as though he was communicating with an invisible audience using sign language. Because he didn't have a regular job he was available when Alice wanted company. It wasn't like she planned to marry him or anything.

"So . . . know ah'm sayin'? . . . this same perv that's on the TV news gave you this and he wants it back enough to pay you five hundred dollars for it?" he asked. "Jesus . . . know ah'm say-ing? . . . this is our lucky day."

"That's right," she said. "He doesn't look like a pervert, but according to the news he is."

"And, like we know, you know, look, he wanted to fuck you because you, you know, look like a little kid."

"I never said that. He was just friendly, is all."

"He wanted to fuck you, a'ight. I think he gave you the little car, like but when you said you wouldn't suck him off in the airplane bathroom, he took it back. So, look here now, you friggin' snatched it out of being angry and scared and like that. Indian-giving son of a bitch likes young stuff. And he has big bucks, right?"

She shrugged. "How would I know that?"

"He has his own damned company. He owns the big place they showed on the TV. How much you reckon we could ask him for? To keep his unproper advances on you quiet. A lot, is how much, know ah'm sayin'? Like I could get my tattoo finished, man."

"The detective said five hundred bucks."

"I figure it's worth like a thousand, you know? Like maybe a lot more than a thou," he said, smiling to show the top row of prominent yel-

low teeth. "That's a starting point for a negotiat-
ing placement. Like see, they say one, you say
naw it gone be more like ten, and we settle right
smack in the middle."

"His investigator gave me weird vibes. I think
I better take the five hundred and get it over
with."

"You got this perv by the gonadies, my
darling. You just say if this pervert don't pay the
five grand, you might jes have to talk to the man
about him putting his hands on your leg. Maybe
saying he'd pay you—know ah'm sayin'?—to
put on a Catholic schoolgirl uniform and let
him fuck you while you sucked on his lollipop."

"It was on an airplane. I doubt he thought I
could get a school uniform on a plane. And how
could he screw me while I did that, like I even
would?"

"Naw, dig this, I mean later on, baby doll. He
gave you that little card with your picture
drawed on it so you could call him and set things
up in a motel, you see. Let your brain create a little here. A real-life eighteen-year-old virgin that
looks more like about thirteen. He wanted to
talk to you. Anybody that wouldn't is a queer,
pure and simple, know ah mean?"

Alice smiled at the compliment. "You think I look thirteen?" Earl was generous with compliments only when he was horny or had an idea about what she could steal, which was about always.

"You call this dude back and tell him he needs to make us a better offer? Then you say you can't be bothered to think about it fa' less'n five grands and you 'ont come off that number even if hell freezes up. He tries to say no, you tell him you are going to talk to the cops about him trying to touch yo' snatch and saying you looked maybe twelve or some shit, and 'bout him wanting to get a motel room and all 'at. Stick to it. I'll be right there to give you like lots of my own love and mental support you need. If he gets rough and tries anything I'll have my dad's gat."

"You'd shoot him if he threatened me?"

"To protect the woman I luz with all my heart? On truth, I would! I gots a three-eighty and I can use it, know ah'm sayin'? And I don't give a flip how big he is, a bullet right between the dude's eyes will make him my size."

Alice took the model car from Earl and tossed it onto the pillows on her bed. Running her hand up his leg, she grasped him through the material and felt him stiffening. She looked up at him, batted her eyelids, and bit her tongue, so he could see its tip. That, she knew from practicing in the mirror, made her look very sexy.

"Oh, yeah. That's what I'm talking about. Hell yes I'd shoot the fucker. I'd shoot the fucker for five grand. Fuckin' A, I would."

"But I'm not worth your risking jail."

"Well, obviously you no *Playboy* beauty. You gots them tooth fences 'n' a roly-poly belly and don't have no tits to speak of, but I luz you anyway." He pressed his splayed fingertips against his chest for emphasis. "See, know ah'm sayin'? To me, you are more or less pretty enough in your own way, and you smart. My mama says, you got a lot to speak for yourself, rich girl or not."

"That so," she said.

"You know I love you, baby doll. You're my girl. I know you be savin' yourself for your husband, but that's gone be me, know ah'm sayin'? I mean you needs to give it up for your man, know ah'm sayin'?"

Alice looked into his dull blue eyes and thought about it.

Tongue tip between her teeth—adorned with gleaming wire—Alice unzipped Earl's pants and freed his rigid member but didn't look at it. She'd seen it before.

"Maybe like later on we can do it. I'm not ready yet. But I'll make you happy."

"A wise man once said, 'A wise man take whats he can get,' " Earl said.

When she began moving her hand on the shaft in the manner of someone chopping at a block of ice with a pick, he closed his eyes and he began moaning his approval softly. She picked up the pace, hoping for a quick resolution.

"Hey!" he said. "This ain't a race. Damn, don't you gots some soothing hand lotion or some shit."

"It makes my hand feel slimy."

"Then relax up on your grips or you gone take my skins off. Know ah'm sayin'?"

"I know what you're saying," she told him.

Alice followed his instructions mindfully, and as soon as she slowed down, he closed his eyes again. This was familiar territory, and she had come to view this exercise with the clinical detachment of a scientist conducting an experiment. As she stroked him, she watched his face carefully, so when he got that weird look and started whimpering, she would know to grab up his dirty T-shirt lying on the floor by the bed.

THIRTY-FOUR

Ward picked up the sheets off the guest bedroom floor and started to put fresh ones on the bed.

The first night he'd spent in that room was after an argument he'd had with Natasha months earlier. He slept in the guest room the night after that in response to her cold silence the following day. Soon they had both accepted the change in sleeping arrangements as though it had been an order from the health department.

There was a gentle tapping on the door and Ward turned. "Yeah."

Natasha opened the door. She had a towel around her neck, and her T-shirt was clinging to her bare torso in places. "I finished five miles on the treadmill. Every muscle I have is screaming.

Look at this," she said, holding out her hands. "No shaking."

"That's great. Maybe it was just stress."

"Ward, what are you doing?"

"I'm just making the bed up."

"Yeah, the FBI screwed up the nice job you did making mine this morning. I saw it before they got here. Thanks for the gesture. I appreciated it."

"I didn't make your bed," he said.

She cocked her head and smiled at him sadly.

"Anyway, it's after six," she said. "I was going to take a shower and make dinner."

"I probably need to shower worse than you do."

She turned to go, then turned back, saying, "With the drought, we shouldn't be wasting water."

"We have a well," he said.

"It still seems wasteful," she said, tilting her head. "Maybe you've forgotten, but the master bathroom shower will comfortably hold two. And there's really no reason to make up the guest room bed, unless you just want to."

Ward stared at her.

"Ward, I'd like for you to come back home to me," she said. "If you want to. I really miss us."

Ward remained frozen, but Natasha crossed to the bed and took his hand in hers and led him from the guest room down the hall to their old bathroom.

Lying in bed an hour later, Natasha said, "The casket. Is it possible the FBI put it there for some bizarre reason?"

Ward felt anger rising inside him. "I don't know. It's the only thing I can think of. It was sick."

"Somebody made it," she said. "It doesn't seem possible that Barney got it from one of his friends and didn't show it to us. It might represent something that had nothing to do with a dead child. You know, like some Halloween deal he got that we didn't know he had?"

Ward shrugged. "I really hope that's the case. I mean, we never inventoried his things, but it seems unlike anything that he would have wanted around."

"I saw where you marked tomorrow on the calendar. We should take some flowers and visit the grave together."

"I thought you marked it," Ward said.

Natasha pulled away suddenly, and turned to face him, going up on her elbow. "You didn't mark it?"

"No, I didn't. I mean, not that I recall. Nights get weird sometimes."

"Like the baseball."

"Okay, so, if I haven't lost my mind, and I didn't make up your bed this morning before I woke up, or put the baseball under the pillow, or take Barney's watch, what does that mean?"

"That I did it and don't remember," she said.

"But I'm the one who loses time, does things I don't remember doing, says things I don't recall saying. But I never saw that casket thing before you found it, and I certainly would never have put it in his room."

"I never thought you did," she said. "What did you do with Buildy Bear? I didn't see him in the guest room or Barney's room."

"I didn't touch Buildy. Seriously."

Natasha sat up and crossed her ankles. "Jesus, Ward. This is too freaky. I had him in this bed night before last. I was sort of feeling . . . I got him from Barney's closet, and slept with him while you were gone. I went to bed last night and he'd vanished. I thought you took him."

"No. Christ, Natasha, maybe I do have Alzheimer's. My mother . . ."

"You're too young for that."

"I hope so."

"Ward, if you didn't do any of those things, and I didn't, then who else? We're the only people here."

THIRTY-FIVE

When his phone rang at midnight, Todd was eating a sandwich.

"Mr. Hartman?" a small, familiar voice asked.

"Speaking," he replied, turning on the recorder and plugging it into the phone.

"I was wondering if you've talked to Mr. McCarty about the . . . you know . . . that little toy car?"

"I have."

"Well?"

"He'll pay to get it back. Have you located it?"

Todd heard a whispering male voice in the background say, "Ten grand." It could be that she'd called the cops and they were monitoring or recording the call, but the cops would not be so dumb as to be whispering instructions to the girl. This was an interesting complication. Hopefully the other person was in for the payoff and cared less about making self-serving waves. That person might keep Alice Palmer on task and they'd resolve the matter expeditiously.

"Yeah, I've found it. I mean, I know where it is."

"And you can get ya hands on it," the other voice whispered.

"I can get it," Alice said. "I don't have it in my hands right now."

More whispering. Todd wished he could tell her to put a hand over the mouthpiece while someone, probably her boyfriend, was giving her instructions. This was strictly amateur time.

"So, what's Mr. McCarty's offer?"

"He said he'd pay a thousand dollars."

"I was thinking like ten," she said nervously.

"Well, Alice. It's one of a kind, which means it is worth something to him but probably nothing at all to anybody else. See, there's only been one owner, and so most collectors don't even know about it, and they would suspect it's a fake and they'd ask Mr. McCarty about it, but if they know about it, they'll know it's hot and know they could never sell it or show it to anybody. But it seems that the man seated beside you for the entire flight told me he saw Mr. McCarty show it to you, then put it back in the briefcase without opening it again. He heard him say he couldn't part with it, but he'd give you one instead. He saw you take it."

"He didn't see shit because he was gone to . . ."

"I know. He was down the aisle at the time waiting for a turn in the lavatory."

Silence.

"Stealing that car, since it is worth more than five hundred, would be grand larceny, a felony. With your record, and since you are an adult now, you could do jail time and we don't want that."

"She could call the police," the male voice blurted. She covered the mouthpiece this time for several seconds but not before he heard the male say, "Tell him the old pervert wanted to fuck you."

Todd smiled. This was entertaining.

"You can call the cops if you want to, and make any accusation against Mr. McCarty you can think of. But extortion is a more serious felony than grand theft, and I have a very credible witness as to everything that went on during the flight. The witness happens to be a retired judge," he lied. "Someone else saw you take the car while Mr. McCarty was away from his seat. There's more, but you are walking a very tight rope."

Silence.

"He's a known pervert," the male voice added. "Just turn on your TV."

"Shut up!" Alice screeched at the young man.

"Good advice, Earl. You don't want to be involved in anything criminal. I can get you two thousand, Alice. Mr. McCarty is not a pervert. I doubt Earl wants to do time for conspiracy to commit extortion, a serious felony. What do you say, Mr. Tucker?"

"How you know my name?" Earl blurted out.

"I know a lot more about you than your name. This is a serious game you're playing, kids. You both have records. If this doesn't end with me paying you two thousand and getting the car, your grandchildren will be visiting you in jail."

A long pause.

"You can't threaten us with no criminal charges. You ain't no cop," Earl said.

Alice said, "Okay. I'll take the two grand."

"I think that would be the smartest move you two could make. Let's set up a meeting that's convenient for you."

"And me," Earl said.

"No, Earl," Todd said. "Like most things, this is way out of your league. You should just go home and wait until Alice calls you."

Doubting that Earl was that smart, Todd planned to keep on his toes. Not that Earl was dangerous, but with the terminally stupid you just never knew.

"How about we meet tomorrow night?" Todd asked.

"Somewhere public," Alice said. "I want to make sure you don't try anything."

"Like?"

"Like ripping me off."

"Alice, I wouldn't dream of stealing from

you. Concord Mills Mall in the food court. Tomorrow."

"Okay," she said. "Tomorrow night. I got classes and other stuff to do in the daytime. Like maybe eight? Bring the money."

"I will. Bring the car."

THIRTY-SIX

While Ward watched Natasha dressing from the bed, his cell phone rang. It was his uncle Mark.

"Morning, Unk," Ward said.

"How are you and Natasha feeling?" Mark asked, his voice rife with concern.

"That would depend on your definition of 'feel,' " Ward replied.

"This is all temporary, kid. I know you were set up and the FBI will figure that out real soon. You gotta keep your chin up. Your father never let the bastards get the better of him, and you're a McCarty."

"Thanks, Unk. I appreciate your faith in me. I wouldn't have been successful without your support and experience. That's a fact and I hope you know that."

"Thanks, kid. But I'm just an old car salesman with a great product line."

"You've always been there for me. I know it and I appreciate it more than I can say."

"You're gonna make an old man cry. Listen, the other reason I called is that I got a call from Flash Dibble a few minutes ago," Mark said. "He asked me to tell you he's as interested as ever to buy the company. He says this virus thing is all a load of crap and he knows you aren't responsible and he is sure you'll be cleared. He thinks that once the company changes hands, its reputation can be salvaged. He also told me that the FBI is going to interview him this morning and he's going to tell them it's a bum rap. His words. He and your father go way back. They were never friends, but they had respect for each other. It's Trey that's the douche bag. Flash is just an astute businessman."

"So how much less you figure we're worth to him now?" Ward asked.

"He didn't say anything about reducing his last offer. We could have Gene feel him out on that. You want, I can talk to Gene."

"It seems like the timing on this scandal is sort of providential for Dibble, doesn't it? I'll be interested in seeing if his new offer is a bit reduced."

"Ward, we both know that at the present, our clients are vulnerable to all of our competition. Being our customers is a potential public relations problem for them, too. This is NASCAR, and moral rectitude, even though it's in short supply, is still a big issue with the fans."

"It's more than a public relations nightmare for me," Ward said, angrily. "You want vulnerability? How about a few years in federal prison? Or being a registered sex offender for the rest of my life?"

"We all know this is a setup of some sort. Flash is one hard-skinned son of a bitch, but if it ends up he had anything to do with this, he'd be destroyed, and the man has hundreds of millions at stake. Even if he wanted to do it to force a sale, I just don't see him risking getting caught doing this."

"There's Trey," Ward said. "I think he's capable of doing something like what happened."

"He's one mean, not-too-bright shit-for-brains. And those are his best points. Still . . . Ward, I don't think he's behind this."

"He wants the company as much as, or more than, his father does. If it wasn't for Trey, Flash could certainly have already bought a company like ours for a lot less. If I get locked up, Trey would get some sort of twisted revenge because I said no to him."

"Ward, this had to have been planned well before you told Trey to his face the deal was dead." Mark asked, "Way I figure it, what can it hurt to keep the options open?"

"Sure," Ward said. "Talk to Gene. I'm curious."

"By the way," Mark said, "we're open again. The servers are clean, and Gene said the feds have what they need. We gotta start doing some damage control. I'm seeing Lee Blackwelder in Charlotte at two. He's expensive, but public relations disasters are what he does best. I'd be right there with you and Natasha, but I think it's best you stay home for a day or two. You need anything, and I mean anything, you call me first. I'll be checking in with you, and I'll call if anything comes up. In the meanwhile, I'm going to be talking to any client who'll take my call."

"I'll call Gene about the Dibble thing. I have to talk to him anyway."

"Your call," Mark said. "I'll follow your lead, boss . . . nephew."

Ward hung up.

He wouldn't sell the company to Dibble for himself, but he had other people to think about. Flash might agree to institute some form of profit-sharing and to not fire employees for a certain period of time. There was also a chance this would somehow work out and Ward would be cleared. All it would take was proving who had come after him. Maybe Todd Hartman could work that miracle. He dialed Gene.

"No news is good news" was how his friend and attorney answered the call. "Wiggins is going to meet with us this morning at ten-thirty. He's informed the assistant federal attorney that if he wants to see you, he will bring you in. Any interviews from here out will only be conducted in his presence. Even so, the FBI may pick you up. You can't trust the bastards. If they show up and want to take you in, call me, or have Natasha do it and I'll call Wiggins. It's likely they'll take it slow and easy and make sure they have their ducks lined up before they move. I get the feeling the prosecutor doesn't have much confidence in the case so far, but that could change at any moment. There's a big commotion to get somebody charged for this . . ."

"What's Wiggins costing me?" Ward asked.

"Twenty thousand retainer for starters. That a problem?"

Ward paused, then forged ahead. "Nope."

"Then bring your checkbook. That pays up through arraignment and plea. The rest depends on what he has to do. This goes to trial, a hundred thousand easy."

"A hundred thousand dollars? Listen—Unk told me that Flash Dibble still wants the company. Flash called him. If you want to, you can see if the offer stands, but if he tries to drop it, it will make me wonder if he's involved in bringing down the value. Keep me posted."

"You change your mind?"

"No, I haven't. I don't know. Let's just say I want to do what's best. And maybe there are other potential buyers."

"Who'd offer less and sell to Flash," Gene said. "By the way, Todd Hartman making any progress on this?"

"I haven't talked to him today. So far, his people have kept the press away."

"See you at ten-thirty, Ward."

"Sounds good."

Ward called Todd's cell phone. It rang four times and went to his voice mail.

When Natasha came in, he filled her in on his conversation with Gene.

When his cell phone rang a minute later, Ward looked at the caller ID. It was Todd Hartman.

"Todd," he said. "We need to talk to you. Something's come up that might be important."

"I was coming to see you with good news. I'll be there in ten minutes."

THIRTY-SEVEN

When Ward opened the front door, Todd was parking his Denali. Leslie Wilde drove in behind him. He waited for her to join him and kissed her on the cheek, and they came to the door together.

"I tried to call," Leslie said, holding up her cell phone. "My battery is dead and I don't have my car charger. I thought I could run errands or whatever you need done. I'm going to take a personal day."

"You don't have to do that, Leslie," Ward said.

"I know, but I really want to help. Cheryl is covering your phone for the day. If it's okay?"

"We both appreciate what you've already done, more than you know. Come on in," Ward said, holding the door open.

"The media vultures are still up there," Leslie said. "It's the same thing over and over on the news. I guess they don't have anything better to put on. It dominated the *Today* show this morning. It's international news. The virus is still spreading, but they've been warning people about not opening the e-mail with the subject 'You have to see this.' "

Ward led them into the den, where Natasha greeted them with a bright smile.

"Todd, what's your good news?" Ward asked.

Todd looked at Leslie. "Maybe we should talk in private," he said.

"No problem. I'll give you guys a few minutes," Leslie said.

Todd said, "It's about the prototype."

"Leslie can hear it," Ward said. "She knows all about it."

"You're the client," Todd told him, smiling at Leslie.

Todd took a tape player from his briefcase and placed it on the table. "I wired myself before I spoke to her."

He pressed down on the play button and the quartet listened to the meeting on the campus of UNCC.

After the conversation played Todd clicked off the machine.

"Ward told me she looks young," Natasha said.

"Yes, she does," Todd replied. "She could pass for twelve."

"And by now she's seen the news, and even before that she was insinuating that she thought Ward made overtures toward her. What if she thinks she can shake him down?" Leslie asked.

"I think we're past that," Todd said.

"Christ," Ward said.

"She's a disturbed young lady with a need for attention," Natasha said. "This could get her some."

Ward asked Todd, "How do we handle it?"

"She was in the middle seat, so I got the name of the man seated beside her on the aisle. His name is Albert Gaines, and he lives down in Rock Hill. I'll talk to him—I'd bet he saw the car when you showed it to her and that he was away from the seat only while you were. And he'll know whether or not you seemed to be coming on to Alice. Sitting that close he'd have to have seen or heard everything that went on."

"Okay," Ward said. "I'm sure you're right. He was right there."

"I spoke to Alice Palmer late last night. She and her boyfriend tried extortion—asking for ten thousand. I told her I'd talked to witness Gaines, and said you'd go two and I wouldn't have them put in jail. Everybody gets what they want. We're going to pay to get the car back. Eight tonight at Concord Mills food court."

"Let's just hope she doesn't decide to call the police anyway," Natasha said. "Maybe she doesn't need the money as much as she needs attention."

"That's possible," Todd said, "but I'm sure her boyfriend just wants a payday."

"By the way, I have someone looking into

Trey Dibble, and I'm trying to find out if Lander Electric has an investigator they use locally, or one their lawyers use. You know which law firm they've retained?"

"I forget the name. Gene's been dealing with them. They're a big firm with offices around the country and two-hundred-plus lawyers. Their North Carolina office is in Durham."

"If you don't mind, I'll call him for that information."

Ward wrote down Gene's phone numbers for Todd.

"This could get expensive," Todd said.

Natasha said, "Whatever it takes, Todd. We'll handle it. Let's just get it fixed as quickly as possible."

Todd nodded, but he didn't seem to be listening. He was looking out through the window at something near the trees. He turned to look at Ward. "I want everybody to just keep talking like you are now. And don't look outside." He reached into his pocket for a walkie-talkie and, holding it in his lap, keyed it.

"Number two," Todd said, as though he was talking to Ward, "circle the house. Slow and quiet. I saw a light flare in the trees, up on the back ridge, ninety degrees out from the living room. Might be a camera."

"Everyone just keep talking, and don't look out the window." Todd looked back toward the kitchen, stood and walked toward the door, turned, and sprinted for the front.

Ward, Natasha, and Leslie sat frozen, as Todd had instructed, until Ward heard him yell out, and he turned to see the investigator running gazelle-like among the trees along the ridge, gun in his hand. Ward also saw the man Todd had called, working his way among the trees on the ridge, coming in from the left side.

Standing, Ward saw Todd signal the other man before sprinting deep into the woods. Five minutes later the two men came walking back, their guns holstered. Todd was wiping dirt from his pants and his jacket.

Ward walked out through the kitchen door and onto the patio in front of the covered pool, Natasha and Leslie following. He saw the two men looking down at the ground. Todd had disappeared below his waist. From a distance, he looked half buried. He reached down and came up with something that looked like a blanket with a man-size hole in the middle.

"Wait here," Ward told the women. He walked swiftly down the grassy slope and up the rise, approaching the two men.

"He got away," Todd said, reaching down into a hole that was about four by six feet wide and a good three feet deep. He lifted out a pair of armored binoculars by the strap and inspected them gently. What Ward had thought was a blanket was actually fine netting stretched across a wood frame with dead leaves attached to the material.

"Mr. McCarty, I'm Bixby Nolan. I work for Mr. Hartman." The other man turned to Ward and nodded.

"Nice to meet you," Ward said absently.

Nolan, wearing black jeans and a T-shirt under a lightweight jacket, was five six, and he looked like a prizefighter. He had a thin scar across his forehead, just above the dark sunglasses, and his blond hair was gathered into a ponytail.

"I didn't see anybody," Nolan said.

"I saw a reflection from these glasses," Todd said. "He ran from the hide when I broke around the house. He was wearing black jeans and shirt and ball cap. Maybe six feet tall with wide shoulders. He vanished into thin air."

Todd reached back into the hole and took out a small, rectangular, flat, dull orange object, which he studied for a moment before he set it on the ground beside the binoculars.

"What's that?" Ward asked.

"See the writing. 'Fine India Made in the USA' stone. For sharpening a survival knife," Todd said. "Stones just like this one come with Randall fighting and survival knives. It fits in a little pocket on the holster."

"That's an expensive knife," Bixby said.

"I doubt the guy was a reporter," Todd said, reaching down and feeling something in the front wall of the hole. He straightened and, climbing out, moved to the backside of the hole and kneeled to look in.

"How do you know that?" Ward asked.

"He's been here for a lot longer than just since yesterday, when the virus hit."

When Ward came around and knelt beside Todd he saw, carved in the clay walls, scores of carefully crafted letters stretched out in long straight lines, stacked to fill the space like a lesson painstakingly chalked on a blackboard. At the base of that wall was a pile of small bits of dry clay, lying where they'd fallen during the carving. Ward realized that the words were, in fact, one word written over and over, and, although they were run together without any spacing, the word was immediately readable because of the capital G every fifth letter. Whoever had been here had time and patience.

Nolan Bixby asked, "What the hell does 'Gizmo' mean?"

"Nothing good," Todd said, with perfect certainty.

THIRTY-EIGHT

"We should call the police," Natasha said, after learning about the hiding place.

"You sure should," Leslie agreed as she poured Ward a cup of coffee.

"What do you think?" Ward asked Todd. "Some nut has been watching our house for a long time. Would Dibble or Lander Electric hire a private eye to spy on us over time like that?"

"This will be under the sheriff's jurisdiction, and the truth is we're only talking trespassing. It might be some private eye. Some of us will do anything to get a result. I think you should call Gene Duncan and see how he thinks you should handle it. Given all that's happened, I think he might want to report it to the FBI. Let them process the evidence."

"There's something else," Ward said. "I was about to tell you when you saw the guy outside. Some weird things have been happening. Some of Barney's things have been moved around over the past week. A baseball from his room ended up in Natasha's bed under a pillow. She thought I did it. A stuffed bear of Barney's vanished from Natasha's room. A watch of his vanished from Natasha's jewelry box."

"And there's no other explanation? Nobody else has access to the house?"

"No. And we found a handmade casket with a figure of a young boy in it in Barney's room. We are sure Barney didn't have that, and we certainly didn't put it there."

"I've been having hand tremors that started about a month ago," Natasha said. "They're getting progressively worse. And Ward's been losing time and doing things he doesn't remember."

"It's like I lose my nights, don't remember dreams, feel dull in the mornings."

"I know it sounds crazy," Natasha said, "but now in the light of everything else that's happened, I'm seriously thinking that we're being drugged."

Todd was silent.

"I can't believe I'm saying this. Look, since our symptoms are very different, I think the drugs we've been getting are as well," Natasha said. "Isn't it possible that someone out there might be giving each of us the different drugs, different ways? Isn't it possible?"

"It's possible," Todd said. "If someone's been in here, he certainly could be moving things and even drugging you both. Maybe he's doing it and watching his handiwork. Yes, it sounds paranoid, but I think you have reason to be paranoid."

"That's scary," Leslie said. "Sitting in a hole for days on end, carving a word into the clay over and over, is way beyond creepy. If the crazy bastard has been coming in here when you weren't home, he could have come in when you were, or hidden in here and . . ."

"Maybe he knows what only one of us drinks or eats. He spikes hers with one drug and mine with another," Ward said.

Todd stared at him and nodded slowly. "So let's see if we can figure out what that might be."

"Well, she drinks wine. I don't care for it," Ward said.

"Daily," Natasha said. "That's the only thing I can think of. I know how far-fetched this is, but it makes sense, doesn't it? Oh, and I drink orange juice and Ward has a citrus allergy."

Todd nodded. "And you, Ward? What's only yours?"

"Scotch. That and bottled water. Natasha drinks our well water. I don't mind the taste, except when I pour it into my single malts."

"Gather up the bottles you have, and I'll take the samples and drop them at a lab I use."

"Shouldn't they get the FBI to test them?" Leslie said.

"You could let the FBI test them. I'm not saying you shouldn't. But I'll do it, too, in case they screw it up or don't actually do it. Are you ready to trust them? They may just think this is a smoke screen designed by Ward to throw them off him."

"I don't trust the FBI," Ward agreed, surely.

"But, on the other hand, if someone's been in and has done that, it might help convince them of your innocence with the virus," Natasha told Ward. "And they might be convinced we didn't spike the drinks ourselves. I mean, there's no real evidence you are guilty of anything. And this same person might have put the virus in your computers. I mean, they have to see that's possible, and would explain everything."

"Why would he be targeting both of us, not just me?" Ward said. "I think we should let the FBI see the hole out there, and if they seem receptive, we can tell them that we think we're being drugged."

"I'll take samples of the wine, the OJ, and the Scotch, and we'll give them the rest and see if we get the same results. They'll have to check it out. It isn't proof that there's someone else doing it, but coupled with the hole out there, it sure gives your lawyer ammunition for reasonable doubt."

"I'm a doctor with access to drugs and compounds," Natasha said.

"But they haven't accused you of anything. Just me," Ward said.

"I'll call Gene," Ward told them. "He'll know what we should do, legally speaking, and he can call the FBI and explain it to them. He can probably get them to come out here."

"And we can see if someone has figured out our alarm system's code," Ward said. "It's a top-of-the-line system and we always arm it when we leave, and at night when we settle in. With all the home invasions around, I figured that because people might think Natasha keeps drugs here they might come to find them."

"Has it gone off recently?" Todd asked.

"No. A few times when we first got it and made stupid mistakes. Not in three or four years, though."

"There should be a record of entries. Even if he entered your code, or somehow added his own, the entries should have registered with the monitoring service," Todd said. "Get me their information and I'll get the log and we can see if it was disarmed when you weren't here. Go ahead and call Duncan."

Ward reached for the portable phone.

"I'll sweep the house for bugs," Todd said, standing. "I carry some sweeping equipment in the truck that'll tell me if there's anything here. And I'll take pictures of the hide and what he left there. And if you'll empty some water bottles and get a funnel if you have one, I can collect the samples."

"But wine bottles have corks," Leslie said.

"A syringe would take care of that," Todd told her bluntly. "We'll know if there's anything in them later today. A toxicology screen doesn't take long, and I'll get it rushed."

Ward dialed Gene.

"I was just about to call you," Gene said, by way of answering.

"You need to come to the house right now," Ward told him.

"What's up?" Gene asked.

Ward said, "We should talk face-to-face."

"Give me fifteen minutes."

THIRTY-NINE

Ward accompanied Todd Hartman as he swept the house and collected three small listening devices from the kitchen, den, and dining area. Someone had been in the house. Todd placed the bugs into a foam-lined envelope.

"These are high-quality bugs—minis that transmit to a receiver. The range is limited to two or three hundred yards at the most. He can place a gatherer inside that zone, and from that device he can transmit anywhere. He's definitely been listening to your conversations."

Todd collected the wine bottles, orange juice containers, and Scotch bottles. He lifted one of the unopened orange juice cartons and, turning it upside down, squeezed it. A tiny stream of orange liquid arced across the room. Someone had been in the house.

"You were right, Todd, he used a syringe," Leslie said.

"Who used a syringe?" Gene asked as he walked into the room, red-faced. After Natasha told him what they'd figured out, Gene accompanied Todd out to the hide. He studied the binoculars, the sharpening stone, and the carvings. Ward saw Gene open his phone and make a call. After five minutes in the heat, they went back inside.

"Todd has pictures of everything so we have a record," Ward said.

"We need to give the remaining liquids to the FBI, but I agree that Todd should definitely have his samples checked. Not that I don't trust the FBI, but they haven't given us any reason to. Lander Electric wouldn't do this," Gene said conclusively.

"The Dibbles are behind this," Ward said. "It's the only thing that makes sense. If not Flash, then Trey is behind it. I know it in my bones."

"I talked to Flash," Gene said. "He said the last offer is still on the table unchanged. Doesn't seem like he's taking advantage of this."

"That was nice of him," Natasha said angrily. She wasn't ready to let a Dibble off the hook.

"Don't you think you could cut him some slack?" Gene said. "If he'd been involved, do you think he would keep his offer firm? Ward, as your attorney and friend, I'd advise you to con-sider his offer. Who knows what else might happen that would negatively affect the company's value."

"Gene, I'm surprised at you," Natasha said. "Haven't you considered that it may be the best way for Flash to distance himself from the dirty tricks? Maybe he knows Trey is responsible and wants to protect him. He knows any damage to the company's reputation won't last once Ward is out of the picture."

Ward stared at his wife as if seeing her for the first time. He had long ago accepted the fact that Natasha was a lot smarter and more perceptive than he was. The knowledge that she was ready to fight the world at his side warmed him and steeled his resolve.

"You ready to let Lander Electric off the hook? They could be behind this. They could have hired this stalker, or investigator—no offense to your profession, Todd—or whatever he is," Gene said.

"Maybe they are responsible," Natasha acknowledged, "but I can't see where the virus, or Ward's innocence or guilt, would affect our wrongful death case."

Ward smiled quietly at her use of the word "our."

Gene said, "Unless they think a jury will believe that a man who can get off looking at
naked children is the sort of nut who would kill
his own son so he could collect insurance, which
there wasn't any, or sue them because of it."
Hearing Gene say that gave Ward a hot, hollow
feeling in the pit of his stomach. And it pissed
him off. And someone had been in the house.
And that terrified Ward McCarty more than he
could possibly have imagined.

FORTY

Todd went to his truck and returned holding
two cell phones. "I have these for you to use.
They're encrypted, so Gene and I can call you
and you can call us without worrying about being monitored. The numbers are on the labels
on the backs. When this is over, you can go back
to using your lines. These'll work with your
chargers."

Ward and Natasha took the cell phones and
looked at the numbers on the backs of the units.

Gene came into the room and said, "What other brand of shit are we going to step into?"

Ward was thinking about Alice Palmer. The girl could certainly add gasoline to the fire that appeared to be no more than coals, and if she went to the federal prosecutor, he might use her as additional proof of Ward's sexual interest in youngsters. Ward was about to mention her to Gene when Natasha did. "Todd, tell Gene about Alice Palmer," she said. "And the missing car."

"Who?" Gene asked.

"I'll let Todd tell you," Ward said.

After Todd ran it all down, he played the tape of his conversation with Alice for Gene. The lawyer shook his head and said, "For pity's sake, can it get any worse? You should have told me this earlier, a lot earlier."

"Isn't that the truth," Natasha said. She was staring out the window.

"I figured Todd could handle it. So far he's batting a thousand."

"It's under control," Todd added evenly.

Natasha said, "I guess that hole out there explains why I felt like I was being watched. Sunday I thought I saw something move out there in the shadows. Jesus, I thought it was an animal."

"Do you have a gun in the house?" Todd asked.

"Of course not." Natasha was incredulous. "Why would *we* own a gun?"

"Well," Todd said, "whatever was out in that hole is the best reason I can think of."

"Ward? With a gun!" Gene said, laughing out loud. "I doubt he knows which end the bullets come out of."

"That much I know," Ward said.

The gun Todd took out of his briefcase was a black steel short-barreled revolver.

"This is a five-shot, thirty-eight-caliber Smith and Wesson," he said. "This is how it works. Pay attention." He pushed forward the textured button on the side of the weapon and held the gun so his new students could see what he was doing as he spoke. "You hold this and push on this side of the cylinder and it swings open." He rotated the gun so they could see that it was empty before he placed five red plastic bullets on the counter, rounded tips pointing up. With measured slowness, Todd took them one by one and placed each into an empty chamber until all were inserted, then closed the cylinder.

"I want you to practice loading and unloading this gun until you can do it fast. The gun will not go off unless the cylinder is closed and the trigger is pulled. The hammer can be cocked manually, or just squeeze the trigger and it fires double action."

Todd opened the gun, ejected the dummy bullets into his hand, laid them on the counter, and closed the cylinder.

"You can safely practice loading and dry-firing with the dummies." He reloaded the gun rapidly. "It isn't good for a hammer to fall on an empty chamber."

"Why is that?" Ward asked.

"In the old days revolver firing pins could break if they didn't strike a primer. The new pins on revolvers are stronger, but every machine has an infinite number of movements before it fails," Todd said. "No sense tempting the laws of metallurgy." He pointed the gun at the refrigerator and pulled the trigger once, then again.

He handed it to Ward butt first.

Ward looked down the barrel.

"It doesn't have much in the way of sights," Todd said.

"How do you line them up then?" Ward asked.

"Don't need to, close in. This has a short barrel, so for all intents and purposes the sights are useless. Just point it like you'd point your finger at something you're looking at and your brain will aim it for you. Natasha, load it and point at the stove."

Ward handed it to Natasha, who held the gun as though it were a dead rat. Gracelessly, she managed to open the cylinder, load the plastic bullets, and close it.

Todd smiled. "Don't put your finger in the trigger guard until you are going to squeeze it. As soon as you decide to use it, point and squeeze like you're making a tight fist. Firmly and slowly, because the gun will go off target if you jerk it. If you imagine that you're aiming at a saucer your enemy is wearing on his chest you'll hit vital organs—heart or lungs. I don't expect that I have to tell you where the vital organs are, Doctor."

"I don't intend to fire it."

"Don't extend the gun. Keep it close to your

body. If you point the gun at someone, fire immediately. Anyone who knows what he's doing can take it from you and use it against you."

"I would never shoot a person," Natasha said with certainty.

"Okay. Then aim to hit something directly behind him and let the bullet find its own path."

"It would go through him," Leslie said.

"If that's the path the bullet has to take, so be it. Natasha, if your target gets the gun, he'll probably use it on you and Ward. Could you kill to save your husband's life or your own?"

"Yes," she said, nodding as she met Ward's eyes. "I would kill to save him. But I'm a doctor. 'First, do no harm.'"

"You're a living woman *first*," Todd said, smiling. "After you shoot the son of a bitch, as a wife protecting yourself and your husband, you can give him CPR as a doctor until the paramedics arrive."

Ward laughed nervously.

Natasha didn't.

"Again. You will only point the gun at someone you have decided to shoot," Todd said, seriously. "Do not hesitate. A man who knows what he's doing can move thirty feet in less than two seconds. A decision to fire through the trigger pull takes an average of three. It's longer if you are a civilian. If that man has a knife he can bat the gun aside and kill you before you can squeeze the trigger. So make the decision when you raise the gun and fire then."

"I'll keep the gun," Ward said.

"That would probably be best," Natasha said. "I'd be thinking about all the gunshot wounds I've tried to repair. The damage it would do."

"Regardless, you should familiarize yourself with the weapon. Just in case."

Natasha pointed the Smith at the stove, closing her eyes; when she pulled the trigger, she jerked visibly at the snap. Natasha handed the gun to Ward, and he did the same thing. He play-fired the gun, killing the windows, the refrigerator, the Mixmaster, the fridge, the stove, and Mr. Coffee. By the end of the session, Mr. Smith and Mr. Wesson were not quite old friends, but they were acquaintances.

FORTY-ONE

The driveway guard called ahead so that when the doorbell rang, the occupants of the McCarty home knew who was at the door. Gene had left and Leslie was out running a list of essential errands for Natasha.

"Agents," Ward said, after opening the door. "Come in."

Agent John Mayes nodded at Ward and Natasha, but Bill Firman looked like a man who was there for a colonoscopy. Mayes wore a wedding band, wingtips, and a cheap suit. Firman had an expensive haircut and manicured nails.

As Todd, Natasha, and Ward watched from a few feet away, the two agents inspected the hide on the hill. While Mayes looked at the same things Firman was looking at, Mayes looked at the McCartys as often as he looked at the hole, the binoculars, the cigarette butts, and the diamond sharpening stone. Finally Firman took out a handkerchief and wiped the perspiration from his forehead. It was ninety-seven degrees and there was not the slightest breeze to stir the leaves.

"So who, or what, is Gizmo?" Firman asked.

"No idea," Natasha said. "He, or it, didn't introduce himself."

"All I know is what everybody knows. That word is slang for electronic devices, widgets, thingamajigs," Ward said.

"Is that a fact?" Firman asked. "And you didn't know this hole was out here?"

"No, I didn't," Ward said.

"Then you wouldn't know how long it has been here?"

"No," Ward said. "We rarely come up here."

"Like to collect firewood in the fall?" Firman mused.

"We buy firewood in the fall," Natasha said.

"We don't even own a chain saw," Ward said. "And we like our trees standing."

"So, Mr. Hartman, you didn't get a good look at this person who scurried out of the hole and fled through the woods?"

"No," Todd said. "I saw a light reflection. I thought it was probably a cameraman sneaking shots. I called for backup, and Bixby Nolan and I converged, but the subject was already running away. I couldn't close on him. He seemed familiar with the terrain, because there's no path, and he was very fast and agile."

"Maybe it was a raccoon," Firman said flatly.

"Your sarcasm is uncalled for, Agent Firman," Natasha said sternly. "Someone has been using this hole to watch our home, which I would think might be of interest to you. Todd Hartman found listening devices in our home, and it's very likely we have been systematically drugged by someone, perhaps the person who was in this hole. If you aren't going to take this seriously, we'll call the actual police. I think they will be more open to investigating this than you seem to be."

"Digging a hole, scratching on the walls, and watching your house. Not federal crimes," Firman said, shrugging. "Who knows who planted those bugs, but breaking and entering even to plant eavesdropping devices and drug liquor supplies are also not federal crimes. And drugs would be easy for you to get your hands on. I saw the toy casket you let your child have. So, I suggest you do call the sheriff, or maybe you could hire a really good private investigator."

"We'd never seen that casket before and it was

not anything our son would have had. We would have seen it in the room. Whoever was in this hole must have planted it to freak us out and your people found it before we did," Ward said angrily.

Todd glared at Firman. "My excuse, if I needed one, is that I've only been working on this for a day. You've got the FBI lab and a lot of support personnel behind you. Maybe we should ask the attorney general to send some actual FBI agents to investigate."

Firman laughed, but Mayes didn't. In fact he appeared thoughtful.

"Agent Firman, there's a medical term that fits you," Natasha said.

Ward knew what was coming because he'd heard this come out of her mouth once before, and he would have said something if he'd thought her contribution might be counterproductive, but he didn't think it could be.

"And what would that medical term be, *Doctor*?" Firman asked.

"Hemorrhoid." Her delivery was perfect.

Mayes laughed.

Firman didn't.

FORTY-TWO

Mayes took samples of liquids away with him in a plastic shopping bag, promising Ward and Todd he'd have them analyzed by the FBI lab. Based solely on Firman's attitude, a speedy response by the lab seemed unlikely to Ward.

Thanks to the tinted windows in Todd's Denali, Natasha and Ward were able to sit up in the backseat without being visible to the few remaining members of the media milling about outside their vans on the road. Nolan and his partner, arms crossed and wearing sidearms and frowns, were keeping them at bay.

"Gizmo," Natasha said. "I keep thinking I've heard that nickname somewhere before."

"So have I," Ward said. "There was a kid in high school who was always building electronic equipment. His nickname was Gizmo. He died our senior year, from leukemia. He won our science fair with a listening device he made from metallic tubes of varying lengths bundled together. The Army actually bought the device from him."

"Him dying pretty much rules him out," Todd said. "Ghosts don't dig holes in the ground and carve their own nicknames into the walls."

In downtown Charlotte, Todd parked in the lot underneath the building where Wiggins & Associates took up half of the fifth floor. Gene was waiting for them in the reception area when they arrived, and he led them back to Tom Wiggins's office. Lawyer Wiggins greeted them warmly and shook everybody's hands. He and Natasha made small talk about the fund-raising for the children's cancer center. Wiggins was involved because he'd lost a granddaughter to bone cancer four years earlier.

"First off," he told them, "they haven't got anything to hang their hats on but theories. What they have might get them an indictment, but I doubt they'll go for one on hunches alone. That doesn't mean they won't arrest Ward if they get him indicted, but for the moment I seriously doubt it. In order for them to convict, they have to prove that you knowingly had the illegal material in your possession, and that you disseminated it."

"Gene's filled me in on the stalker and the possible drugging. Obviously, someone released this virus on purpose, and it appears they set you up to take the blame. Mr. Hartman can verify the facts, and based on his expertise and reputation, his word should carry weight."

Todd, seated to one side, nodded.

"Computer experts are going over the virus and we should have everything figured out except for whoever planted it. Someone has been accessing porn sites using your office computer for over a year. From what I have been able to put together using what the prosecutor shared with me, someone used your computer many times over the past ten months to visit unsavory sites. Usually when you were there, according to the receptionist's time sheets."

"How is that possible?" Ward asked.

Todd said, "It can be done remotely, using spyware programs."

"Todd probably knows more about this than I do, but I am told the program can be tracked back to the originator," Wiggins said.

"Good," Natasha said.

Todd nodded his agreement.

"Your son Barney died, what, about a year ago?" Wiggins asked.

Natasha said, "Today is the one-year anniversary."

The meeting lasted less than thirty minutes, but Gene assured Ward and Natasha on the way out that they'd be billed for an hour.

FORTY-THREE

Filled with outrage that clinched his stomach like a vise, Ward pressed down hard on the pedal and tossed *The Charlotte Observer* into the trash can's open mouth, letting the lid slam shut.

Natasha rubbed his forearm. "They only say you are the CEO of RGI, and that the virus originated from a computer in your office. Nothing we can do about it. It's all just innuendo and speculation."

"Innuendo sucks. Unk gets the mud splashed on him, too," Ward said. "I sure as hell can do something about it. I'll cancel our subscription."

Natasha laughed. "That'll teach them."

"Perception doesn't go away."

"They'll find out who doc'd the box," Natasha said.

" 'Doc'd the box'?" Todd asked.

"I think it sounds really techy," Natasha said. "A play on . . . you know."

Todd laughed easily.

"I've really missed your sense of humor." Ward smiled, leaned over, and kissed his wife. "I've decided that I'm going to sell the company." He looked up into Natasha's eyes, waiting for her response.

"To Dibble?" Natasha asked, taking a sip of water.

"It's the only offer on the table. With the money we can move and start over somewhere. Maybe Seattle." When he said it, he had a thought that rocked him to his core. *And leave Barney here?* He wondered if the same thought hit his wife, because he saw her eyes lose their focus for a second. Or was she thinking about the partnership offer from her old professor?

"I just can't picture Trey Dibble running your father's company. I'm afraid I'm going to have to vote against it."

"I think Dibble is behind the virus," Todd said.

"I don't think it's Lander Electric. Except for your son's accident, they're squeaky-clean. This is just business with them, and with Dibble it's probably more personal than business. Everything I've found out about Trey Dibble tells me he's one seriously ruined bowl of fruit. He hangs with some pretty rough customers—some of which are known drug dealers and one connected to organized crime."

"I have no choice, Natasha. You've seen how people look at me, how your own patients turned against you. How many of our many friends have showed up at the driveway or tried to see us to show their support?"

"The problem is my patients' parents," Natasha said, smiling sadly. "My patients like me."

FORTY-FOUR

Security in the downtown condo complex was hardly more than a showy illusion designed to make the owners feel secure and intimidate amateurs. Only the cameras in the lobby, the elevator cabins, and the main hallways were monitored by staff security. Watcher overrode the alarm on the fire door and fried the circuits in that camera without worrying it would be discovered anytime soon.

Watcher wasn't even breathing hard after climbing twenty-three floors of stairs. Once in the service hall, he slipped to the rear door that opened into the kitchen of Trey Dibble's penthouse. The expensive and complicated lock on the steel security door slowed Watcher less than ten seconds. Once inside, he heard the voices of two men radiating from the living room. Watcher moved to the door and listened.

"The FBI saw me earlier this morning. I figured they'd come see you."

"Well, why didn't you call and warn me?" Trey whined.

"I told them to check you out," Flash said. "If you did have anything to do with that virus, you're going to prison with my blessings."

"I have to have the six hundred thousand today," a third voice chimed in.

This voice reflected some anger, but that was covered over by fear.

"As I said before, Mark, I will advance it to you in a personal transaction. But the deal has to go through. That's a lot of money."

"You'll get it back," Mark Wilson said.

"Ward is not going to sell to me," Flash said. "But if you say you can make it happen, I believe you, Mark. You're both a horse trader and his uncle. And you know better than to try to screw me."

"He'll sell," Mark said. "He's in a box, thanks to your son."

"Thanks to me?" Trey snapped.

"That fucking virus. What were you thinking?" Mark demanded. "We all know that was your doing."

"Me?" Trey asked. "I didn't have anything to do with it!"

Flash said, "In my son's sole defense, he isn't that imaginative."

"He could have paid somebody who is," Mark said. "Who else could have had any reason to pull that shit?"

"The FBI is convinced Ward did it," Flash said. "I told them I didn't believe it for a minute, and I don't. This will blow over and they will catch the mentally challenged person who did it."

"I bet Ward did do it," Trey said. "Why would anybody else? It's a friggin dumb-ass move, and unproductive for our benefit."

"If you did this, I'll turn you in myself," Flash repeated. "Mark, I want RGI, and if I don't get it, I have friends who will collect the six hundred thousand. Do we understand each other? If Ward finds out the six hundred thousand is missing, how are you going to get it back into the bank without admitting what you did? What are you going to tell him?"

"I'll explain that I borrowed it for an emergency and I'm paying it back," Mark said. "He'll be pissed, but he is my nephew. He knows I love him."

"Remember that stock is worthless, due to adverse public opinion," Trey said. "RGI's reputation is total shit. I think we should cut our offer in half."

"Our offer?" Flash laughed mirthlessly. "How much of *your* money is on the table here? This is my money we're talking about. Until you have some money that isn't mine to put in, keep your damned business advice to yourself. Mark, three months and I expect repayment in full. I have a certified check in my pocket, and a promissory note form. You sign and you can walk over to the bank to cover your problem."

As Watcher listened, he looked at the granite countertops, a bottle of cooking oil, and an idea formed in his mind.

Five minutes later, Flash and McCarty's uncle concluded their business and left the condominium together.

Watcher waited a few seconds before he strolled into the living room.

Trey sat on the couch sucking on a lit joint, which he held in his chubby fingers like a cigarette. He wore a Speedo, his jewelry, and nothing else.

"Trey," Watcher said.

The joint flew into the air and Trey twisted on the couch to look back over his shoulder at Watcher.

"FUCK!" Trey blurted. "How did you get in here? You scared the shit out of me. I thought the goddamned FBI had circled back." He slid off the couch and rushed to the joint smoldering on the thick area rug. Lifting it up, he smashed the place where it had been with the sole of his foot.

"The back door was standing open."

"Fucking Tami." Trey snorted. "She took the trash out and the dumb-ass whore forgot to lock it."

"Where's she now?"

"The FBI said they wanted to talk to me so I sent her out to Belk to look at shoes and told her to stay out for an hour. Then Daddy called and said Mark Wilson was outside and they were going to meet up here. I told him the FBI was here, and he said to call when they left and he'd have Mark wait in the restaurant across the street and to call when they left. Hell, Daddy sent them here to bust my balls."

Trey winked. "I told them the opposite of what Daddy did. He said Ward was no way a pervert." Trey laughed in a nervous burst. "I told them Ward was light in the loafers."

Watcher nodded.

"The FBI is after McCarty, and how. The virus thing was brilliant. But my dumb-ass old man isn't smart enough to offer less. Sometimes he amazes me. Business is business, and I'm sure as hell not going to let anything color my judgment when I take over."

"All tooth and claw," Watcher said. "You're

twice the businessman your old man is. You'll do what has to be done."

Trey hit the joint again. "Tooth and claw. I like that. So can we trust your computer genius to keep his pie-hole shut?"

"His lips are sealed."

"My old man better never find out I was involved. I swore to God I wasn't. This geek. How can you be sure he won't turn on you? The FBI told me their lab techs can trace the guy who did it."

"They may track him down. But he'll never tell them anything."

"How can you be sure he'll do time without turning on you?"

"Because he's left the country," Watcher lied, smiling. "You paid me to be thorough."

"Best fifty grand I ever spent. You handled the situation. We get RGI and I don't need to know any more than that. That's all. Maybe if you get popped, you'll trade up for me. Believe me, I've thought about it. Maybe you should have killed the geek, not sent him out of the country. He might come back."

"I brought him over from Europe. He's French. Hates America. Uses aliases and doesn't know you exist. You paid me cash so there's no proof I've ever done anything for you. That gives you total deniability. The only way you'd be connected to the geek is if the FBI found his business card on you and a phone that's linked to one he had." Watcher smiled at Trey.

Trey smiled back and pointed with the smoking joint. "That's why I hired you. A man shows up with a plan, you listen, and if it makes sense, you bite. This deal is about done, and I'm so happy with the virus that I'm gonna give you a retainer as a consultant when we get RGI. The virus was a great idea, even if it was yours."

"I'm not doing this for money, Trey."

"What you doing it for, the kicks?" Trey asked, offering Watcher the joint.

He shook his head and said, "It's more complex. It was in my best interest to drop Ward McCarty."

"Whatever," Trey said, disinterested. "No more needs to be said. He's a spoiled prick. Not like he worked to build that company. He inherited it. Okay, you get what you want and so do I. I like what you do, and I want you watching my back here on out and helping me climb up the ladder tooth and claw. Just remember, you don't ever tell me nothing more about how you work the miracles I need. Next we deal with my old man," Trey said, winking. "If the old guy needs to go for a swim, you up for hard-core?"

"Tooth and claw," Watcher said. "I'm going to go. You should lock the door behind me."

Trey took a hit from the joint and followed Watcher through the door. He didn't notice the bottle of cooking oil lying on its side on the counter or that the contents had pooled on the terrazzo floor until his feet went out from under him. Trey's last thought was probably that Watcher was grabbing him to keep him from falling, not in order to guide the back of his head into the sharp edge of the granite countertop as he fell.

After Watcher checked for Trey Dibble's pulse, and didn't find one, he looked at the pad by the telephone. He pressed Dibble's prints onto it, and placed Bert's business card under it so it was barely covered and the cops would have to try not to see it there. There was just one more connection to Bert that Watcher had to handle.

Going back into the living room, Watcher placed his disposable cell phone between the cushions of the couch. It was the phone he'd used exclusively to talk to Bert Marmaduke over the past three weeks. On the way out of the kitchen, Watcher took the plastic bag containing the knife he'd used on old Bert from his pocket, and dropped just the knife into the garbage can, making a loud metallic noise when it hit the bottom.

Just as he was closing the door, he heard the front door open and close. He left, and was opening the stairwell door when he heard Tami Waterman's scream.

FORTY-FIVE

According to the news reports, the virus was still creating havoc around the world, but other stories had started receiving more and more play, so the virus in turn received less.

At a little past one, Ward walked past the kitchen where Natasha and Leslie Wilde were sitting across from each other at the counter, talking and laughing like schoolgirls.

Leslie had come to the McCartys' house to drop off the bags of groceries she'd purchased from the list Natasha had given her earlier that morning. She sat on a stool at the counter while Natasha put them away. She had also brought them a laptop computer from the office, in case they wanted to check e-mails. The last thing Natasha wanted to do was open a computer and look at e-mails.

"God, I'll be so glad when this is all over. How's that for stating the obvious?" Natasha said. "I believe it's aged me ten years."

"This will all be over soon," Leslie told Natasha. "And you look marvelous. It will all work out, you'll see."

"I hope so." Natasha lowered her voice. "So, Todd Hartman is quite a guy."

"And attractive, smart, and handsome," Leslie said, smiling.

"And a professional," Natasha said. "That's important."

"Yes, he's employed," Leslie said. "And did I mention handsome?"

"I think you might have."

Natasha's dealings with Leslie had always been pleasant, though superficial. She had spoken to her on the phone untold times, but until this mess started she had never spent more than a few minutes talking to her face-to-face. They had never been socially connected, and Natasha intended to change that. Of all of their so-called friends, none had sent messages of support. Of course, due to a lack of computers to retrieve e-mails, the fact that the phones were off, and the guards at the driveway, there wasn't an easy way for their friends to get in touch.

Leslie said, "Ward seems much more relaxed today."

Natasha looked at Leslie. "Ward is finally putting things into perspective. He's decided that life has to go on. I think if there's one good thing that has come from this virus mess it's that this helped us both see that we still have each other."

"I should go back to the office. If you need anything, call me."

"I will, and thank you, Leslie."

Natasha walked her out to her car, and waved until she was out of sight.

FORTY-SIX

The gun Earl Tucker twirled clumsily was a .380 semiautomatic Walther PPK.

Alice held out her hand. "Let me try it," she said, beckoning.

Earl held the gun out butt first, but when she reached for it, he flipped it in his hand and aimed the barrel at her.

"That's an old Western trick that Marshal William Earp was famous for."

"You mean Wyatt Earp."

"S'wat I said."

"You said *William* Earp."

She grabbed the gun from Earl and turned it over in her hands.

"You think I don't know Wyatt Earp? Was a tongue slip, is all that was. Know ah'm sayin'?"

"Only a retard would think it was William."

Earl put his face close to Alice's ear. "How would you like to be porked by a real cowboy?"

She pushed him back onto her bed and aimed the gun at a picture on her wall. "A real cowboy wouldn't give his gun to a girl."

He sat up and held out his hand. "So, give it back."

"Let me hold it," she said.

"You don't even know how to use it."

"Show me."

"Nah."

"You don't know how to shoot it, do you?"

Earl frowned. "What chu talkin'?"

"How does it work, then?"

Earl took the gun and, reaching into his pocket, he took out a loaded magazine. "You push this clip up inna handle, pull back the doohickey and let go, an' she's ready for action. Know ah'm sayin'?"

"I get it." She looked at the empty handle and reached out for the loaded magazine. "Okay. Let me load it."

"Naw, it's too dangerous. Girls don know shit about guns."

"If you ever want me to milk big Earl again," she said, waving her fingers and smiling seductively.

"Ah-ite," he said, handing her the magazine.

She inserted the magazine and aimed the gun at the picture again, whereupon the magazine fell to the carpet.

"You have to puts it all the way in," Earl whined, handing it back. "Listen for it to click. And grab the top and pull that part back so it sticks the bullet in the barrel. And then you just pull the trigger, see ah'm sayin'?"

Alice followed Earl's instructions, pointed the gun at the large jar filled with pennies sitting atop her dresser and pulled the trigger. The jar seemed to evaporate and a spray of hundreds of copper coins filled the air, then landed and bounced on the hardwood floor. Alice's ears rang and she looked at the smoking gun as though finding it in her hand was a complete and baffling surprise.

"Oh-my-god," she said, grinning widely.

When Earl didn't answer, Alice looked back at him and noticed a stream of blood running down from his forehead, down his nose, and dripping onto the front of his extra-extra-large white T-shirt emblazoned with a picture of a sneering 50 Cent.

"Earl!" she screamed. "Oh, shit!"

He turned his eyes to her.

"You're bleeding!"

Earl put his hand to the tip of his nose, looked

at the blood on his fingers, and, with the un-
yielding stiffness of a falling tree, hit the wood
floor so hard his head bounced.

FORTY-SEVEN

"You friggin shot me in the head!" Earl yelled.

"No, I didn't," she said, dabbing Earl's forehead with a cold and blood-smeared washcloth.
"I only shot my penny jar. What the bullet did after that was just physics."

"What?"

"A body in motion—like a bullet—remains in
motion until acted on by an outside force, like
gravity, friction, or a jar of pennies. Either the
bullet hit you after its energy was about used up,
or more probably a piece of glass or a penny did.
It's a prick. Stop whining and I'll put a Band-Aid
on the boo-boo."

"Any fool know she can't shoot a gun inside a
house. Know ah'm sayin'?"

"It was an accident. My ears are still ringing so
bad I can hardly hear you."

"Damn, I'm lucky it didn't split my danged head open and get me in my brains."

Alice laughed. "You didn't even feel it, and it barely cut you. It was probably a piece of glass."

"See, maybe I should go to an emergency room and get a real doctor that knows medical stuff to look at it," he said angrily.

"Duh! They have to report gunshot wounds to the cops, you know. How you going to explain that? It's a ganked gun, right?"

"I said it was my dad's."

"I know what you said, Earl. But you never tell the truth. Where'd you really get it?"

He went into a sulk, which meant he'd been caught in a lie he couldn't think his way out of.

She opened the medicine cabinet, found a Band-Aid, and put it over the cut. "We better pick up all those pennies and the glass before my mama gets home and has a flying shit fit."

"I don't do no housework," Earl said. "She don't even come in here."

"Well, there's always a first time. So, can you show me where the safety is on that gun?"

"I'm a' be the one holding the piece," Earl said.

"Why?"

"'Cause like, I know how to work the safety. And you couldn't shoot the dude anyway."

"I shot you, didn't I?"

"But he won't be holding no jar a' pennies."

FORTY-EIGHT

Ward was seated at the dining room table when Gene called him.

"You sitting down?" Gene asked.

"As a matter of fact I'm eating a late lunch. We're going to get Todd to take us to the cemetery in a little while."

"Trey Dibble is dead," Gene said.

"What is it?" Natasha asked.

"Trey Dibble is dead," Ward told her. "No, that doesn't make sense, Gene," he said into the phone.

"What happened?" Natasha asked.

Ward hit the speaker button and held the phone in front of him.

"You're on speaker so Natasha can hear. What happened?"

"A secretary in our office has a sister who works for EMS. It appears to have been an accident. Trey slipped and hit his head on a countertop and died, probably almost instantly. His girlfriend found him an hour ago in his kitchen. The weird thing is, homicide detectives arrived there before EMS or the police."

"But it was an accident?"

"I know. It can't be right. That would mean Tami called homicide before she called EMS. In case you don't know how these things work: You call nine one one and dispatch sends an ambulance, and the fire department, and the cops. Cops take a look, and if EMS or the officers suspect foul play, then they call in detectives. That takes time, even if it's somebody famous. The detectives arrived before the others. This is beyond weird, and the secretary might have gotten it totally wrong, but I'm trying to find out more, and as soon as I can, I'll call you."

Ward hit the speaker button again and turned to Natasha.

"He's right. Unless they were in the building anyway, they'd be an hour or better getting their act together and going to the scene."

Ward's phone rang again and Ward flipped it open, said hello, and listened.

"Sure, Nolan. Let him through."

A minute later, Ward opened the door to find his uncle standing on the stoop smiling like a used-car salesman who'd come to tell them their credit had failed muster so he was repossessing their new car.

"Unk," Ward said. "I didn't expect you. Come in. I've got a lot to catch you up on."

"I wish I didn't have to bother you, Ward, but I came to tell you something that's, well, it's somewhat delicate and I thought we ought to talk about it face-to-face. You got a minute?"

"Sure," Ward said, opening the door and stepping back to let his uncle in. "Natasha is inside."

"It concerns both of you."

The two men walked into the living room.

"Natasha, Unk has something to tell us," Ward said.

Natasha crossed to hug Ward's uncle. "Hello, Unk. Want something to drink?"

"No, thank you, Natasha," Mark said. "This is difficult for me. I don't know how to begin."

"Sit down," Ward said.

When Mark sat, his tenuous smile vanished altogether.

"I just . . . deposited six hundred and thirty-five thousand dollars back into the account it came from. I stole it from the company."

Neither Ward nor Natasha said anything.

Mark put his head in his hands and cried.

After a few awkward seconds, Ward walked over and put a hand on his uncle's shoulder. "I don't understand."

Natasha went to the kitchen and returned with a tissue. "What are you talking about, Unk?" she asked.

"I embezzled money from our own damn company to cover gambling debts. I've been taking money for the past eleven months. I tried to stop, but . . ." He sobbed. "I put it all back an hour ago."

Mark wiped his tears.

"My gambling. It just somehow got out of control. I was way down and I tried to double up and catch up. It was crazy, but I was desperate to pay these people. The more I tried to catch up, the deeper I went into the hole. Then, to get even with these men, I borrowed from a loan shark and bad got worse. I always intended to put the money back. I took cash as I had to have it."

"Why didn't you tell me early on?" Ward asked him. "We could have fixed it before it got serious."

"Ward's right," Natasha said, firmly.

"It's my stupid pride. You had so much on your plate without my trouble. I'm so sorry."

"It's all back," Ward said.

"To the penny. It was wrong, but I did make it right."

"Right," Natasha said thoughtfully. "I'm not so sure. Unk, where did you get the money to put back?" Natasha asked.

Mark looked up at her, tears in his eyes. "It's all over," he said.

"That might depend on where you got the six hundred thousand to pay back," she said.

"A loan," Mark said.

"From whom?" she asked him.

Mark said, "It was a personal loan. What does that matter?"

"What did you use for collateral?" Ward asked. "Was it a loan from Flash?"

Mark managed a crooked smile.

"I mean, who else has six hundred grand available they'd loan you?"

Mark nodded.

"Did he take your stock for collateral?" Ward asked.

"You know I can't assign or sell my stock."

"I know that, but did he take it?"

"You think I'd lie to Flash about that? Commit fraud?"

"I know that the way my dad set it up, you can only sell your stock to me, at current value. In case you die, since you are divorced from my blood aunt, I would automatically get it after paying your estate fair market value."

"If you died first, would I have to sell your stock to Unk?" Natasha asked.

Mark shook his head. "No. It only works one way. You or Ward are blood, and you can sell whenever to whomever you choose. That was all Wardo," Mark said. "He set it up like a wall to protect his line, so he and his heirs would always control the company. I agreed to it and it's never mattered to me. When we started the company, I didn't know what it would be worth down the road. Nobody knew what NASCAR would do.

Except Wardo. He always knew. He was the one with vision. I was always just a salesman."

"But it mattered later, when the company became successful," Natasha said. "You must have resented how Wardo set it up then."

"No, I loved him like a brother. I made him a lot of money, but I never felt shorted. We both worked hard, but he had the original idea, and he got the ball rolling before I came on. I only had to take orders from eager buyers and watch it grow."

"So if you didn't use your stock for collateral to Flash," Ward asked, "what did you use for collateral for the loan?"

"When you sell the company, I'll get the six hundred thousand off the top of my end. I guess since you'll never sell, as an alternative, you could buy me out and I could pay Flash back from the proceeds of the transaction. I mean, I'm sure you don't want to ever see me again after my betrayal."

"No," Ward said. "I don't want to buy you out. I do that and I'd have to hire a sales manager, and I'd be incurring debt I don't need. I'll sell to Flash Dibble at the price he offered if he'll agree to take care of our employees the way I would have. He'll agree. He won't like sharing profits with employees, but he'll see it's smart business because they know what they're doing."

Mark nodded.

Natasha spoke. "If Ward sells, and it's fine by me if he really wants to, he should take the video game out of the company. I'm sure you won't mind signing it away, Unk. He was just cutting the company in out of the goodness of his heart. He'll reimburse RGI for any money it put into the development."

Mark looked surprised, but nodded. "It was Ward's idea, and he's the one who should own it. I never had anything to do with it. It's only right. Why should Flash get his hands on it?"

"Flash doesn't know about it, does he?" Natasha asked.

"No, he doesn't. I didn't tell him."

"Because if you did, it might explain why he wants RGI so badly, all things considered. It might explain a lot that's been happening." She didn't elaborate, but Ward certainly understood.

"I don't want the company. Maybe Barney would have wanted it if he'd lived, but . . ." He looked at Natasha and smiled. "I know what is important."

"But if Flash doesn't keep Trey away, he could destroy RGI." Mark ran his fingers through his hair.

"Trey Dibble is dead," Ward said.

If Ward had been holding a baseball, he could have slipped it into Mark's mouth without touching teeth.

FORTY-NINE

From the den, a fuming Natasha watched Ward and his uncle seated beside the pool in lounge chairs, talking as though nothing had happened. Despite what he'd told his uncle about selling to Flash Dibble, she knew Ward was deeply hurt and torn, and that he wouldn't say that to his uncle. Instead, he would suffer without venting, as usual. She watched for several minutes before she could stand it no longer and stormed outside.

When she approached, Mark looked up at her and made the mistake of smiling one of his patented isn't-the-world-an-oyster smiles.

"Unk," she said. "I just wanted to say a couple of things."

"Sure, Natasha," he replied. "You can say anything to me. We're family."

"Family. I'm glad you feel that way." She saw Ward turn his eyes out toward the woods.

"Gambling is a sickness and I'm going to get help so I never do it again," Mark added.

"Okay . . . Unk, I refuse to dismiss this by agreeing that you have a disease you should treat, and just letting it go. What you did is unforgivable, because Ward loves and trusts you like a boy trusts his father and you repaid that by betraying him in the worst way. Not because you stole money from him but because you took advantage of him at the lowest point in his life. If he hadn't been grieving for our son, I doubt you would have dreamed of stealing from him, or known he wouldn't be paying attention to the books."

Ward turned back to the conversation, suddenly interested.

"I loved Barney," Mark said. "His passing affected all of us deeply."

"Don't you dare use our child's death as an excuse for your behavior. If only for the sake of his memory, and our grief, you should have never taken the first nickel. If Wardo was alive and you had pulled this crap, he would have prosecuted, and he would never have forgiven you as Ward seems able to do. That's because Ward is a better and far kinder person than his father was."

"You aren't saying anything that I haven't told myself a thousand times," Mark said. "I do love both of you."

"You've put Ward in the position of sacrificing to help you, even though you have been working against his interest by plotting with the Dibbles. Don't you dare deny it. While selling the company will bring you both a lot of money, I do not believe he is going to sell because he wants the financial freedom but to pull your ass out of a fire you made."

"Flash knows about the game, doesn't he?" Ward asked.

Mark shrugged and stood. "I don't know for sure, but I think he might. I guess I should go."

"Yes, I think that's a good idea," Ward said, standing. "I'll tell Gene to tell Flash as soon as the time is right. If he still wants it, without the video game."

"Maybe Flash Dibble will let you work off the loan by selling cars for him," Natasha said.

"I deserve that," Mark said. "If there's anything I can do."

"I can't imagine another thing you could possibly do for us," Natasha said firmly. Her hands had been planted on her hips since she'd confronted Mark Wilson. At that moment she was furious with him, but she could never hate him, or anyone else. Neither she nor Ward had ever learned how to do that. And she knew that wasn't a bad thing; it just made them vulnerable.

As soon as his uncle was out of hearing range, Ward stood and said, "The truth is, I'd love to just sketch and paint and lead the reflective life of the artist."

She laughed. "You should do exactly that, if that would make you happy." Ward reached out and took her hand, and kissed her gently.

"You make me happy. Thank you," he said. "I've never seen you so pissed off. Truth is, I should have said what you said to Unk. I just couldn't bring myself to do it."

"That's okay, darling. Confrontation is what wives are for," Natasha said.

FIFTY

Just after Mark left, Ward and Natasha took a quick shower together, which led to them ending up in bed afterward, drying themselves in the twisted sheets. If the phone in the den had chimed a minute earlier, it would have interrupted their passion. The doorbell rang.

Ward got off the bed, slipped on his boxers, and put on his robe.

"Where's that gun?"

Natasha put her fingers through her hair, thinking. She frowned. "I put it in the top drawer. I'm getting dressed."

Ward went over and opened the drawer, looking in at the revolver and the bullets lying beside it. He lifted the gun and opened it, dropping in the five bullets. Putting the pistol into the pocket of his robe, he went to the front door without seeing who had called.

With his right hand gripping the weapon in his pocket, he opened the door to Agent Mayes, whose Crown Victoria was parked behind him. He had a laptop computer under his arm. The guard behind them had his phone in hand, mouthing that he had tried to call ahead.

"Agent Mayes," Ward said, taking his hand out of his pocket.

"Is this a bad time?" Mayes asked.

"No, what can I do for you?"

"I thought I'd come by personally and give you some news."

"Where's your partner?" Ward said.

"Agent Firman is tying up a few loose ends," Mayes said.

"Please, come in," Ward said.

Natasha came into the den wearing a loose-fitting T-shirt and jeans. She leaned against the fireplace, arms crossed, staring at the FBI agent.

"Agent Mayes brought some news," Ward said.

"It appears that you were right about Trey Dibble framing you." Mayes stood as if behind a lectern.

"Early this morning the police caught some underage kids with meth. They said they got it from this computer tech named Bert Marmaduke. The police went to Marmaduke's place and, armed with a search warrant, went in. Somebody had killed Marmaduke. In their investigation, they uncovered evidence that Marmaduke had designed the computer virus. They also found evidence that pointed to Trey Dibble's involvement with Marmaduke in the virus, and Dibble had to be investigated as a suspect in the murder."

"That's why homicide detectives were at Dibble's place before EMS was," Ward said.

"How did you know that?" Mayes asked, surprised.

"Rumor our lawyer picked up," Natasha said.

"Anyway, we know Trey paid Marmaduke to design the virus, and he killed Marmaduke to keep us from finding him through the hacker. The police found the murder weapon in Trey's garbage can, the phones they talked on, cash at Marmaduke's with Trey's prints on it, and more. Assistant Federal Attorney Walker should be calling your lawyers to give them the news."

"That was thoughtful of you," Natasha said.

"Look," Mayes said. "Agent Firman and I were just doing our job, and there was never anything personal about it. The FBI doesn't apologize officially, but I wanted to apologize."

"Not officially, naturally," Natasha said.

"I wish I could do that."

Natasha said, "You wouldn't want to put a human face on the FBI."

"Look, we followed the evidence, and it ran right to you. But when it went off in another direction we followed it. I know how hard this was on you."

"Really?" Natasha said. "I somehow doubt you do."

"One thing. We don't know who the guy in the hole was, and maybe he's gone for good . . . Do you have a gun?"

"Yes, we do," Ward said.

Mayes said, "I think you should be careful."

"The guard is staying for a while," Ward said.

"Agent Mayes," Natasha said. "The name Gizmo is something I'm sure I've heard before. I mean, everybody's heard the word, but I think I've heard it before in some context other than normal. It feels like something related to my practice, but I can't place when or where I heard it," she said.

"When you do remember," Mayes said, taking out his card, "call me. Any time, day or night."

"Look, we appreciate your concern, we really

do," Natasha said, "but we just want to get on with our lives."

"By the way," Ward added. "Can you inform the press, off the record if that's what you have to do, that I've been cleared?"

"I think I can do that. Unofficially."

Fifteen minutes later, Natasha was behind the wheel of her Lexus, waving at the security guard, who waved back as she and Ward rolled by. The crowd amounted to one TV van, which was aimed the wrong way for a full-blown chase sequence. Besides, the reporter and a cameraman had set up the camera for a taping. The sides of the road were littered with empty water bottles, soda cans, and fast-food sacks, to the point that it looked as though a packed garbage truck had roared by with its rear door open.

"I guess we don't need guards for the press any longer," Natasha said as she pushed down on the accelerator.

"Looks like the party's over," Ward said. "Thank God."

"You can say that again."

"Looks like the party's over. Thank God."

FIFTY-ONE

Her hair wet from a long, hot shower, Alice stood looking into her closet trying to decide what she was going to wear to the "toys for bucks" exchange at the mall. She thought about Earl when she looked at the box on her dresser where his gun was hidden.

The question was whether she'd dress comfortably, as always, or maybe dress up like a serious businesswoman. It was business she was going to be doing. Two thousand dollars for a little toy car whose doors and hood didn't even open up. For that kind of money there should be a little toy driver who moved his hands and head and maybe even changed the toy oil. It was mind-blowing that anyone would pay that much money for a toy. Alice dried her hair, feeling she deserved the money for, if nothing else, keeping it safe.

The car reminded her of visiting her father and his bimbo wife, a Vegas Barbie whose boyfriend was plastic surgeon Ken. She'd already had her lips pumped up so she looked like she lived in a beehive. Alice's three-year-old half brother was an annoying little dork with a nose that ran constantly. He couldn't talk without yelling demands at the top of his shrill voice.

Alice's mother had new breasts, probably thinking that with the bigger breasts she could hold a man, or some other silly shit. She read brochures about face-lifts, buttock inserts, and all manner of cosmetic-enhancement nonsense. Alice knew it was a waste of money, but there was no way to convince Delores Palmer, who had the money to waste. If her mother didn't think she could have the pert figure of a sixteen-year-old, Alice could be driving a nice new BMW convertible instead of a shitty little beater.

Alice decided to dress formally. She stretched on a tight pair of black designer jeans her stepmother had bought her in Vegas, a crisp black T-shirt sporting a Jolly Roger where the skull had been replaced with a silhouette of a doughnut, and lightweight socks with yellow bathtub ducks on them. She slipped on a pair of dark gray sandals.

Going down the stairs, Alice heard odd sounds. Slipping to the kitchen door, she looked in to see her mother lying on the butcher-block island, with her skirt hiked up and her legs spread. Her blouse was open and her new and very erect breasts were exposed for the benefit of Bruce Benning, a neighbor who had just turned seventeen. He lived five doors down and had mowed the lawn since spring. Alice herself had flirted with him on several occasions over the years, but to no avail. Now, standing on tiptoe, his shorts a nylon puddle on the floor, he thrust his hips, driving himself in and out of Delores Palmer, his gaze moving between her breasts and his member's mesmerizing vanishing act.

Furious, Alice turned and went to the den and started to go out through the French doors, thinking she'd slam the door to jar the couple. With her hand still on the handle, a thought occurred to her and she looked at the telephone. She crossed over to the table, punched in 911, and waited for the operator to answer.

"Nine one one. What is the nature of your emergency?"

Alice cupped the receiver and whispered, "Hurry, help me. I'm afraid . . . he's going to rape me."

She set the phone down, leaving the connection open so they couldn't call back and spoil

everything. The best thing about living in a good
neighborhood was that there were lots of cops
with not much to do.

Delores Palmer might figure out Alice had
called them, but whatever shit she caught would
be worth it. Her mother knew Alice was home,
since her car was in the driveway. Delores conducted her life as though she was a busy, single
woman without a worry in the world . . . or a
child.

Alice went out the door, closing it gently
so her mother wouldn't be disrupted. Alice
imagined that the interruption would be much
more impressive when accomplished by armed
police officers peering in at the fuck session
from the freshly mown backyard.

FIFTY-TWO

Standing in his bedroom, Watcher slipped on
black jeans and a long-sleeved black T-shirt. His
flashlight and the Randall lay side by side next to
his black sneakers.

Watcher's mind locked on a memory three years old. One cold night, after spending two adventurous hours in bed with a young sergeant's wife, Ross had just fallen asleep when Watcher slipped out of the man's closet, overpowered the older man, tied him up, and gagged him. He wrapped the naked man in a sheet and carried him, kicking and twisting, out to his waiting car. Watcher drove to an abandoned house trailer ten miles outside Fayetteville. After lashing the sergeant to a kitchen chair, Watcher had gone back into the bedroom and led in his own wife, who began sobbing when he tied her into a chair facing her lover.

Sergeant Ross begged Watcher to let him live, and cried that he was sorry about the affair. Picking up a section of heavy iron pipe from the counter, Watcher broke both of the man's knees with two swift blows. The sergeant's screams reverberated on the cheap paneling and leaked out through the broken windows, carrying over the vacant fields surrounding the trailer.

Watcher had next taken up a propane torch and lit it. Evelyn was new to violence and was certain that she was going to soon follow the sergeant's fate, so her screams were even louder than her ex-lover's. The sergeant was a fit man of forty, which helped him last two hours while Watcher first played the torch over his naked extremities and then went to work on his torso, neck, hair, and finally his face. Thick smoke and the unmistakable smell of cooking meat filled the trailer to the point that it was difficult for Watcher to see through it.

The last thing Watcher did was turn off the torch, shake up a can of spray-foam insulation, and push the plastic straw into the barely conscious man's throat. Pressing the trigger mechanism, Watcher heard the hissing as the foam shot out, filling Ross's throat with the yellow foam that expanded rapidly, oozing back out of his mouth and nostrils. That done, he removed the sticky surgeon's gloves, slipped on a second pair, and smiled at his wife, who looked at him with terrified eyes. Roughly, he tied rope around her knee, then pulled the loose end behind the chair and tied it around her other knee, opening her legs wide.

"Evelyn, my darling slut," he said emotionlessly, aiming the straw's tip at the exposed target. "Could I interest you in a refreshing douche?"

FIFTY-THREE

The gates into pastoral Oakwood Cemetery faced Church Street in Concord. Behind the painted iron fence, narrow asphalt roads serpentined among gently rolling hills lined with stone monuments dotted with evergreens, boxwoods, and stately oak trees. Barney's grave was located just to the left of his grandfather's in the family plot where McCartys had been buried since 1918.

Natasha parked under a large oak at the top of a hill.

Ward reached to the floor for the flowers purchased from a florist on the way, leaned over to kiss Natasha, then opened his door and stepped out into the afternoon heat to the buzz of insects.

They walked hand in hand between the rows of graves to the familiar cluster of headstones. Still clutching hands, they stood before the newest stone and gazed down. The grass was brown due to the drought. Dried flowers crumbled in a vase that leaned against the granite base of Barney's headstone. Ward handed the new flowers to Natasha and she replaced the dead ones.

"It's so nice here," she said. "Peaceful."

"Barney, we love you," Ward said, his voice choking. "We'll always love you."

"He knows that," Natasha said, squeezing Ward's hand. "He knows."

Ward took Natasha into his arms and together they wept softly.

"Maybe we should come here more, together," Natasha said.

"He isn't here," Ward said. "Barney is in heaven. I truly believe that. He isn't in there," he said, looking at the grave. "But we can visit this place . . . for us."

They stood holding each other for ten minutes. Ward kissed Natasha gently on her lips and put his forehead against hers. Taking her hand, Ward led his wife back to the car.

FIFTY-FOUR

When they returned, the TV van was gone. Ward stopped beside the guard standing near the throat of the driveway and rolled down his window. The guard, a tall, wide-shouldered bald man, smiled when they stopped. He had a black garbage bag in his hand, fairly full by the look of it. The street looked pristine compared to only hours earlier. Several bags were already filled and lay side by side near the NO TRESPASSING sign the guards had put up around the property.

"We can pick up the garbage," Ward told the guard.

"Gives me something to do," the guard said, smiling.

"Looks pretty quiet," Ward said. He noticed calluses on the man's strong hands. The black uniform looked uncomfortable in the heat. There was a large survival knife on the gun belt. The man's eyes weren't smiling in concert with his lips.

"Word's out that you're not news anymore," the guard said. "That FBI agent told the media creeps they were wasting their time and could call Tom Wiggins if they wanted the scoop. They checked it out and hauled ass. I'm just waiting around to be officially dismissed. Todd said with the hole behind your house, you might want some protection until you don't." He put a hand on the gun at his side. "I'll make sure nobody bothers you guys."

"I guess you should hang around a little while," Ward said.

"I'm not going anywhere as long as there's a threat. We'll leave the go-away sign," he said.

"Thanks," Natasha said. "We really appreciate it. I don't know your name."

"People call me Thumper. Y'all have a nice evening. As long as I'm here, you won't be in any danger from any hole-dwelling creep."

Ward pulled away, rolling the window back up as he went.

"Somehow I don't feel any safer," Natasha commented. "He is sort of . . ."

"I know," Ward answered.

Ward parked the Lexus in the garage and went into the house, closing the rolling door behind them.

"Sometimes I wish we had a big dog," Natasha said.

"That's doable," Ward said. "How about a wolf?"

"I was thinking more like a Labrador," she said. "Or a golden retriever."

"So, what do you want to do with the rest of the evening, after?" she asked him.

"After what?"

She put her arms around his waist, and kissed him. "If you'll follow me, young man, I'll show you what."

FIFTY-FIVE

Alice Palmer pulled up in front of Earl's ramshackle house just as the sun was going down. The Tucker home was in a downwardly mobile subdivision off Brookshire Boulevard. As Alice pulled up she saw a girl leaving the porch steps, walking away without looking back at Earl. Earl stood at the porch steps and ambled slowly to the Toyota like an old man shuffling in fast-moving water. He opened the door and slunk into the car, buckling his belt slowly.

"Heeeey now," he said.

"Are you drunk?" Alice demanded, furious that he could get loaded when something this important was going to be happening and she needed him watching her back.

"I just had a couple beers an' some little weed is all. Know ah'm sayin'? Ah'm chillin', babykins."

"You're drunk as hell," she said angrily. "You know how important this is to me!"

"It's a deal to me, too, you know," he replied sluggishly. "Show me tha moneeeey!"

"Shit," she said. "I don't believe you. You are such an asshole."

"Come on, baby doll. It's my money too-we-oooowe."

She stared at him as he turned slowly and stared at her, his eyes bleary and unfocused. There was something red, which looked suspiciously like lipstick, smeared on and around Earl's lips, on his pocked cheeks and his chin.

"Know I love you, baby." He placed a hand on

her thigh and moved his fingers between her legs. "See ah'm sayin'?"

"Never mind," she said, grabbing his wrist, lifting his hand, and putting it onto his own lap. "Keep your hands to yourself."

"You sure know how to hurt a man's pride. Mens got they needs, Brenda."

"Brenda? Who the hell is Brenda?"

Earl squinted, waved his hand dismissively. "I said Alice."

"No, you said Brenda. I'm not high. I heard you distinctly."

"Naw, baby. I never said no Brenda, know ah'm sayin'? That gal was at the house wasn't Brenda. Jus' some friend of my sistah. In fact, wasn't no gal up in there at all."

"No, I don't know what you are saying. Why do you always talk like some inner-city Americo-African thug? Do you know what I am saying?"

"So, I been thinkin' on how all I'm gonna spend the two grands."

"Is that right?" Alice said.

"Firstest, we go gets my tat completed up, know ah'm sayin'? Then I gots my eye on niss fat chain what's ultra hot. And some kicks that on be mean time fo' tha feets. You wants yo man to be kickin' it cool. Look, baby doll, two grand ain't all that much bread. We gots us a major opportunity here to score a lots more."

"What the hell are you talking about?"

"We ain't settlin' for no two. We gettin' a whole ten. Know ah'm sayin'? We put the three-eighty up that cracker's nose and tell him ten, Brenda."

Alice cut the wheel to the right and back hard to the left twice before pulling to the shoulder.

"Whasup? You driving crazy."

"Do me a favor, Earl."

"Like what?"

"Get out and make sure my back tire isn't going flat. The car is driving funny. Let me unbuckle your seat belt," she said.

She undid his seat belt.

Earl grinned dumbly. "I ain't gots to get all the way out, on account I can lean out and see up under at the wheels." He opened the door, turned in his seat, leaned out, and put his head down close to the ground, stretching to look under the car.

Alice swung her legs up and, pivoting around, planted her back against the door. When her feet connected, Earl flew from the car and landed limbs akimbo, facedown in the gravel. Alice roared away, leaving him lying beside the road. In the rearview she saw him turning his head to watch her.

She slammed on the brakes, opened the door, got out, planted her hands on her hips and yelled, "Walk home, you stupid ass! And screw yourself!"

She would have to just get used to the idea of doing this all alone. After all, she only had to hand over the little car and she could do some shopping at Game World with her reward money.

FIFTY-SIX

Todd arrived at the enormous mall early. In a plain envelope in his front pants pocket, Todd had twenty crisp one-hundred-dollar bills. In a second envelope he had an additional twenty crisp fifties. With someone as squirrelly as Alice

Palmer, he had to hedge his bets. This had to end tonight.

After parking, he locked his Colt 1911 in his glove box before climbing out and locking the doors. Pocketing his keys, he walked toward the entrance, joining the throngs filtering into the building.

Hartman made his way to the food court, ordered sesame chicken at the Hunan kiosk, and sat down with his back to that restaurant to eat a leisurely meal and wait for Alice Palmer to show up. From his vantage point he could keep his eyes on both ends of the enormous open space, packed with hundreds of tables and chairs. During the peak hours scores of trash receptacles were emptied every ten minutes, and the tables were filled with patrons. It was a perfect place as public spaces went. At least this way even a wing nut like Earl shouldn't be a potentially dangerous variable.

FIFTY-SEVEN

Natasha poured herself a glass of wine from the bottle they'd purchased on the way home from the cemetery. She opened Leslie's laptop on the counter and waited for it to power up. She heard the TV come on and a few familiar bars of music flowing from the den.

"It's about the virus," Ward yelled from the den. "Breaking news!"

She rushed into the room to stand beside her husband while the newscaster explained that the child-porn virus was planted on the computers at RGI by a saboteur. The announcer said the FBI and the Charlotte police department would be holding a joint press conference the next morning, but that RGI had been cleared of all accusations.

"All right!" Ward hollered, hugging Natasha. "That's it. Damnation be gone."

For ten minutes Natasha read her e-mails. About half of them were from people that were furious because her computer sent the virus to theirs. She was careful not to open any e-mails with attachments since the virus was still out there, and probably in some of those e-mails.

The other half of the e-mails were from people saying they knew Ward didn't have anything to do with the virus. It was warming to read those. She had e-mails from her parents, and other members of her family in Washington and Oregon, expressing their support. Her mother asked for Natasha to call them as soon as she could because her phone stayed busy. There were several "call me's" in the stack. All of her partners (except for Dan Wheat) had e-mailed saying they hoped she'd let them know if they could help in any way. They were all time-dated before Ward had been cleared.

And even though she and Ward hadn't discussed it since Barney's birth, they could have another child, and she hoped Ward would be up for that, because she most certainly was. No child could ever replace Barney, but they had plenty of love to give a new child, or children. She smiled at the thought of another McCarty.

Gizmo. The odd word kept rattling around in Natasha's mind, because she was sure she'd heard it before under circumstances related to her practice, even though she couldn't zero in on an image her memory could replay. Maybe, because the word was a source of anxiety, she was imagining it meant more to her than that. The nearly hieroglyphic decoration was obsessively executed and had to have taken untold long hours of concentrated effort to accomplish. The five letters had been as uniform as letters chiseled into a tombstone by a stonemason.

She looked down at the legal pad, where she had written the word out and doodled circles and stars around it, trying to trigger something solid.

She had the feeling that if she could just remember, she'd know something crucial.

She was about to turn off the computer when she had an idea. She went to Google and typed in the word "Gizmo." There were eleven million, eight hundred thousand and seventeen hits. She shook her head slowly as she pondered the mountain of hay that might contain the needle she was searching for.

She typed "Gizmo" and "Charlotte NC." There were ten thousand and seventy-one hits. When she added the word "Obituaries," there were fewer than three thousand, still an unmanageable number. The first one was:

. . . survivors are her father, Richard M. Morrison, Sr., of Harrisburg, NC; her aunt, Glenda Eudy, and husband, Clint, of Greensboro; and her cat, Gizmo.

Natasha smiled strangely. Why, she wondered, had she added the word obituaries? That seemed odd. The second one was:

Oct. 14, 2003, at the Community Medical Center in Scranton after being suddenly stricken. Arlene loved her babies: her dogs, Cody, Cindy, and Gizmo.

It seemed to be a popular name people gave their pets. *Perhaps,* she mused, *having a pet named Gizmo could be hazardous to your health.*

She had a thought. Since it was *her* memory, she added NorthEast Medical Center, Concord, and there were only five. She had read through two entries, when she saw something in the third that made her blood run cold.

FIFTY-EIGHT

When Gene Duncan called, Ward was watching the news as a commentator said that the RGI virus was designed by a thirty-year-old Charlotte resident named Bert Marmaduke. The newscaster said that suspect Marmaduke had been murdered the evening before his body was found, but gave no cause of death, and made no mention of Trey Dibble's connection to the event. Ward was wondering if the media people refrained from mentioning Trey because Flash's advertising dollars kept the regional TV stations solvent. He figured it was just a matter of time.

Presently, Trey's death was reported, as accidental. There were interviews with several NASCAR-involved individuals, whose comments were probably less than honest, each saying something on the order of what a unique individual Trey Dibble had been. Flash Dibble was reported to be in seclusion, and his assistant said that he and his wife wanted to thank everyone who had offered their prayers and consolation.

"You seen the news?" Gene asked.

"I have."

"Flash called me," Gene said. "He asked me to pass on his deep sorrow for his son's actions. He told me to tell you that he didn't have any idea about any of it. He still wants RGI and said he'd like to keep it just the way it is. He also mentioned that he might be open to a partnership involvement."

"Jesus, Gene, he's still able to think about business?"

"What can I say?"

"Call him back. Tell him to work with you and get the deal drawn up for my signature. Tell him I'll stay through a reasonable transaction period, but maybe Unk would be open to something more permanent with him."

"Did you just say what I thought you said?"

"Yes. The sooner the better. You can figure out how to spend your commission now. But the video game is not part of the sale."

"I don't know why that would ever come up. He doesn't know about it."

That was something Ward was no longer sure of. It was possible that his uncle had told Flash about the game, and that was why he wanted

RGI so badly. It didn't matter, because if Flash backed out, Ward would continue to run RGI as he had before, and he'd keep Unk in place and pay Flash the six hundred thousand his uncle owed him. Ward wanted everybody happy because, for the first time in a year, he was.

Gene continued, "Oh, yeah, and the most amazing thing of all. Are you sitting down?"

"Yes, I am. Would you get to it?"

"Tom Wiggins told me to tell you there's no charge for his services."

"That's very generous, but I want to pay him for his time."

"He thought you'd say that. He said you could send a check for twelve hundred to his favorite charity."

"The children's oncology center. Tell him it's as good as in their account."

"I will. Okay, buddy. I'll call Flash and I'll get on the deal as soon as I hang up."

"So, why are you still talking to me?" Ward clicked off the phone and tapped it on the back of the couch.

He looked up to see Natasha standing in the doorway. "That was Gene. He . . ."

Ward stopped because he knew Natasha wasn't hearing a word he said. She was staring at him, a look of horror on her face.

"What?" Ward asked. "Natasha?" He jumped up and ran across the room, taking her by the shoulders.

"Gizmo. I know who he is."

"Who? How do you know him?"

"I killed him."

FIFTY-NINE

It was dark when Alice lucked out and found a parking spot very close to a towering green painted metal sculpture resembling blades of grass. She wondered if it was designed to make people see what it felt like to be insects. It seemed to her that lots of things in society were designed to make people feel less significant than they were.

Alice walked toward three young men smoking cigarettes near the entrance. She straightened as she approached, and measured them for attractiveness. Two of the boys were sort of fat, and all three were wearing baggy shorts and T-shirts with smart-ass messages printed on them. There was one guy who was taller, and skinny—just her type—and she made eye contact with him. He looked over at her and his eyes lit up, so she slowed.

"Hey, good looking!" he said, smiling. "Where you been all my life?"

Alice stopped and smiled widely, keeping her lips together so her braces didn't show. And she waved.

"Looking for you," a high-pitched voice replied from behind her.

Alice turned to see three girls closing from behind, and, as they passed Alice, the boys straightened and posed like models in anticipation.

"You're late," one of the fat boys said to the girls.

Alice felt embarrassed, disappointed, and invisible. And she felt anger growing within her.

She slumped, tightened the grip on her black cloth carry bag, and strode purposefully into the entrance, the sounds of youthful laughter closing on her back in rhythmic waves. She heard one of the girls say, "That little kid thought you were talking to *her*!"

Alice walked slowly past the shop windows, pausing here and there to check out merchandise, imagining owning some of the items and picturing as well how ownership of each would make her feel. In a matter of minutes she found herself nearing the food court entrance and the smells of a hundred food items hit her like a wave. She skulked on, clenching the strap of her bag like someone was going to grab it and take off running.

Alice checked herself out in a dark shop window, and what she saw made her wonder why the boys hadn't been attracted to her. She looked younger than she was, and she supposed they had imagined that she was too young for them, but she was prettier than any of the other girls had been by a mile.

She thought about Mr. McCarty and how nice he'd been to her, and she had been sure that was because he was attracted to her. He deserved to have his toy car taken, since he was a sexual predator. Everybody knew it. In fact he deserved to be punished, and giving her his money—which was just to keep her from telling the cops that he tried his moves on her—was him being afraid of additional proof that he was guilty of being an old pedophile.

She braced herself and walked into the food court, scanning the tables, looking for the man who'd stopped her on campus.

After a few seconds she saw him seated at a table, waving just his fingers at her. She hesitated a few seconds, then nodded and walked over to him.

SIXTY

Natasha led Ward to the kitchen and showed him the obituary.

Louis A. Gismano, Jr., seven years of age, died of complications from injuries sustained when he was struck by an automobile on April 3, 2005, at **NorthEast Medical Center**. Louis, known as **Gizmo** to friends and family, was the beloved son of U.S. Army Sergeant Louis Anthony and Evelyn Gismano of

Fayetteville, N.C. Burial services are being handled by
Sullivan's Highland Funeral Service in Fayetteville.

"Jesus," Ward said. "You knew him?"

"He was hit by a car. The driver was a drunk,
a boy named Howard Lindley. The child was
brought to the emergency room. I'd have to
look at his records to be sure, but I remember
that he had multiple fractures, and internal
bleeding, so I went in to address the bleeding. I
removed a ruptured kidney and his spleen. After
surgery he was in critical condition, but he
should have lived. They put off setting the fractures to allow him time to gain strength, and
there was too much swelling to address that anyway."

"You just said you killed him," Ward added.

"I didn't murder him, but I missed something
that wasn't immediately apparent in the initial
workup, or during my first surgery. He was unconscious, and there was a damaged wall in his
aorta that blew out. They rushed him back into
surgery. I cracked his chest but there was nothing I could do. The father didn't get to the hospital until after the child died. I wasn't there
when he arrived, but I got a call and was on my

way to explain what had happened, but before I got to the ICU, security stopped me. They'd called the cops, so I never talked to the father. I was told not to talk to him, and I was also told he was screaming, 'Gizmo. You bastards murdered Gizmo!' "

"I remember that," Ward said, remembering how upset his wife had been at the time.

"A panel of physicians reviewed the case, and they ruled that there was no contributory negligence. Nobody could have known about the weak wall in his aorta, and there was no evidence to support a malpractice suit. I never heard another word. I'd forgotten all about it. I mean, I did the best I could given what was known."

"What made you remember?"

"I don't really know. I queried Gizmo first. Next I added obits and then NorthEast Medical Center, because something told me my memory of the name was connected to my practice."

"He was a soldier. Jesus. It's got to be him in that hole."

"Yes," she said. "What if he still believes I killed his son?"

"I'll call the police," Ward said.

"Call Todd," she said. "Let him call them. He'll know what to say that will get their attention. He'll know what to do."

SIXTY-ONE

Todd stood as Alice approached the table. She sat down across from him and smiled nervously.

"Hi," she said. "You found the place all right."

"Yes," Todd said.

"I mean, of course you did." She laughed nervously. "Of course you did. Duh, you're sitting here." She hit herself on the forehead with the butt of her hand. "What was I thinking?"

"And you found it," Todd said.

"I come here sometimes. They have a great place called Asphalt Jungle, and they've got super cool shit. Clothes, jeans, and skateboards they build from the parts you want. I don't skate, but I have friends who do."

"Did you bring the model?" Todd asked, wanting to get this over with.

His cell phone vibrated, so he took it out and

looked at the caller ID. It was Ward McCarty. He put the phone away. He'd call him back as soon as this was over.

"Yeah, I brought it. You know, he's a pervert. Tell me why I shouldn't call the police."

"Well, a couple of reasons . . ."

"I know, I could get in trouble. You said that, but what about all those kids? I've been thinking it over. Even if I did get in trouble for like taking the car, he's a pervert and I doubt the cops would charge me."

"Alice, first off, the FBI and the cops know he's not guilty, because they know who did it. More importantly, we have a deal, and we've held up our end. Mr. McCarty's son loved that car and the boy died in a terrible accident, and Mr. McCarty carried the car around with him because his son loved it and he loved his son."

"Kind of like a memento," she said, a look of suspicion crossing her features. "Is that the truth?"

"Absolutely."

Alice opened her bag and looked in. She took a note card out and studied it.

"What's that?" Todd asked.

"He drew this picture of me on the airplane," she said, showing it to Todd.

"It's good," Todd said.

"I forgot all about it," she said. "He's a good sketcher. You think I look like this?"

"Yes." Todd glanced from card to person, back and forth. "It shows a you I haven't seen before."

"Seriously?"

"Yep. In the picture, you look innocent and sensitive. And you look vulnerable, and there's intelligence, humor, and mischief in your expression. I guess he drew you the way he saw you."

"I make good grades. That's never been hard for me. And I can do some mischief shit. I did something earlier tonight that would be considered that exactly."

Todd said, "He obviously thought you were a nice person. So why would you want to do him harm?"

"I don't. You think I made up that he wanted to screw me. I thought that's probably why he drew me so . . . I don't know. Because he wanted to hook up with me. I guess maybe he *was* just being nice."

"I think he liked you because he thought there

was something likeable about you. I doubt he ever imagined you'd do what you did. He's the kind of guy who would be kind to a young person traveling alone. You told him your parents were divorced and you were shuttling between them."

"No, I didn't," she said, but her eyes wandered around the space.

"He was kind to you because that's the kind of man he is. He thought you were vulnerable, and maybe in pain over the fact that you felt betrayed by your parents. There was never anything sexual in his mind, and I think you know that."

"I don't know anything like that!" she snapped. "And you don't either. You're just trying to make me feel bad."

Todd took the envelope out of his pocket and placed it on the table in front of her.

"This is yours." But he purposefully kept the envelope pinned under his hand. "It's two thousand," Todd told her.

"You want the car now?"

"I think we've arrived at that point."

She reached into the black carry bag and removed the small blue car and placed it on the table, wheels down, and pushed it across the table. Todd lifted his hand, picked the car up, and examined it.

"It was already scratched," she said, taking the envelope.

"You can count it," Todd said.

"I trust you." Alice stuffed the envelope into her purse and looked around the food court.

"So, where's Earl?" Todd asked, placing the model in his jacket pocket.

"I don't know, and I don't care."

"You could do better," Todd said. "I'm sure you know that."

Her face suddenly felt hot and she snatched the drawing and tore it up into small pieces and let them flutter to the tabletop. "You don't know me. You've got your little piece-of-shit toy car." She stood up and grabbed up her tote bag.

"Good luck," he told her.

"Fuck you," she replied, and stormed off out of the food court.

SIXTY-TWO

Alice was around the corner in the corridor when her cell phone started ringing. She pulled it from the pocket of her jeans and looked at the ID. It was Earl.

"What, Earl?" she said.

"Where you at?"

"If it's any of your business, I'm at the mall."

"Doing the deal?"

"Maybe. You still drunk?"

"Naw, did you ask for ten like I said?"

"No, I did not. I agreed on two. More would be dishonorable."

"Damn. A'ight, that's cool. So, see ah'm sayin', you coming to get me so we can do what we said. You know, gets me my money, the tat and stuff?"

"*Your* money?"

"Well, it's like mostly mines, in it? Was me gots the gun. Who negotiated the deal? Who said ten grand so as you ended with two not some measly five hundred? Who'd you shoot in the fuckin' head?"

"I don't know, Earl. I'm thinking that I should keep the entire two thousand."

"Without me you'd be lucky to have anybody fuck you through a hole in a wall, you no-tit loser bitch. If you couldn't make a fist around my pecker, you'd be worthless."

"Whatever," she said, fuming. "But if I'm the loser, how come I've got the money and you're the one sitting on your front porch?"

"Who're you calling a loser?"

"Maybe the loser who's a penniless freak with the IQ of a mollusk."

"Don't you dare try to fuck me!"

"Why would I bother, when you're doing such a great job of fucking yourself? We're done, and if I ever see you again, even by accident, I really am going to shoot you."

She snapped the phone closed and laughed. When her phone rang again, she started to ignore it, but she wanted to say a few more things.

"You evil little monster! You horrid bitch!" the voice hissed.

Alice felt her cheeks reddening, and her stomach felt hot and hollow. The female voice was distorted by cold fury, but Alice had heard this same tone often enough since childhood.

294 JOHN RAMSEY MILLER

"You miserable ingrate."

"What's wrong, Mother?" Alice managed to say, using the most innocent voice she could muster.

"You've ruined me," her mother hissed.

"What are you talking about?"

"Nine one one ring any bells?"

"That's the emergency police and fire number."

"Do you have any idea what you've done?"

"If you'll calm down before you blow out a vein or something and tell me what you're talking about . . ."

"I'm talking about the police coming into my house with their guns out and handcuffing the lawn boy! You've really done it." Her mother's ranting was now accented by sobs.

Fuck it. "Were you two still fucking when the cops came?"

"They were going to *arrest* me!" Delores snapped.

"You aren't in jail though, are you?"

"No, I'm not. He's seventeen. How could you?"

"How could you screw a boy younger than me in my own kitchen while I was home? You deserve to be arrested for child molesting. And I hate you, you bitch."

"I'll put your things on the back porch. Maybe you can go live with your father, but he doesn't want you there either. We have given you everything, and you've given nothing but pain in return. You are a self-centered, hateful, evil little troll, and you've never done one unselfish thing in your life. So we got divorced, it happens, and you decided to punish us for the rest of our lives. That's over, Alice, for good."

"I'm not the reason you got divorced, so don't try to make me feel guilty. You hate me because you think I'm ugly, and you are so friggin' beautiful."

"Talking to you is a waste of breath. I can't tell you anything the professionals couldn't tell us. Lawyers and shrinks, all a waste of my time and money. Good-bye, Alice. And I wish you good luck, because you lack any personality or capacity to care about anybody but yourself."

The phone went dead.

Alice wanted to laugh because the cops had caught her mother screwing a kid in the kitchen. She wished she had a film of it to watch.

I'm an evil monster?

She's the monster.

She never loved me.

I never loved her. Screw her.

I've got money.

I can get an apartment, and I can get a job.

I'll show her.

Alice left the mall, walked to her car, unlocked it, and climbed in. She put the bag on the passenger seat, cranked it, and just sat there, thinking. Her mother was wrong. She'd done lots of unselfish things. Lots. Alice tried to think of one, but nothing came to mind.

"I gave Mr. McCarty his little toy car back when I didn't have to. That was unselfish. Totally unselfish," she said.

She let her eyes wander to the black carry bag and, reaching in, took out the envelope to count the money. She wouldn't spend any until she got an apartment and cable TV. Two grand would be enough.

She counted the bills twice. Though she was, you didn't have to be a math major to know that twenty fifty-dollar bills didn't equal two thousand dollars. Why did people always think they could fuck her over?

SIXTY-THREE

Todd Hartman placed the model car in his glove box, tucking the Colt into the center console. He opened his phone and dialed Ward McCarty, who answered on the second ring. "Hartman," he said. "You just called?"

"Todd, Natasha remembered something. She knows who Gizmo is. Gizmo was the nickname of a child who died after she operated on him four years ago."

Todd listened intently as Ward told him the story.

"I'm leaving Concord Mills," he said. "I'll get what I can on Louis Gismano and we can figure out what to do when I get there. In the meantime, you stay in the house. I'll call Thumper, and I'll get some more people back out there to cover the house. I'm twenty minutes away. Keep the phone lines clear. Load the gun I gave you, keep it with you, and turn out the lights like you're going to bed so, if he's around, he can't see in. I'll call the sheriff's department on the way and get a unit out there. Make sure the house is locked up tight."

"Okay," Ward said. "I can do that."

"Is Natasha all right?"

"She's upset."

"Tell her to relax. We'll deal with this Gismano. Don't worry. I mean it."

Todd hung up, cranked the car, and raced out of the parking lot. As soon as he got on Bruton Smith Boulevard, he dialed Thumper.

"Thumper, block the driveway until I get there. The stalker is a vet and I have no idea what his level of competence is, so watch your ass. I'm going to make some calls so real help's on the way."

As he drove eighty miles an hour, Todd picked up the Colt and clipped the holster onto his belt.

SIXTY-FOUR

Leslie Wilde turned into the McCartys' driveway and was coming around the first turn when she saw the truck parked across her way. A powerfully built man, dressed entirely in black, stepped from around the truck, his hand resting on a handgun at his side. She had never seen this guard before. As he approached, Leslie fought the urge to roll up the window. This guy was big, and his eyes as intense as a prison guard's in a riot. A film of sweat coated his face, and Leslie's eyes were drawn to the large knife strapped to his left thigh.

"Who are you, and what's your business here?"

"I'm Mr. McCarty's secretary. I came to bring the McCartys a bottle of champagne. To celebrate that he's been cleared."

The guard leaned down to better see inside. "Wait, you're Mr. Hartman's girlfriend."

"The McCartys don't know I'm coming. I brought a bottle of champagne to surprise them," Leslie repeated. She held up the bottle. "I'll just give it to them and go. I thought you guys would be gone."

"All I know is Mr. Hartman told me there's a stalker around who could be dangerous and to block the driveway. He's sending more guys back here. Not necessary to send me help. I can handle any stalker that shows up around here."

He chewed his lower lip and nodded. "I'll call the McCartys and let them know you're here. If

they say to, I'll move the truck and let you in."
The guard lifted his cell phone and called a num-
ber, and said, "Mr. McCarty, Leslie Wilde is here.
She's got something for you guys."

The guard listened to Mr. McCarty's response
and closed his phone.

"He says to come in," the guard told her. "Go
slow and I'll follow to watch you until you're
safely inside."

SIXTY-FIVE

"Leslie, you shouldn't have," Ward said, taking
the chilled bottle from her.

"Don't be silly. You guys have to celebrate."

He closed the door and led Leslie back to the
den where Natasha was sitting on the couch. A
single candle in a holder set in the fireplace offered the sole illumination for the large room.

"Why are all the lights off in here?" Leslie
asked. "Looks like you're having a séance. I figured you'd be dancing."

"Todd told us to keep the lights off so anybody outside would think we were sleeping."

"Leslie brought champagne," Ward said. "I'll get some glasses."

"That was thoughtful of you," Natasha said, crossing to kiss Leslie on the cheek.

"It's French," Leslie said, smiling. "That makes it real champagne."

"Todd's on his way." Ward said. "He should be here any time now. We think the man who was in the hole out there could be a man who blames Natasha for his son's death."

Natasha told Leslie about her Google search that found Gizmo, and the story about the child's death.

"Of course you didn't, but if he thinks you murdered his child, that's what matters. Some medical review board says you didn't screw up and kill the boy, but maybe he believes it was a cover-up. Even if a panel of doctors decided you didn't kill his son, everybody thinks doctors cover up for each other the way cops do."

"That wasn't the case," Natasha said. "I operated to save his life. I was totally focused. It's what we couldn't have known that killed him. We could have saved him if there had been some way to know about that damage. He was hit by a car. There was a lot going on, besides the ruptured kidney that I removed, and his spleen . . . I stabilized him. But there was a weakened place in his aorta that blew after surgery. The wall split open and by the time we had him back in the OR, he . . . I did everything I could."

"You aren't a heart surgeon, are you?" Leslie said.

"I'm not, but there was no time to get one in, and one of the best testified that nobody could have saved the child given the circumstances. The rip was six or seven centimeters long—"

"There's something else. Something strange," Ward interrupted. "A young man named Howard Lindley was driving the car that ran over the boy."

"Who is Howard Lindley?" Leslie asked. "Wasn't he the boy who got high and murdered three of his friends?"

"Yes," Natasha said. "Same young man."

"Howard Lindley's father is a well-connected attorney, and Howard got probation for that hit-and-run, so what if Gizmo's father wasn't happy about that and set him up by killing his friends? What if he was watching Howard like he's been watching us, and made it look like Howard snapped and killed his friends? Howard is in prison for murder. He murdered his friends in a blind rage, no recollection of any of it. It's possible, isn't it? That he was set up? The courts failed to punish Gismano's son's killer. For any man that's got to be hard to handle."

"It's scary," Leslie said.

"Gizmo's father was there at the hospital. Where was his mother?" Ward asked.

Natasha thought for a moment and said, "I don't know."

"You never talked to her?" Leslie asked.

"No. I suppose someone from the hospital staff dealt with her and her husband. After security told me he'd been arrested, I went back to other surgeries I had scheduled."

Natasha started crying. "If I could have saved him, I would have done whatever it would have taken. All I can tell you is I did the best I could. It's how I do things."

SIXTY-SIX

Natasha and Leslie were seated on the couch.

Everyone's heads snapped around as there was a loud tapping on the front door.

"Probably Todd," Ward said. "I'll let him in." He took the gun and went to the door. Looking out through the tall glass panel beside the door he saw Todd looking down at his cell phone. Todd put it to his ear, took it away, looked at the readout, and closed it.

Ward opened the door, holding the gun behind him.

"Is Thumper in here?" Todd asked.

"No," Ward said.

"His truck was blocking the driveway. I tried to call him, but I don't have a signal. Turn off the porch light."

Ward cut the light. "He walked Leslie in ten minutes ago. I saw him outside when she got here. He told her he was going to take a walk around the property," Ward said.

"Bixby and two other guys are on the way

from Charlotte." Todd looked at his watch. "They should be here in an hour."

Ward locked the door and followed Todd to the den, putting the revolver on the mantel.

"Hello, Leslie," Todd said.

"Todd. Want a glass of champagne?"

"No, and before I forget . . ." Reaching into his jacket, Todd took out the prototype and handed it to Ward, who studied it in the candle-light.

"Any problems?" Ward asked.

"None, but I found out a few things since we last spoke. First, the Scotch was laced with Rohypnol. The drug in Natasha's wine is a hyper-tension drug whose main side effect is tremors."

"Rohypnol—the date rape drug," Natasha said. "That explains Ward's time lapses and memory loss, and the other drug accounts for my shaking hands."

"The alarm logs don't show anything, so he figured a way around it to plant the drugs and play mind games with you. Now, Gismano. I called a friend of mine at Bragg, who, it turns out has an open file on Louis Gismano, and was interested that he might be hiding out around here."

Ward sat down in the chair.

"Sergeant Gismano was Special Forces, which isn't good for us. He was in for twelve years. He was married in '98 to Evelyn Merrit, and Louis Jr. was their only child. Gismano served with distinction in the second Gulf War, and in Afghanistan, where he received the Bronze Star. Shortly after his son died, he left the service, and nobody's heard anything from him since. My friend told me the driver of the car that killed his son had insurance that settled for half a million dollars. Louis took the money and dropped off the radar."

"What do you mean?" Natasha asked.

"Nobody's heard from him or his wife since he left the Army. The wife's parents filed a missing-person report on her, and they believe Louis killed her. He thought she betrayed him. They both vanished. The mother said Evelyn was having an affair with a sergeant named Ross, who also disappeared from his apartment. The missing sergeant—a Special Forces training officer—made a career of sleeping with the wives of men overseas, and if he is dead, the list of suspects would be lengthy. Gismano started out as a communications specialist, but in Afghanistan he killed three Taliban honchos with a knife during a mission."

"So, he's a serious threat," Ward said.

"A very scary individual," Todd said. "If he thinks Natasha killed his son, we have to take this very seriously. I'm no match for this guy, and neither are my men."

"So what can we do?" Natasha asked. "Can we reason with him?"

"Well, this guy probably isn't looking to dialog. If he's made up his mind, that's it."

"And he's probably unbalanced," Leslie added.

"Probably," Todd said. "I'm going to ask the military at Bragg to put some of their people on finding him. It's a long shot, but I still know people there and I think they might like to nip this in the bud themselves. Men like Louis Gismano are forces of nature, and can only be handled by men just like them."

"Anything you can do will be greatly appreciated," Ward said. The thought of being targeted by a man like the one Todd described was truly terrifying.

"It's cold comfort, but he might not actually be intending to harm you," Todd said. "We know he's been watching you for a long time.

He could have poisoned or killed you in a number of ways if that was his intention."

"If he means us no harm," Natasha asked, "why would he be here at all? If he blames me for his child's death, what else could he be after?"

"He is a surveillance expert. Likely he's been collecting intelligence."

"But you said he's a killer," Leslie said. "That Sergeant Ross he may have killed was Special Forces, wasn't he? The military thinks he killed his wife, too, don't they?"

"My friend said Louis's wife was in a motel room with Ross when their son was hit. Evelyn's sister was with the boy. Betrayal isn't something Gismano would take lightly. And a betrayal that he thought killed his son . . ."

"But it wouldn't have been the mother's fault. I mean, she obviously trusted her sister with the boy."

Todd looked at Leslie and shrugged.

"Howard Lindley ran over Gizmo," Ward said. "He got a slap on the wrist for the hit-and-run. That had to have pissed Louis off."

"He was on drugs when he hit the child," Natasha said.

"Howard Lindley, the driver of the car that killed Gismano's son, was convicted of murdering three of his friends. He said he was framed," Ward said. "I think Louis killed Lindley's friends and set it up so he'd be blamed."

"That's pretty far-fetched," Todd said.

"Is it?" Ward asked. "Is it more likely that the kid snapped and suddenly killed his friends?"

"I followed the trial," Todd said. "The kid was guilty as they come. He bragged to people on several occasions about running over Louis's sister-in-law and his son. He said he knocked the kid out of the ballpark."

"Can you find out what Louis looks like?"

"When I get the files," Todd said. "My friend's e-mailing them from Bragg. All I know is he's six feet tall, weighs one seventy-eight, and was bald when last seen. The boys will be here soon. Until then, we hunker down," Todd said.

"You can use my computer," Leslie said.

Todd typed and watched the screen, and frowned. "No server."

"It was fine a little while ago."

"Your wireless is DSL, right?"

"Yes," Natasha said.

Todd opened his phone again, saw that there still was no service, and snapped it closed.

"Where's the landline?"

He picked up a remote unit from the bar and tried to make a call.

"What's the matter?" Leslie asked.

"It's dead," Todd said.

"The line?" Ward asked.

"Yes," Todd said. "Probably cut."

Ward picked up his cell and it also had no signal. "I don't have one either," he said.

"Why is there no cellular signal?" Natasha asked. "We always have a great signal here. There's a tower a quarter mile away. How could anybody cut that line?"

Todd took out his own .45 and said, "I'm going to go outside, find Thumper, and wait for the men to get here."

"You didn't answer Natasha," Ward said.

"It's possible the signal is being jammed," Todd said.

"Louis Gismano," Ward said, looking at the revolver. "Jesus."

"It's possible," Todd said. "Keep the doors locked and stay right here with the women. Louis Gismano is good, but he isn't bulletproof.

If he gets in don't talk to him. Just shoot before he gets within ten feet. If he starts moving toward you, fire. I just need some makeup."

"How well do you know Thumper?" Leslie asked Todd.

"He's worked for me on a few occasions, why? He seems very adept."

"He's sort of creepy, and he was wearing a big survival knife a little while ago," Leslie said.

"A survival knife?" Todd asked, frowning.

"Security guards don't need survival knives, do they?" Natasha asked.

Todd shook his head. "You're sure it wasn't a flashlight case or something?"

"It's a large knife," Ward said. "I saw it, too."

Todd slipped off his shirt, exposing a black T-shirt. He went to the fireplace and reached down and began to rub his hands on the fire-blackened stone. He began smearing the soot onto his arms, his face, the back and front of his neck. When he was done, he wiped his palms off on the front of his jeans.

"I'm going to go out and get a signal," Todd said. "Two hard taps close together followed by a third after three beats is me. Anybody else, don't open the door."

"Okay," Ward said.

When Todd slipped outside, Ward locked the front door behind him. Through the window, Ward couldn't see anything, but he imagined Todd, gun at his side, walking up the driveway. He moved back into the den where the candle, set in the fireplace, illuminated the women's faces. Natasha had the prototype in her hands, rolling the tires absently.

"I bet you wish you hadn't come," Natasha said to Leslie.

"Don't be silly," Leslie replied. "We're safe with Todd here."

SIXTY-SEVEN

Alice huddled at a public phone kiosk, hunched over the "M" section of a phone book, her finger finding the exact address she wanted. She used her GPS to find her way to his house. Her indignant anger grew as she drove slowly past the McCartys' mailbox three times before she made up her mind to drive in. When the narrow driveway turned she stopped, her path blocked by a black pickup truck. She got out of her car and knocked on the empty truck's window. She couldn't see anybody around. What idiot would park that way so nobody could get in? Enclosed by the trees, the property beyond her headlights was dark and creepy. It reminded her of one of the many horror films she'd seen over the years. She told herself movies were not real, but she was.

Thinking better of her late-night visit, Alice started to turn around. Backing between two trees, she was jolted when her rear tire fell into a hole. When she tried to pull forward, the car wouldn't move. She gave it more power and the wheel spun loudly, but it didn't budge. She slammed her palms against the steering wheel and cursed.

Turning off the lights, she threw open the car door and rooted in her black tote until she found her cell phone. She flipped it open and was greeted by her lighted screen and an absence of bars. "Fuck!" she yelled, stamping her feet on the floorboard.

Alice cut the motor, climbed out of the car, slammed the door, walked to the truck, and stood there in the darkness listening to the buzzing of the insects. An overcast blocked what moon there was, and she stood there afraid and confused.

In the darkness, she could barely make out the asphalt driveway that ran through the woods beyond the truck, and she cursed silently because she didn't have a flashlight in her car.

Taking the black tote bag from the passenger's seat in the Corolla, she went around the truck, moving away from the stuck automobile, opening her cell phone to give herself some illumination.

Walking cautiously, she rounded the next bend and was beginning to be able to see better as her eyes grew increasingly accustomed to the darkness.

She heard a noise off to her right—a slight rustling sound, like a wolf stalking her—and she held up her cell phone, straining to see what had made the noise. In the weak light Alice could just make out something reflecting the bluish glow in the leaves. She moved cautiously, inching toward the shape.

She heard a door closing and turned toward the sound. She didn't see any light from that direction, but to her left she could make out a shape over the rise—a roof? Hearing footsteps behind her, Alice started to scream, but a strong hand closed around her mouth as an arm cinched her waist, and she was lifted into the air, kicking off her sandals in the process. She kicked against her assailant, hitting his legs with her heels, but to no effect.

"Shhhhhhhh," the man whispered into her ear. "Cut the crap."

Alice closed her eyes and the fast-moving man carried her like a doll toward the house.

SIXTY-EIGHT

Even with the gun in his hand, Ward had never felt so helpless. The weapon should have given him a sense of control, but it felt like a metal toy. He tried to imagine himself aiming the gun at Louis Gismano and pulling the trigger as Gismano ran at him, knife raised, but the image ended with Gismano dodging the bullets and killing Ward, then everybody else in the house.

The idea of Gismano killing Ward didn't bother him one tenth as much as the image of him killing Natasha and Leslie.

Todd was their only hope. If Gismano wasn't stopped—if he escaped—how long would it be before he returned? They couldn't pay for protection forever, and if Todd's contacts couldn't find him, who could? He thought about a monster defiling Barney's room and his memory by stealing the bear and leaving a casket with an effigy of their dead child lying glued in the small black box. Ward breathed deeply, willing away his nausea.

Natasha sat on the couch, her arm resting lovingly on his back. Leslie sat in a leather chair, staring at the flickering candle in the fireplace. He heard Todd's musical rap on the door. Natasha jerked, straightening.

"That's Todd," Ward said, standing.

He moved to the front door just as Todd knocked again, tapping out his signal authoritatively.

Ward opened the door to the sight of a girl suspended in the air, floating, but he realized that the blackened investigator Todd was supporting her weight, his blackened hand over her mouth. Seeing her was such a surprise, it took Ward a second to put the child into context.

"Alice?" he asked. At the sound of his voice, Alice opened her eyes and abject fear changed into pure relief. The hand left her mouth.

"Mr. McCarty, make him put me down!" she said. Todd pushed by and entered the house, carrying her past Ward, who, after locking the big door, followed them into the den.

"Who's this?" Natasha asked.

Todd released Alice, who stood barefoot, looking first at the women, and back at Ward.

"What are you doing here, Alice?" Ward asked her.

"Alice Palmer?" Natasha asked.

"There's a truck blocking your driveway and I got stuck trying to turn around, and I came up the driveway and this psycho kidnapped me."

"Why are you here?" Todd asked her.

"Because he stiffed me." She looked accusingly at Todd. "Did you think I wouldn't notice, ass bite?"

"Stiffed you?" Todd was genuinely perplexed.

"You gave me one thousand dollars, not two."

Todd reached into his pocket and took out an envelope. Opening it, he shook his head and showed it to her. He laughed awkwardly. "I'm sorry. You're right. I gave you the wrong envelope. This one was supposed to be yours."

"You ought to give me both of them then," she said, holding out her hand. "Since you inconvenienced me and kidnapped me you should pay another thousand."

"I agree," Natasha said. "Give her the three thousand and let her go."

Alice looked at Todd. "So, why are you all sooty, and why's it like so freaking dark in here?" she asked, shoving the envelope into the black carry bag. "Can you like call somebody to come get my car out of that hole?"

"Our phones aren't working," Ward said.

"Mine didn't work either," she said, putting her black cloth bag on the couch. "Why would you live where you can't have a phone?"

"How did you get here?" Ward asked her.

"I got your address from the phone book," she said. "I have a GPS."

"Did you steal it?" Leslie asked.

"My mother bought it for me for my birthday so I wouldn't get lost. You know," she said, looking at Leslie, "you could be nicer. You don't even know me."

"What you did was unforgivable," Leslie told her. "You took advantage of Mr. McCarty, and you caused the McCartys both a great deal of unnecessary anxiety."

"My bad," Alice said.

"Alice," Ward said. "You came at a terrible time. There is a man outside who wants to kill my wife."

"Which one is the wife he wants to kill?"

"I'm both," Natasha said dryly.

"Nice to meet you." Alice chewed on a fingernail for a second. "And he could have killed me?"

"Yes," Todd said. "I doubt he wants to kill you, but since you're here, who knows. He won't want to leave any witnesses."

"So you like saved my life?" she asked Todd.

Ward nodded. "He probably did."

"Gismano won't harm her," Leslie said. "Will he, Todd?"

"He's not killing anybody tonight," Todd said. "I'm assuming Thumper either is neutralized or isn't who I thought he was."

He took his Colt from its holster. "I'm going to work my way away from here until I can get a signal, and make some calls. I need to give my guys a heads-up on what we're facing here now and get some deputies with guns out here."

"Maybe you should stay here until they come." Natasha said. "If we stay together, with you and Ward armed, wouldn't that be preferable to splitting up?"

"Maybe Natasha's right," Ward said.

"I agree," Leslie said.

"We're not voting," Todd replied. "Gismano could kill my guys if I don't warn them. If Thumper is Gismano, he could ambush them because they know him. Whatever his plan is, I need to short-circuit it. There's a definite range on jamming devices. So, once I get out I can make the calls, and even if we don't stop him tonight, it'll be over for now."

Ward followed Todd to the door.

"I'll go around and make my way to the subdivision back there. Even if the cell doesn't work, there are phones in the houses. It's probably safer than trying to go to the road down the driveway. I suspect he'll be out there waiting for one of us to try that way. I'll knock on the door when I get back."

In the darkened garage, Ward triggered the roll-up door closest to them. He waited until

Todd, .45 in hand, bowed down and slipped out into the darkness before he rolled the door back into place.

SIXTY-NINE

Ward looked out across the backyard from the dark kitchen. He thought he saw a shape moving fast up the slope beyond the pool. In the den Alice had seated herself on the hearth. She was staring into a candle.

"This candle is about shot," she said. "You got any more?"

"Yes," Natasha said. "In the kitchen. I'll get one."

"I'll get it," Leslie said. "Where are they in the kitchen?"

"The drawer next to the fridge," Natasha said. "There are a dozen or more."

When Leslie came back, she lit a long candle from the dying one, and pressed it into a vacant ring in the candleholder. Ward noticed the large butcher knife in her hand.

"Just in case," she said, holding up the knife so the blade caught the light. "I, for one, will not go gently into that good night."

"Not a bad idea," Natasha said. "What time is it?"

Ward glanced down at his watch. "Ten," he said.

"Do you have a flashlight or anything, besides that candle?" Alice asked.

"Yes," Ward said, "but we don't want the guy out there to be able to see what we're doing in here."

"God, this is all so freaky, don't you think?"

"Yes, Alice," Natasha said, looking at Ward. "We certainly do."

"So, you're like a little-kid doctor? And what're you?" she asked Leslie.

"I'm a secretary," Leslie said.

"Oh," Alice said. "So you're like a typer?"

"Yes," Leslie said. "And also a filer, and a phone answerer."

"Cool," said Alice. "How much money do you make?"

Even in the low light, Ward saw Leslie roll her eyes.

"You know, my mother went off the deep end

and I need some funds quick, so I sure could use a job."

"Too bad we don't have any jobs that entail stealing our inventory," Leslie said.

"So, Mr. Hartman told me your kid died," Alice told Ward. "You didn't tell me that. You definitely told me you didn't have any kids. I remember stuff like that."

"I didn't want to go into it at the time."

"When did he die?"

"It happened a year ago today," Natasha said.

Ward thought about the circle around the date on the calendar in the kitchen.

"If you'd have told me the truth, I wouldn't have taken his toy car, you know. I'm not heartless. I'm basically a good person." She took a picture from the mantel and held it so she could see it in the candlelight. "Is this him?"

"That's him," Ward said. "His name was Barney."

"He was a cute kid. Let me ask you something," Alice said. "You remember drawing my picture on the plane?"

"Yes, I do."

"Well, something happened to the picture.

And I really liked it a lot. What I wonder is, could you like maybe draw me again?"

"I'd be happy to," Ward said.

Alice looked at Natasha. "He can really draw people good. Did you know that?"

"Yes," Natasha said. "Ward's a very talented man."

"Well, he should draw all the time. He could like sell pictures of people. He could make some money drawing like kids and stuff. I really wish I hadn't torn it up. It was just because that investigator dude pissed me off. Do you mind me talking so much? I mean, I could shut up."

"No." Natasha smiled warmly. "It's distracting."

"So, do you like living out here in the middle of nowhere?"

"Most of the time the inconvenience is convenient," Natasha said.

"That doesn't make any sense," Alice said.

"Well, when you're out here, it takes effort and energy to go anywhere. So instead of going to stores and spending money when you get bored, you don't leave home. And it's isolated, which is a good thing most of the time."

"But like if you need the cops, like now,

they're a long way off," Alice said. "Wild animals make me nervous. Not to mention murderers running around in the woods. Why is a killer trying to kill you?"

"He thinks we did something to him, which we definitely didn't do."

"Like what?"

"He thinks Dr. McCarty killed his son," Leslie said.

"I thought *your* son was dead?" Alice said, confused.

"Our son died because of an accidental electrocution. The man outside's son was hit by a car, and I operated on him. There was something else wrong; and he died from that. He didn't die because of anything I did, but because I didn't know he had something else wrong. There was no way for anybody to know."

"So, just tell him that," Alice said.

"He wouldn't believe it," Leslie said.

"Is he crazy?" Alice asked.

Leslie said, "Seems pretty obvious he's past the reasoning stage."

SEVENTY

Cupping his hands to keep light from leaking, Louis Gismano used his penlight to look at the picture of Gizmo one last time. "This is for you, little guy," he told the picture. Placing the photo in his front pocket, Louis stood from his crouching position and raised his hands over his head to stretch his arms and loosen his tense shoulder muscles. He had just dragged a warm corpse, now lying at his feet, deep into the woods. Opening the dead man's cell phone, he broke it in half and, winding up like a major-league pitcher, threw it off into the woods, hearing it shatter against a tree trunk.

For the past twenty years Louis had exercised religiously, even doubling up on his repetitions since leaving the Army because if a man ever slows down, his reflexes rapidly go to shit. He'd seen it happen, and slowed reactions meant the difference between life and death—a bullet slamming home because you didn't move fast enough, or a sudden scraping of the tip of a blade nicking the inside of your spine as it sliced through your neck.

Someday no amount of exercise or vitamins would help maintain his speed, strength, or reflexes. Often he tried to look down the road at his life-to-be, but he could never see anything of it. Before Gizmo's death, he often pictured himself watching his son grow up, saw Gizmo joining the military to follow in his father's footsteps, driving a car to take his girlfriend on a date; he imagined Gizmo's bachelor party, and the grandchildren he would have bounced on his knee, taught to shoot a gun, use a knife. After Gizmo died, there had been nothing in the future.

Gizmo had been full of life and laughter. Louis's wife had been a good mother to the boy, except for that one lapse in judgment that had cost their son his life. Louis told himself that he cared that she had screwed Ross only because it had put their son in a position to be killed by some worthless punk. That had sealed her fate, more than the betrayal of their vows. That betrayal was something he understood. He'd slept with a lot of other women to satiate his needs, and what was a little sperm toss-and-catch between friends? He could have forgiven her, and allowed her to live, had it not been for what her actions had done to Gizmo. Everybody who had a part in his son's murder had to pay for that involvement, even the woman who had given birth to him.

This was just another war.

In war you fight and you win, or you die trying.

In war there are casualties.

In war there is justice.

In justice there is truth.

Louis moved rapidly around to the garage, unlocked the garage door electronically, and using his back silently raised the door two feet and rolled beneath. Before cutting the landline, he'd called the alarm company, posing as their local installer, to tell them the system would be offline from ten until around midnight. He had prepared for his mission, as a good soldier would. He pulled out his knife and, moving from car to car in the dark garage, stabbed each of the twelve tires, releasing the trapped air in a dull whoosh.

There were now three women and one man

inside the house waiting for Todd Hartman to rush in and save the day. But Hartman was gone, and the only other person the people inside the house would ever see on this earth was Louis Gismano.

He was still crouching behind the BMW when the lights inside the garage suddenly came to life, so he froze, holding the knife at the ready.

Seconds later, when the garage lights went out, Louis moved to the kitchen door and stared through the glass into the house. He saw the golden pulsing glow from the candle in the den visible through the kitchen doorway. Knife in hand, he readied himself to move into the house and get on with the task at hand.

SEVENTY-ONE

Ward sat holding the gun in one hand and Natasha's hand in the other. Alice was seated with her legs bent under her, playing an electronic game in a chair to one side of them, her face illuminated by the small screen. She was absorbed in the whistles and beeps. Leslie sat with her ankles crossed on the ottoman in front of her chair, absently tapping the blade of the butcher knife on her thigh. She was glaring at Alice.

"I should take a walk around and check the doors," Ward said.

"Take the gun," Natasha told him.

"You keep it," he said.

"No, I insist," Natasha said. "It freaks me out."

He walked through the kitchen to the garage door. Turning on the light inside the garage, he stared out at the vehicle closest to him—Natasha's Lexus—and his heart sank when he noticed that the two tires he could see were flat. Gismano had flattened the tires of the vehicles. If they had already been flat when Todd had slipped out, neither had noticed in the dark.

"Shit," he said.

"What is it?" Natasha said, startling him. She had come up behind him.

"Nothing," he said, flipping off the light. He led her back to the kitchen.

"Obviously it isn't nothing," she insisted.

"I was just looking at the cars. Silly since the driveway is blocked. That's all."

"That isn't all," she said. "I know you, Ward. What else?"

"He punctured the tires of your Lexus, probably all three cars. I couldn't see the Beemer or the Toyota's tires, but I assume he got them as well."

"We have to get Alice and Leslie out of here. They aren't involved in this," Natasha said. "It isn't fair for them to be in danger. It isn't fair for you to be either."

"I'm with you about them, but I'm sticking with you. He's our problem, and with Todd's help we'll get through this. And I do have a gun. That's an edge. Isn't it?"

"One thing," Natasha said. "He got into the garage, and we know he's gotten into the house before. So, can't he do it again?"

SEVENTY-TWO

"Don't you think it's like really weird?" Alice asked. "That this shit happens on the anniversary of your son's . . . you know . . ."

"Barney's death," Natasha said. "Yes, it's an unpleasant coincidence, to say the least."

"That does seem very odd," Leslie said.

"Maybe it isn't a coincidence at all," Ward said. "If this Gismano character has been watching us, he knows what today is."

"He marked it on the calendar," Natasha said wearily.

"Maybe this Gismano guy set all of that up," Leslie said. "And timed it all for the anniversary. Tonight."

"You ever think what if he killed your son?" Alice said, without looking up from the Game Boy screen.

"He didn't," Leslie said reflexively. "Barney died from faulty wiring. Nobody killed him. It was an accident. This guy Louis loved his son. I doubt he would murder an innocent child."

"Leslie's right," Ward said, wondering if

Gismano could have rigged the wiring to electrify the place where Barney stepped, wet from swimming in the pool. It was too monstrous an act to consider. Or could he have done it believing that Ward or Natasha would be killed, and he hadn't considered that the boy might be the victim? No, Ward couldn't believe that kind of indifference to a life so precious was possible. He and Natasha had never considered that possibility, and the investigators would surely have found evidence to point to tampering, and they hadn't. The ground-fault interrupter hadn't been put on the line and saturated ground had allowed the electricity to find its way out through a bare spot in the insulation and kill his son. Barney had not fallen into a trap that had been set for Ward. Ward's heart palpitated at the thought.

Ward also let himself wonder if the virus might have been a killer's doing and that the hacker's and Trey's murders were committed by the ex-soldier to cover his trail. Not that it mattered now.

Ward said, "Right now we just have to keep him at bay until help gets here, which should be very soon. Todd will get word out and his guys are on their way here." And he wondered if Todd had indeed made it out to a good signal.

Leslie said, "Can we talk about something else? He's just a crazy man, and talking about him won't get rid of him. We have to figure out a plan to kill him."

"Did you guys ever have a séance to talk to your son? Maybe he like has an idea. Séances are so cool."

SEVENTY-THREE

Ward opened the .38 and looked at the candle's reflection on the brass circles, the contrasting silver primers in their centers. He closed the cylinder carefully, hearing the positive snap of steel on steel as it locked back in place.

Sitting in the silence, he heard a squeak over Alice's Game Boy that was so slight he almost missed it. The women heard it, too, and turned toward the sound. His house had been built using expensive hardware throughout, but even the best metal hinges, when not lubricated regularly, would make a noise when opening.

"Natasha, take Leslie and Alice to our bedroom and lock the door," he whispered. "You can escape through the window. Once I know he's in here, I'll yell."

"Maybe it's Todd," Natasha whispered back.

"No, he'd knock," Ward whispered.

Alice turned off her Game Boy and looked at Ward. Without saying anything, Leslie took the butcher knife, Alice lifted her tote bag, and they followed Natasha out of the room, moving fast down the hallway.

Ward blew out the candle, got behind the chair, and aimed the .38 at the kitchen door thirty feet away across the dining table. He heard the bedroom door slamming shut behind the women. He blinked and waited for his eyes to become fully accustomed to the darkness.

Using the back of the chair to brace his extended hands—one gripping the weapon, the other under the butt—Ward felt his gun hand shaking. Never in his life had he been in mortal danger. He knew Louis Gismano was in the kitchen; to get into the rest of the house he had to come through the kitchen door, which Ward could just make out. Once through the door Gismano's choices were to make a hard left turn to the foyer, or come in the darkness straight toward Ward through the dining area. When Louis left the kitchen to come into the den, he would be in range. The only problem was that Ward had never fired a gun at any living thing before.

"Louis," Ward said in a louder than conversational tone. "I know why you're here. What happened to your son was a terrible tragedy, but it wasn't my wife's fault. There are people with guns coming any minute. You can just go," Ward said, his voice breaking up slightly. "I have a gun. I don't want to shoot you, but I will if you don't give me any choice."

He jumped at the sound of Natasha's voice drifting eerily out from the kitchen. "Little guy, Mama loves you so very much."

He knew the recorded voice came from the stuffed bear that had been stolen.

Ward wondered if his mind was playing a trick on him, or if there was a figure filling the kitchen doorway.

Rage replaced his fear, and remembering Todd's instructions, and trusting his instincts, Ward let his brain tell his hand where to send the bullet, and he slowly tightened his grip, squeezing the trigger back evenly. For a split second when the trigger broke, his hand jumped, bright light filled the large space, and the explosion deafened him. In the flash Ward saw a man standing there. As Ward's eyes adjusted, he was sure the door frame was now empty.

"Shit," Ward said.

He was answered with a loud, eerie burst of laughter and Natasha's recorded voice: "Little guy, Mama loves you so very much."

SEVENTY-FOUR

Holding hands, the three women strode in controlled panic down the hall in the dark, entering the master bedroom. Natasha slammed and locked the heavy door after them.

"The killer is in the house?" Alice asked.

"Not now," Leslie snapped.

"Well, excuse me for asking questions," Alice shot back. "There is a maniac after me."

"Sorry, Alice," Natasha said. "Why in God's name are you two here? It isn't fair. We have to get you both out safe."

"What about you?" Leslie said, holding the knife down by her side.

"He wants me," Natasha said. "Worst case, he gets me. Go, you two. Out the window. Go to the road and flag down a car, or turn right and go to the subdivision and call the sheriff."

Taking the window crank in hand Natasha started turning it counterclockwise and the window began to slowly open out. As she was about to get it open enough for them to get out, there was an explosion, loud even through the solid door.

"Ward!" Natasha cried out.

"Was that a gun?" Alice asked.

"Ward must have shot at him," Leslie said, hopefully. "Maybe he got him?"

Or maybe he shot at Ward. "Leslie, you and Alice go now! Get away while he's in here."

"What about you?" Leslie said. "I'm not going anywhere."

Alice went to the window and looked out. "It's a long way down," she said. "I could get hurt jumping down there."

"You could get killed in here," Natasha said. "Now go. You, too, Leslie."

"You're not coming?" Leslie asked, incredulous.

Through the door the women heard the killer's muted laughter.

"Ward needs me," Natasha said. "I won't leave him. Give me that knife and go."

"You want the knife?" Leslie asked.

"What, are you going to fight a killer?" Alice asked.

"If need be," Natasha said.

"But you're a doctor," Alice said. "What do you know about killing people?"

SEVENTY-FIVE

"Nobody's coming. Hartman never made a call." The odd, lilting voice came from the kitchen. "The doctor has to pay for murdering my son."

A sinking feeling captured Ward when he knew that Todd hadn't made it out. But, he thought, Todd had already called for backup, and Louis had no way to know that.

"Todd called for help," Ward called out in the darkness.

"Ward, I never made any calls. I hope you can forgive me for deceiving you. I never called my guys. But I want you to know I did tear up the check you wrote me."

"Todd?"

The voice changed, became instantly recognizable. "No, I'm Louis Gismano. I've only been Todd Hartman, P.I., for three years. Hartman was a buddy of mine from Bragg. Nice guy, too, if a bit simple. He was an MP from Muncie, Indiana, who married a sweet gal from Australia and moved to Sydney. We stay in touch. I got his birth certificate and switched our fingerprints and DNA records. He's a successful private investigator because I put in a lot of legit hours, when I wasn't watching you two, or Howard Lindley."

Ward was still aiming at the doorway, but his hand was shaking worse than before he'd fired the gun.

"You came damn close to doing me serious injury, Ward," Louis said from the kitchen in a loud voice. The light came on in that room, startling Ward. "I've had worse, but for your first shot at a man, it wasn't far off, really. And in the dark and all. I'm impressed. I didn't know I was such a good teacher."

"I'll come closer next time," Ward said. "You can still leave."

"And miss the sight of your intestines steaming on the floor between your wide-open legs?"

"I will shoot you," Ward called. "And next time I'll kill you."

"You had your chance and you blew it," Louis said.

"But I have four more chances and you'll have to show yourself."

"No, Ward. Take my word. That was your only chance. I just didn't think you could shoot that accurately, even accidentally. Beginner's luck, that's all. I've been bit worse, and I'll survive this little nick."

"You've left some of your DNA on the floor, I bet. I guess that's a good thing for me, but not so good for you."

"I'll tidy up before I leave, Ward. Amazing what a little bleach can do to mess up those DNA tests. Ward, you'll get much better accuracy if you cock the hammer before you fire again."

"I'll try that," Ward said, cocking the hammer,

the sound remarkably loud. Louis chuckled in response. His voice sounded strained.

"Why fight it?" Louis asked. "You're no killer.
Tell you what. I'll make it fast for you. What do
you have to live for? Your son is dead. Your wife
is a baby killer. I'm good with a knife. It won't
hurt at all. Promise."

Ward said, "Your son died, but it had nothing
at all to do with Natasha. You know her. You
have to know that she did everything in her
power to save your son. And for all of your
snooping, the only way you missed that is because you are blinded by your thirst for revenge.
I will kill you to keep her safe."

"You're an idiot, Ward," Louis said. "And
you're starting to piss me off defending that
murdering slut."

"There's only one murderer here."

Ward knew that the longer he talked, the farther away the women would get. Maybe Louis
would kill him. Hell, he probably had no chance
to survive. After he'd seen that the tires were cut,
he and Natasha agreed that if Louis came in, she
and the others would go to the bedroom, lock
the door, and go out the window. Even after

Louis killed Ward, the lock was good and would slow him.

"So," Louis said. "Should be just a minute or two, now."

"Until what, Louis? What happens next?"

"I bet you think your wife and the girls got out the window. Don't you know I plan for contingencies? Your wife can't escape this house, Ward. You think I'd leave that to chance?"

Ward sensed he was missing something obvious. He was startled by the sudden light in the hallway and he turned his head without moving the gun from where it pointed. He saw three female figures enter the hallway together and start walking toward him. He thought his eyes were playing tricks on him. Alice was leading the women down the hallway. Natasha was at her side, and Leslie was just behind them. They were almost in the den when Ward saw Leslie holding the knife against Natasha's side.

"Put the gun down, Ward," Leslie said, making sure Ward could see the blade. "I will kill her."

"What the hell are you doing, Leslie?"

"She killed Gizmo," Leslie Wilde said, flatly. "He was our son."

An icy hand closed around Ward's heart. That

was what he'd been missing. So Louis hadn't killed his wife after all. It had been Todd who told them the authorities thought he'd killed his wife. The authorities probably weren't looking for Gismano at all.

Louis called from the kitchen, "Ward, don't tell me you're surprised."

We're all dead, Ward thought.

SEVENTY-SIX

Special FBI Agent John Mayes was at home in Harrisburg, North Carolina, having just arrived there, when the phone rang. He looked at the ID and opened the phone.

"Where are you?" Bill Firman asked him.

"I just got home," he said. "Where should I be?"

"You know that duct tape the techs found under McCarty's BMW?"

"What about it?"

"I'm looking at the lab report, and there was a fingerprint on it."

"That's great," John said, stifling a yawn.

"Maybe not. The print belonged to Todd Hartman."

"And?"

"The lab said that tape's been under the car for a very long time. You remember how ratty and filthy it was, right?"

"Yeah."

"The fingerprint's been there since the tape went on. It was on the sticky side. According to McCarty, he hired Hartman the day before the virus thing happened, right?"

"I believe he said something to that effect."

"That brings up some questions, don't you think?"

"I'll talk to the McCartys," Mayes said. "First thing in the morning."

John Mayes hung up. As he stood there looking at the plate his wife had put on the table, his mind started turning that revelation over in his head. He decided that he should call the McCartys. He dialed all of the numbers he had, and each time the phones went straight to voice mail. He put his phone back into his pocket and looked at his watch.

Maybe he should take a run out there and

make sure everything was all right. And at the very least, Todd Hartman had some explaining to do.

He dialed his partner's number and Firman answered.

"Bill, I tried the McCartys' phone and they didn't pick up."

"I suspect they're talking to people, or celebrating. I would be."

"Well, I expect you're right. I'm going to eat dinner, and then, if they still don't answer, I'll probably take a ride to Concord and let McCarty know about the tape. Maybe he hired Hartman longer back than he told me."

"You want me to go with?"

"No. Get some rest. I just don't want to leave it until the morning."

Mayes hung up, and lifted his fork. The idea that Todd Hartman, a respected investigator, might have been up to no good was crazy. He needed some sleep, and family time—not three more hours in the field.

He set down his fork, and even before he stood, his wife had picked up the plate and put it back into the oven.

SEVENTY-SEVEN

Evelyn Gismano turned on the lights in the living room and Louis strolled into the dining room holding a wad of blood-soaked paper towels against his right forearm. He had sliced the long sleeve of his T-shirt from the cuff to his shoulder to get to the injury. The 1911 was holstered at his side, and there was a large survival knife in his belt. Ward kept the gun trained on him, but he may as well have been pointing his finger.

"Ward shot you?" Evelyn asked, a note of concern in her voice.

"He sure did," Louis said. "You're no more surprised than I am."

"You're working for Mr. McCarty," Alice said. "Isn't this like a conflict of interest?"

"You should have gone home," Louis said. "You're in a world of shit here, Alice. And I was starting to like you."

"My mother kicked me out," Alice said, frowning. "And I didn't know you were a psycho."

"Sit down," Louis told her, as he sat in a dining chair resting his wounded arm on the table. Taking the large knife from his belt, he drove the tip an inch into the dining table.

"Ward, put your gun down and plant your ass in the chair. Get his gun, Evelyn."

Evelyn grabbed Natasha and placed the butcher knife against her exposed throat.

Ward stood, placed the Smith on the hearth, and moved away, sitting down in the chair he'd just used as a bench rest.

"You should have loaded blanks, Louis," Evelyn said.

"Hindsight is twenty-twenty." Louis shrugged.

Alice sat on the couch, holding her tote bag to her chest like a baby.

Natasha sat down beside her and put a protective arm around the girl's shoulder. Ward didn't see fear in the young girl's eyes, just something more like fascination. Natasha appeared more concerned than afraid.

Evelyn Gismano reached over and picked up the handgun from the hearth. Aiming in the general vicinity of the trio, she walked over to stand by the table, handing Louis the Smith & Wesson, which he absently tossed on the table beside the erect Randall. He took the bloody paper towels from the wound and his wife looked at it, frowning. There was a deep channel cut into the bottom of his forearm, and the exiting bullet had laid his elbow open.

"I should look at that," Natasha said.

"I don't think so," Evelyn said. "You've done enough damage to us."

"It looks like it shattered your elbow," Natasha said. "You'll have to get medical attention."

"It'll be fine," he said, dismissing her. "You're far more dangerous to other people than your pantywaist husband."

"That's a bad wound. It could get infected. I can clean it and mitigate the future damage. You could end up losing the arm. And it is going to hurt a lot."

"Shut the fuck up," Evelyn hissed.

"Get some warm water, Leslie," Natasha said. "You have to clean it. I can stitch it, and at least slow the bleeding. I have some medical supplies."

"You're worried about me?" Louis asked, snorting derisively.

"You're getting blood all over," Alice said. She opened her black carry bag.

"Don't sweat it," Evelyn snapped.

"So, can I play my game?"

Everyone looked at Alice quizzically. "You want to play a video game right now?" Louis asked slowly.

"I was winning. It's no skin off your ass. It relaxes me. Plus your fucked-up arm is making me want to puke."

"Forget it," Louis told her.

Evelyn said, "You just sit there like the amazingly stupid and ugly fucking toad you are. I ought to just shoot you in that ass-face and put the world out of its misery."

"You could just say no," Alice said, frowning. "You don't have to be such an asshole."

"Actually," Louis said, "we should thank Alice for being a little thief. She helped me get in here earlier than I'd planned. I was planning to use the virus as my entry into the McCarty household. Just like Howard's party at the lake, the gods smiled."

"I hope you bleed to death," Alice said. "People like you are why the world is so fucked up. And if you didn't know it, your wife's a total psycho bitch. I can't believe anybody let her have a kid in the first place."

Ward let his eyes pass over the fireplace tools, trying to think of something he could do, some weapon he might go for, when he got a chance. His eyes went to the prototype on the mantel, and he thought about Barney, his mind forming an image of his son laughing with everything he was—laughter that took over his entire being. *If I die, I will be with Barney.* Death held no fear for him. But he had to mess with Louis a little, because Louis wouldn't expect that from him. Ward needed to play for time. He had to muddy the waters for Louis the way Louis had muddied them for Ward.

"So, Louis," Ward said, "how much longer does Leslie—Evelyn—here have?"

Louis's eyes fixed on Ward, as did Evelyn's.

"Unless you lied about her screwing Sergeant Ross."

"Fuck you, Ward," Evelyn snapped.

"That was why Gizmo was out there to be killed by Howard Lindley. Way it looks to me, you killed his three friends and set him up to go to prison. Those young men were sons, just like Gizmo was yours. If you'll kill three totally innocent young men, are you really going to let Evelyn off the hook for what she did? Obviously she's alive now because you needed her to get close to us, but seems like she's just deadweight now."

Louis's eyes sparkled, and something like a smile crossed his tight lips.

"Shut up, Ward," Evelyn snapped.

"Your wife knows I'm telling the truth. She's a very intelligent woman. You blame her as much as, if not more than, you blame Natasha."

"She's my wife," Louis said after a too-long silence. "She was Gizmo's mother. She knows I love her. She's in this every bit as much as I am. Isn't that right?"

Evelyn nodded once, but her eyes remained uncertain.

"I forgave her for the affair, after I showed her the error of her ways."

Evelyn smiled nervously. "Sergeant Ross seduced me like he seduced a lot of other women. He was evil. He deserved to die for it."

Ward shrugged. "You'd know Louis better than I do. Maybe he has really forgiven you because he still loves you despite how you helped to kill Gizmo. Perhaps he doesn't still think

about you in bed getting your sweaty jollies
while your son wandered into the path of
Howard's car. Maybe you can believe we're going to be the last objects of his revenge. I'm
thinking if he can really believe that Natasha
killed Gizmo and that she didn't do everything
in her power to save him, and he can still kill
her . . . Or is this all just an excuse for him to kill
and torture innocent people? It seems evident
that there's no stopping place, just pauses in the
process. Louis may miss Gizmo. Maybe he loved
him and he's been driven to this by grief and he
isn't just another sociopath who's using Gizmo's
death as an excuse. But I think he likes killing. It
gives him pleasure. Best case, he's insane."

"Shut up," Louis said, wincing as the pain hit
home. "You don't know what the hell you're
talking about."

"No? What's the body count in your son's
name? Six? Seven? More? We'll make it what,
nine? You know Natasha tried to save Gizmo,
don't you, Evelyn. If Lindley hadn't hit your
poor sister, you think he'd have let her live?"

"It won't work," Louis said, pulling the survival knife from its resting place and gripping it
in his bloody left hand to point the tip at Ward.

"You're not going to save yourself by making up this psychological mumbo jumbo. You're a dead man."

Ward didn't intend to shut up. "You don't feel anything, because psychopaths can't feel anything. You kill so you can, but there's no lasting satisfaction in it. And it's your only purpose. There's no stopping place. Everybody is responsible for your son's death except you. Everybody but you should die. So why did you start sleeping with that sergeant, Evelyn? Was it because you never felt loved? We're all just cardboard targets in Louis's world. He wants you to believe he loved your son, but what kind of love allows him to paint his son's legacy in blood? What kind of a meaningful monument is it? Natasha has spent the past three years saving children and raising money for a children's surgical center at the hospital, while he's spent the past three years killing people. Louis wants to kill Natasha, and his selfishness will do harm to innocent children, all like your son, for decades to come."

"Bullshit. You're suing the people who killed your son," Evelyn said. "That's revenge, just so you'll get hundreds of thousands of dollars."

"The people responsible for killing Barney

should pay for their mistake, but that money is going to the hospital in our son's name so something good can come out of our loss. We want to honor Barney's memory long after we're gone. You'll kill us and we'll be together with our Barney. What will Gizmo's life have counted for?"

"I'm going to gut you like a fish," Louis said evenly. "While Natasha watches."

"I suppose you can't believe in life after death," Ward continued. "We do. If there's life after death, maybe Gizmo is watching you. He must be proud of his parents."

"You're using bullshit psychology on us," Louis said. "It won't work. Trying to divide us against each other. It's good, Ward, but she loves me. She loved Gizmo."

"She's scared shitless of you," Ward continued. "She's doing this because she knows that until we're gone, she's safe. Slipping that disk into my computer, getting close to feed you information on us. Doing her part while you snuck in and drugged me at home, and screwed with our heads. Once that's over, she knows you'll only have her left to punish.

"You're going to get caught," Ward said,

finally. "You'll see. And you're going to hell, and you won't ever see your son again because he won't be there."

"Enough of this bullshit," Louis said. He flinched and closed his eyes tight for a second.

Evelyn looked at her husband and back at Ward. Ward had gotten to her, but how much good that would do was impossible to gauge.

"Shoot the kid," Louis said, opening his eyes. He put down the blade, grabbed up the gun and held it out to Evelyn, butt first. She looked at it, bewildered.

"What?" she asked.

"Shoot the toad," he repeated. "You hate the bitch and she has to die. Or do you want me to do all the work myself?"

Evelyn's eyes reflected horror. "Me shoot her?"

"Take this, go over there, and put the fucking gun to her forehead and blow her brains out. Do it now!"

"I . . . can't do it," she said, her eyes darting around the room.

"You've never killed anybody," Ward said. "He wants the satisfaction of seeing you be like him."

Louis flipped the weapon in his left hand to grip it. "You can't? You can't? Yes, you can, and you will!"

"She didn't do anything," Evelyn protested.

"Did the boys in Lindley's cabin? Did you ever say, 'They didn't do anything'? No, you said it was a good thing. Alice is an annoying little thief. And she's a witness. Do you want me to let her go so we can watch her testify against us?"

"You can do it," Evelyn said. "You know how."

"I taught you to shoot. But you don't mind if I kill her?" he asked.

Evelyn nodded. "Please."

Louis aimed the gun at Alice, who pressed herself against Natasha, and squeezed the bag tighter to her chest.

Natasha held her tight, protectively. "Alice never even heard of Gizmo until she came here and we told her. She's as innocent as Gizmo was."

"Collateral damage," Louis said.

"Like those teenage boys at the lake," Ward said. "Like Trey. You killed Trey, didn't you? And that hacker you hired. And Thumper?"

"Yes, I did. Now shut the fuck up." He turned

to his wife. "Are you going to take this gun and shoot her?" he demanded.

"No," Evelyn said. "I won't do it. I can't, Louis."

Louis winced, opened his eyes, and seemed to be weighing something for several seconds.

"I let you live in the trailer, because you promised you'd do whatever it took to help me pay back the bastards who killed Gizmo. Against my better judgment, I didn't use the torch on you, didn't fill you with spray foam. This is my reward?"

"You know I love you, Louis. I've proved that. But I can't and I—"

As she spoke, Louis turned the muzzle from Alice and fired. The bullet passed through the base of Evelyn's neck, ending her words, and punched a large hole in the window behind her. The thick double panes of glass around the hole formed a spiderweb of tiny cracks around it.

Evelyn looked at Louis, bewildered, and collapsed. Natasha screamed out, and Louis stood, aiming the gun at her.

"You bastard!" Ward yelled.

Louis waved the gun. "I ask her to do one little thing and she refuses. In all this time she's never done anything but sit back and keep her hands clean. She never loved Gizmo. She never loved anybody but herself. Totally selfish."

"Let me help her," Natasha demanded, straightening.

"She's beyond help," Louis said, unloading the gun and putting it back down on the table. "I think we should get this finished."

He picked up his knife and came into the den with blood streaming down his arm, dripping off his fingers.

Ward sprang from the chair and grabbed the poker. He raised it up like a major league batter and moved toward Louis. Blood dripped rapidly to the stone floor, the rug. Crouching, Louis held the knife in his left hand. Except for his hair, his bright teeth, and steel-blue eyes, the coating of ash totally obscured his features.

Louis pounced like a cat and was on Ward so fast he didn't have time to swing the poker. The knife passed through Ward's left shoulder, striking the bone as it went through the tissue.

Louis sprang back, balancing and waving the blade in a figure eight. Ward swung the poker, missing by a foot.

Natasha lunged from the couch and jumped on Louis's back, wrapping her arms around his neck and applying pressure.

Without so much as swaying, Louis snapped his head back and connected with Natasha's forehead, with a sound like a hammer striking a coconut. She collapsed behind him in a heap.

Despite the weakness in his shoulder, Ward raised the poker and swung again, stepping into the blow to close with Louis. Louis seemed to vanish as he ducked the poker's wide arc, moved in, and swung his blade, opening Ward's shirt and releasing a gout of blood through the sliced fabric. Ward dropped the poker as he fell backward against the fireplace. His right arm on the stone mantel for balance, Ward felt the prototype against his hand and gripped it.

Meeting Louis's eyes, and drawing strength from the victorious smile on the killer's lips, he mustered all of his strength and threw the car as hard as he could.

When the prototype hit Louis an edge found a bright blue eye.

Louis bent and cursed, putting the back of his knife hand against the damaged eye for a second before he looked back up at Ward with a bloody, orbless socket.

Ward was aware of Louis lunging, and he felt a new pressure high in his chest as the blade entered.

Ward, no longer able to stand, slid down the front of the fireplace.

Louis looked at Ward and fixed him with one-eyed unbridled rage. The knife in his hand flipped to change position, the back edge of the blade resting against his forearm, preparing to finish his opponent.

Ward put his hands reflexively to his stomach, and felt something warm and substantial, and knew he was holding in part of his intestines. He could feel hot blood running down across his groin and he couldn't catch his breath.

Louis looked at Ward's wound, and said, "Don't die yet."

Louis turned.

On the couch, Alice had drawn her legs up, holding her knees, the tote bag trapped against her. Ward couldn't hear the screams, just the odd sound of wind, like a hurricane, rushing through his mind.

Below Louis, a stunned Natasha raised herself

up on one arm. Louis grabbed her hair with his bloody right hand, and looked at Ward, who was trying in vain to get to his feet.

"Watch," Louis hollered, placing the blade pointing down at the base of her neck just behind her collarbone.

"No!" Ward yelled, his eyes locking on his wife's. They were wide open in terror, but as he watched they closed once, then opened and she smiled weakly at him. Her final expression was one of acceptance, and sadness, but there was no fear there.

And behind Natasha he saw Alice looking into her tote like a woman searching for a tube of lipstick.

"This is for Gizmo," Louis said.

Ward was aware of the first notes of Louis's laughter.

He saw the muscles in Louis's arm tighten, but Ward managed to lunge and grab the end of the blade with his right hand, squeezing as hard as he could.

Ward felt the pressure of the blade biting into the meat and tissue, wedging into bone as Louis pushed down.

Ward looked up and met Louis's amused gaze.

He felt the blade moving down, the tip penetrating Natasha's neck, and he squeezed harder. The knife seemed to rise for an instant. Ward pulled the blade toward him. Louis gritted his teeth and snarled as he muscled the blade back to Natasha's neck.

Ward was blinded by a bright flash, and an aura around Louis's form. The killer's features evaporated. Louis released the knife. As Louis/Todd fell sideways, Ward saw a small gun in Alice's hand, a thin plume of smoke rising from its barrel.

Ward raised his hand and saw that the knife was still there, wedged fast, covered in his own blood.

Washed with a feeling of well-being as he fell backward, Ward was filled with the sensation of floating, and he realized that, even though he hadn't felt himself connecting with the floor, he was on his back looking up at the light fixture.

Sound faded, and Ward's head was filled with a continuous dull tone like that of a struck gong. As he stared at the dimming ceiling, Natasha suddenly loomed over him, a thin line on her neck oozing blood in a wide ribbon. She was crying and he could feel the pressure of her hands, first on his cheeks, and then on his violated abdomen.

He couldn't hear what she was saying, because just over her left shoulder he saw a golden circle growing, and from within it, Barney's smiling face.

Barney's hands seemed to reach through his mother's shoulder, and Ward's hands rose to take them. The child's hands were as warm and real as they had been before he died. Ward's own hands were now bloodless, the right one undamaged as Barney pulled his father up from where he was lying.

As Ward rose, he turned his head to look down on Natasha's back, her head turned down over a body he recognized as his own. The physical Ward McCarty was splayed on the floor beneath her, seemingly floating in a rapidly expanding pool of blood that looked like black water.

SEVENTY-EIGHT

Natasha stared into her husband's open eyes through a veil of warm tears. His pupils were fixed and dilated.

"Oh, Ward, don't leave me," she called, cradling his bloodred face between her wet hands.

"Is he dead?" Alice asked.

Natasha eased Ward's head down and began giving him chest compressions. After a dozen, she put her fingers to his throat and felt a faint pulse, then nothing.

"No, he's still alive."

Natsaha gathered her thoughts. "Alice, on top of the refrigerator—bring me the black case!"

Alice tossed the gun to the couch cushions, ran, and returned in seconds with the case in her hands. Natasha opened it with bloody hands and turned on the defibrillator, purchased after her son's death.

"Now, look under the sink and get the trash bags. In the utility room there's a roll of duct tape in the cabinet over the washing machine.

Bring those to me," Natasha ordered in as calm a voice as she could manage. "Can you do that?"

"Sure I can," Alice said, rushing from the room.

Natasha felt the blood flowing freely from Ward's open wounds, but she had to get his heart beating, and it might, at least until he had lost so much blood that his heart was starved.

"Oh, Ward, please stay with me. Please don't leave me."

SEVENTY-NINE

Alice found the garbage bags and rushed to the utility room. In the collection of tools in the cabinet over the washing machine, there was a large roll of gray tape, which she grabbed up and carried from the room.

When she turned the corner she ran headlong into a solid mass holding a gun. It grabbed her with its free hand.

Alice screamed.

From the den, Natasha yelled, "Alice!"

"FBI," the man yelled.

"Get the fuck out of the way," Alice hollered, struggling to break away.

The man released her and she ran back to the den, jumping over the body of Evelyn Gismano and handing the bags and tape to Natasha, who had pulled Ward's wet shirt up over his chest. Agent Mayes rushed into the room behind her, then froze in place as he took in the scene. Before he did anything to help, he moved from Evelyn to Louis Gismano, checking each for a pulse. Natasha glanced up and noted his presence with relief.

Taking a plastic bag, Natasha laid it over the open wound and said, "Agent Mayes, grip him under his shoulders and lift him up for me."

The FBI man put his gun in its holster, and did what Natasha told him to do.

Alice stood back as the man and Natasha raised Ward's torso, and she watched as Natasha pressed his guts into the cavity, placed the trash bag around her husband's stomach, took the roll of tape, and, with difficulty, secured the bag in place.

"There's no cell signal," Agent Mayes told her. "And the driveway is blocked."

"We have to get him to the emergency room," she said. "We can't wait for EMS or he'll bleed out."

"My car is up the driveway."

"Can you carry him?" Natasha asked.

Mayes knelt, picked Ward McCarty up from the floor, and carried him. Passing the front door he began to run, with Alice and Natasha at his side. Natasha had the defibrillator case under her arm.

"Stay with us, Ward," the FBI agent said.

The man put Ward in the rear of his car, then ran around and pulled him completely inside.

Natasha climbed in the backseat and kneeled on the floorboard. The agent slammed the doors and, as Alice Palmer climbed into the passenger seat, he placed a blue light on the dashboard, flipped it on, and roared out in reverse, turning the heavy sedan out onto the road. He jerked the shifter down and peeled rubber heading down the highway. A mile down the road, he picked up his phone and dialed 911 without looking.

"Please hurry," Natasha commanded.

"I'm hurrying as fast as I can," he replied, the

speedometer passing rapidly through eighty miles an hour.

"Don't you like have a siren?" Alice asked him. And she realized, to her amazement, that she was crying.

EIGHTY

When Ward opened his eyes slowly, the first thing he saw was Natasha, sitting beside the bed holding his left hand.

"Welcome back," she said, wiping away a tear from her cheek.

He turned his head the other way to see Alice Palmer asleep in the reclining chair by the window. There were small droplets of blood, like freckles, dotting her lax features.

A tall, stooped man in whites, with a gleaming bald head, finished checking the machines. Ward looked across the bed, fixing him in his gaze. He recognized the man, but couldn't seem to remember his name.

"Ward, you're in the hospital and you're fine.

Don't try to talk. You need to rest and gain your strength. Your injuries are very serious, but you're going to be fine."

Ward tried to speak, but all that came out was a croak.

"Don't try to talk," Natasha said. "You're safe. We're all safe."

"I was dead," Ward managed to say. "I was with Barney," he told her. "I really was."

"Your heart stopped," Natasha told him. "But just for a few seconds."

"I saw . . ." Ward started. "I saw you put the garbage bag around me. I was watching from . . ." He tried to point up, to remember more, and did. "I was with Barney and I saw you leaning over me trying to help me."

Natasha's perplexed expression reflected confusion, but he was sure she believed him.

"You have to get some rest. You can tell me about it later."

"We repaired everything, Ward," the doctor said. "You're stable, and your vitals are getting stronger by the minute."

"Thank, you, Scott," he said, his voice cracking with gratitude. Scott Boggs was the doctor's name and his son had played Little League with

Barney. Ward's right hand was throbbing and he looked down at the encasing bandage. He remembered the knife. "My hand . . ."

"There's extensive damage to your hand. Dr. Levingston, our orthopedist, took a look at it, and he's going to operate to reattach the tendons when you're stronger. Hopefully the nerves will grow back together in time."

"I understand," Ward said. "Thank you, Scott."

Boggs put a hand on Ward's shoulder and squeezed gently. "You are so welcome, Ward. Mind your wife and get some rest. We'll manage the pain, and get you back on your feet in no time."

"It could use some pain management," he said.

"We're on top of it," Natasha said.

A nurse had come in and Natasha stepped back to let her take her place. The nurse raised a syringe, looked at it, and inserted it into the IV tube culminating under the bandage on Ward's hand. As she depressed the syringe, Ward felt a cool sensation in his right hand as the pain faded.

He was aware of Natasha kissing him on the cheek as he floated away.

EIGHTY-ONE

Outside the overcast sky was cooling the summer air, and a pair of deer grazed without fear on grass near the tree line. FBI Agent John Mayes stood in the McCartys' den watching the FBI's crime scene technicians gathering evidence. The case wasn't federal, but Mayes had decided that the least the FBI could do was process the scene to make sure things were done right, and the local authorities would be able to close the case as soon as possible.

He turned to see into the kitchen where Dr. McCarty sat looking out the window, her hand trembling as she brought a bottle of water to her lips. The rectangular bandage that covered the sutured knife wound on her neck was visible—that would be lasting evidence of the events of the night before.

Alice Palmer sat on a stool beside Natasha, playing her video game, lost in her own thoughts. The odd young girl had killed an extremely dangerous man, and had she not done so, she and the

McCartys would be dead. And maybe he would have even killed Mayes.

The sheriff's deputy had driven the women back to the house. Mayes had arrived a few minutes earlier, so the two could give their official statements. Mayes and Firman would get Ward McCarty's side when he was no longer in and out from painkillers.

Alice had remained at Dr. McCarty's side, and she'd been a comfort through the long morning hours while Ward McCarty had been in surgery.

Dr. McCarty locked eyes with Mayes. She smiled weakly and nodded at him. She'd gone without sleep since the morning before, had gone through hell the night before, and had been in the OR observing her husband's touch-and-go surgery until ten that morning. She had only left him after he was out of surgery and had spoken to her. Despite the circles under her eyes, they remained bright, though worried.

John Mayes closed his notebook and signaled Bill Firman. Together, they walked into the kitchen.

Alice broke her concentration on the tiny screen to look up as they entered. Just for a second, though. The girl seemed no worse for the ordeal she'd been through, but he thought she might be in shock.

"Alice, this is FBI Agent Bill Firman," Natasha said.

"Okay," Alice said.

"This won't take long," Mayes told the women.

"That's fine," Natasha told him. "I'd like to get cleaned up and get back to the hospital as soon as possible."

"Me, too," Alice said, without looking up. "I stink like a pig."

Alice's video game emitted a series of musical notes and she smiled broadly before turning the screen toward Dr. McCarty.

"I beat it," she said, proudly.

"That's good, Alice," Dr. McCarty told her, smiling.

Alice turned the machine off and placed it on the counter. "You can give it to one of your sick kids or something."

"I had your car pulled out of the hole. You can go whenever you like," Mayes said.

Alice shrugged. "I told my mother I'd come home tomorrow. I thought I'd stay around to keep Natasha company—if she wants me to, I mean."

Dr. McCarty placed her hand on the girl's. "That's absolutely fine. My parents are coming in tomorrow, but until they get here, I could use the company."

Alice beamed.

"Dr. McCarty," Mayes said. "We need to get an official statement if you feel up to it."

"Should I have Gene Duncan here?" she asked.

"You don't need him," Firman said, then almost sheepishly added, "Naturally that's strictly up to you. We just want to help you through this."

She looked at Mayes, and he nodded.

"I feel up to it now," she said.

Firman said, "So, this is what we have already. Alice came to see you after the model car thing. She'd found the car on the airplane ride and returned it to Mr. Gismano, who was posing as Todd Hartman. She came here to talk to Mr. McCarty about a job."

"That's good," Alice said.

"Louis killed the guard outside. Evelyn Gismano, whom you believed was Leslie Wilde, had a gun, the .38, which she left near the couch. After Louis Gismano shot his wife, he was trying to kill Dr. and Mr. McCarty with his knife. Acting in fear for your lives, Alice picked up Evelyn's gun and shot Louis. Total self-defense. End of story."

"That's right, isn't it, Alice?"

"No," she said, rolling her eyes at the ceiling. "I told you already. I brought that gun in my bag and—"

"I think you are mistaken," Firman interrupted. "That misconception on your part might be problematic for you, Alice. There are legal ramifications as to the gun, which is a weapon that was stolen in a burglary."

"By Earl Tucker. I said that. I gave you his address."

Alice looked at the frowning agents and at Natasha.

"But we agreed you were mistaken, because of the excitement," Mayes said. "Remember?"

"Okay. But Earl deserves to be arrested. Anyway, I saw Leslie . . . Evelyn, with the gun. She was brandishing it all around the house. What a total bitch."

"That's all we need," Firman said. "Isn't that right, Agent Mayes?"

Mayes closed his notebook and pocketed it.

"Okay, whatever. Could I like go take a shower?" Alice asked. "I mean you obviously don't need me to tell my story, right? Just do me one solid and leave in the part where I say, 'I killed the fucker and I'd do it again.' Okay?"

"In fear for yours and the McCartys' lives, you killed the fucker and you'd do it again. Got it," Firman said, shaking his head.

Dr. McCarty leaned over and put her arm around the young girl's shoulder. "Alice," she said. "You go take a shower. Pick out something to wear from my things. Whatever suits you."

"Cool," Alice said, smiling. "It won't fit though."

After Alice left the kitchen, Mayes said, "She's going to need some psychiatric help."

"I agree," Natasha said. "Her mother and I will see to it."

"Strange kid or not, it was a brave thing she did," Firman said.

"Yes, it was. She's odd, I'll give you that, but she's intelligent in so many ways. I guess she's just a teenager. By the way, Agent Mayes, I never did thank you for showing up last night."

"Wish I'd gotten here sooner."

"If you hadn't come, Ward would be dead," she said. "There was no way we could have waited for an ambulance."

"Dr. McCarty," Bill Firman said, looking at Mayes before looking back at her. "I want to officially apologize for being such a hemorrhoid."

EIGHTY-TWO

Thirty-six days later, Natasha parked her Lexus in the garage and held on to Ward's arm to help support him as they entered their home through the kitchen. Her parents had left the day before to return to Seattle. Having them there had been a comfort, but Ward was fully able to walk short distances on his own, despite the painful tightness in his chest and abdomen. The operation on his hand had restored partial use of the fingers, although there was no feeling in them. Therapy would restore some measure of use, and some of the feeling could return in time, but the doctors agreed that his fine-line drawing days were done.

He looked around the living room and was pleased that there were no signs remaining of the events that had put him in the hospital. Except for the new carpet and the gray wool curtains on the windows, it was just the way it had been before.

Slowly, Ward sat down on the couch, and Natasha handed him the remote. "You hungry?"

He tossed the remote aside and took her wrist. "I'm starving, but not for food."

"Not now, big boy," she said, laughing.

"Why not? Doctors said I could exercise."

"Walking is what they had in mind," she said, laughing and pulling her hand away. "Besides, you might embarrass our friends."

"What?"

He looked where she was pointing, and laughed at the sight of the wave of smiling people coming up the hallway.

EIGHTY-THREE

On a crisp January morning Natasha stepped up to a podium set on risers outside Carolinas Medical Center—NorthEast under the new sign: THE BARNEY MCCARTY PEDIATRIC SURGICAL CENTER. The bright sunshine cut the chill off the soft winter breeze.

She looked out at the crowd of doctors, nurses, technicians, local politicians, businessmen, and lawyers, some of them friends of hers and her husband's. With the laughter of several children—a good number of them patients—rising into the air, Dr. McCarty gathered herself to speak.

"I want to thank each and every one of you for coming today. This wing, which we are here to dedicate, stands behind me due to the unselfish donations of a great number of people whose money helped us make it a reality."

The crowd applauded wildly. Someone yelled out, "And the video game sure didn't hurt!"

"I guess I should mention that the sales from my husband's video game, which I hope all of you own, were certainly a big help, and will ensure that this center will be able to help children without the financial means to cover their care. That is all the more appropriate since most of our patients play video games, Ward's included."

The crowd laughed and applauded.

"As most of you know, this was a dream of ours that you shared. We wanted to do this in memory of our son, Barney, who, as most of you are aware, died tragically in childhood four years ago." She felt on the verge of tears, but fought it. "But it was more than money that built it. This dream was paid for with love, creativity, and hard work, as well as the generous donations of so many people."

She looked out and saw a beaming Flash Dibble. His wife, a perpetually frowning fireplug of a woman a few inches taller than her husband, was wearing a long mink coat. Natasha wasn't crazy about the man, but he had generously contributed a million dollars to the unit, and pledged five more to be paid over that many years.

Ward's uncle Mark and his aunt Ashley stood behind the Dibbles, smiling proudly. In the spirit of his many second chances, Ashley had taken

Mark back after he divorced Bunny. Natasha also saw FBI agents John Mayes and Bill Firman near the back of the crowd, and Tom Wiggins, along with Howard Lindley's parents, who'd happily made a six-figure donation since the McCartys' and Alice's testimony had freed their son from death row.

Natasha paused until the applause ended. "So today, I know that my son, Barney, is here with us in spirit, and his love will live on inside this building, and every child and parent who passes through these doors will have a better opportunity to live healthier, happier, longer, and more productive lives."

Natasha jumped when something grabbed her legs from behind and she looked down and laughed. Bending, she lifted the small child and anchored him on her hip before continuing. She cut her eyes back at Ward, who shrugged.

"Obviously my son thinks I've said enough."

There was more resounding applause and laughter.

"So, if we can move this inside you'll find hot coffee, fruit punch, and an assortment of cakes and cookies. Our staff and volunteers will be happy to guide you through the building. We're open for business starting this afternoon, and this facility will be open as long as there are patients who need the services. Thank you again."

Carrying the child, Natasha walked over to receive a kiss from Ward.

"Sorry about the interruption," Ward said, "but Palmer's strong as a bull. He broke loose and I couldn't catch him."

"Like you tried," Natasha said, laughing.

Gene Duncan smiled at them, and put an arm around his wife, Lucy, who was seven months pregnant. "You did good, Dr. McCarty," Gene said, simultaneously hugging her and the child.

"Ward should have given the address," she told them.

"Nobody would have heard me over the sound of my knees knocking together. All I did was write checks. Natasha did the work."

Alice Palmer stood beside the Duncans, smiling, showing an even row of straight teeth. Her long blond hair was tucked behind her ears, and she wore a cashmere coat open to show off her dress, accented by a pearl necklace with matching earrings.

Natasha handed her son to his father, kissed

the boy on his forehead, and said, "You are your father's son, Palmer McCarty."

"That he is," Gene agreed, smiling at the child, who stuck out his tongue and made a loud, particularly wet raspberry sound.

"Be nice, Palmer," Ward told the boy.

"Come to Aunt Alice." Alice reached out to take Palmer, but he slapped at her playfully, shook his head, and buried his face in his father's chest.

"Palmer McCarty!" Alice chided. "You know you want to come to me. Natasha," she said, "that was a beautiful speech. Jeez, I almost always cry at this happy shit."

And with that, Natasha hooked her arm in her husband's. They melted into the wide line of people filing into the new building past the life-size bronze statue of a nine-year-old boy who, while holding a model car in his delicate hands, greeted the passersby with an angel's smile.

ABOUT THE AUTHOR

JOHN RAMSEY MILLER's career has included stints as a visual artist, advertising copywriter, and journalist. He is the author of the nationally bestselling *The Last Family; Too Far Gone;* and four Winter Massey thrillers: *Inside Out, Upside Down, Side by Side,* and *Smoke & Mirrors,* and is at work on his next book.

A native son of Mississippi, he now lives in North Carolina with his wife, and writes full-time.

If you enjoyed THE LAST DAY,
pick up one of these gripping thrillers,
also by John Ramsey Miller.

SMOKE & MIRRORS

TOO FAR GONE

SIDE BY SIDE

UPSIDE DOWN

INSIDE OUT

THE LAST FAMILY

Available from Bantam Dell at your favorite bookstore.

Visit our website at www.bantamdell.com
Visit the author at www.johnramseymiller.com